THIRD
MESSENGER

THIRD MESSENGER

ELLSWORTH JAMES

THIRD MESSENGER

iUniverse books may be ordered through booksellers or by contacting:

iUniverse
1663 Liberty Drive
Bloomington, IN 47403
www.iuniverse.com
1-800-Authors (1-800-288-4677)

ISBN: 978-1-5320-6467-8 (sc)
ISBN: 978-1-5320-6468-5 (e)

Library of Congress Control Number: 2018914752

Print information available on the last page.

iUniverse rev. date: 12/27/2018

For Kathleen
F.A.T.E

PROLOGUE

Guyama Village,
In The Rain Forest Of Guatemala

The Paragon team lay hidden in the jungle. The seven-man unit was heavily armed, considering they were about to invade a primitive village whose inhabitants defended themselves with tiny bows and stone knives. Each man wore body armor, and all carried high-caliber assault rifles. The team burrowed into the undergrowth as their leader, a burly man named Jones, belly crawled to the jungle's edge and stared into the village.

Jones cocked his head to listen, hearing only the buzzing of jungle insects. He gazed a long minute at the cluster of reed huts. The hair prickled on his neck as he analyzed the situation. Finally, the guard exhaled and made a decision.

Jones raised a fist and motioned his team forward. The men crept into the village and approached the first hut, then Jones raised his weapon and stepped inside. The tiny room was dark and smelled of death. Jones flipped on an LED headlamp. He slowly rotated his head and ran sharp eyes around the interior, studying the scene. He saw signs of a hasty evacuation. The hut's window holes still held their thatch plugs. Something had torn away the woven blanket that covered the entrance. Jones knelt at a fire pit, staring at the glowing coals.

The attack came at night. The villagers had made no effort to fight their attacker. They had run in terror from it. Jones stared thoughtfully at his surroundings then carefully backed from the hut.

A pair of scientists stood at the jungle's edge. The men wore stiff fatigue uniforms and Kevlar vests, and their flushed faces were shiny with sweat. They watched nervously as the guard approached. Jones jerked his head towards the village, and the two men picked up their gear bags and stepped into the open.

There was a shout, and a Paragon guard emerged from a distant hut, urgently waving. The men jogged to the flimsy reed structure. Jones moved aside and allowed the scientists to enter. He stuck his head inside, then drew a hissing breath. The scene was revolting. The hut's interior was painted with blood. Coals from the fire pit were scattered and smoldering.

A grim-faced scientist named Joseph Hermann put a handkerchief to his mouth and squatted to inspect the carnage. The other man pulled a field microscope from his backpack and set it up in the doorway. He rummaged through a medical bag and handed Hermann a packet of slides.

"Two bodies," Hermann said, scraping at a wound with a scalpel. "An adult female, maybe eighteen." He gently turned her head and saw the woman's throat had been torn out. "Cause of death would be a severed carotid." The man nodded towards a bloody clump of flesh lying nearby. "That was an infant." He took a blood sample from the woman and transferred a droplet onto a slide. He handed the specimen to the other scientist.

The Paragon guard was inspecting the back wall. "Something knocked down the wall," Jones said. "Came inside and took the baby, then killed the mother when she tried to fight it."

The security man gazed at the grisly scene. "You know what did this, Doc?"

"No idea," Hermann answered brusquely. "What about the rest of the villagers?"

Jones sighed and pushed back his cap. "They took off in a hurry. Panicked and ran, from the looks of it. Their weaponry's gone, so I'd say they've abandoned the village." Jones jerked his head towards the jungle. "Somebody's hanging around out there. Probably this lady's husband. I'll send a couple of men after him, but we won't get near him."

"Don't worry about it," Hermann said.

"I thought he could tell us what happened here."

"Leave him alone."

The Paragon guard shrugged and said nothing more.

Hermann's broad face was grim as he went to the microscope and peered into the eyepiece. He studied skittering molecules, then raised his head to stare at the devastated hut.

"Well," he said, "this is officially a fucking disaster."

He looked at the security man. "Clean up this mess. Burn the hut. Contact Bohanon. Tell him to get his ass down here right now."

"Shouldn't we notify Houston?"

Joseph Hermann looked at the man as if he were stupid.

"No notifications," he said.

PART ONE

The Tikal Project

CHAPTER ONE

Lindbergh Field
San Diego California

The plane made a sharp banking turn and rolled into final approach as the blue Pacific hove into view. Will Connors glanced out the window and watched San Diego's sprawl appear beneath him. He emitted a weary sigh as he considered what awaited him on the ground. Today he would join the company of men who would not welcome him, in search of something he was unlikely to find.

A battered valise sat between his legs. He reached into it and removed the letter. It contained a Houston postmark and the letterhead of Steele Pharmaceuticals. Connors ran his eyes down the document. He had been invited to travel to the jungles of Guatemala, where the company was operating the Tikal Project. The company was claiming a discovery that would change the nature of human life. Connors had accepted their offer to join a team assigned to inspect it.

The cabin erupted in a flurry of activity. Flight attendants scurried about, bells chimed, and trays returned to upright positions. Beyond a skid-marked runway, he could see the

1

white-capped water of San Diego Bay. A narrow strand of beach served as a sinuous dividing line separating the pristine ocean from the intrusions of man. Connors watched as the runway reached up to embrace the aircraft, and a minute later they rolled to the terminal.

The girl had planted herself in front of the stream of disembarking passengers and was bouncing like a frenetic cheerleader. Her sun-bleached hair was pulled into pigtails, and a rectangular nametag embossed with the logo "NOVA LABS" rode above the swell of her chest.

"Doctor Connors?" She widened the Pepsodent smile and pointed at her nametag. "I'm Dana Watters from Nova Laboratories. I'm here to welcome you to San Diego and escort you to the meeting." Her words tumbled out in a rush, and the ingenuous act lightened Connors' mood a notch.

She grabbed the garment bag and led him to a waiting limousine. Connors dropped his lanky frame into the leather back seat and lowered the window to half-mast as the limo pulled into traffic. Triangular sails dotted the blue-green bay. Streams of ornamental citrus lined the boulevards. The sidewalks were crammed with tanned people in bathing suits rushing past on skates. Everyone was blond, and every other car a convertible. He smelled the briny air and felt the swirling bay breeze cool his forehead. He turned to the young woman.

"Have the others arrived?"

"Everybody but one. Mr. Travers from Nova's been here all week. So has the security guy, Mr. Bohanon. Doctor Shimota flew in from Connecticut last night, and Doctor Wilkinson from the FDA's here." Dana frowned and bit her lip, staring at a clipboard. "That leaves Doctor Rodgers. I don't know about her itinerary. I assume she'll be here today."

Connors nodded and turned to stare out the window. The limousine was rolling through the grounds of the sprawling Beachcomber Hotel. The place was lush and green, and he had the sense of traveling through a tropical jungle. They followed a winding road past clusters of bungalows scattered among the greenery. The vehicle stopped in front of the conference center. Dana led her guest to the door, insisting she'd take care of his registration and bag. Connors walked inside.

"Connors?" A group of men was seated around a long conference table. One jumped to his feet. Wayne Wilkinson held up an imperious hand as he gaped at Connors. The fleshy folds of the man's face tightened into a look of malice as he ran a hand through his mane of white hair. Connors felt a flush of irritation heat his face, but he ignored Wilkinson and found a seat at the table. He pulled out the Tikal report and leafed through it.

Wilkinson directed his venom at the man fidgeting behind the lectern. "What happened to Bernard?"

"Doctor Bernard was forced to withdraw," Bob Travers replied. He tugged nervously at the tie encircling his fleshy neck. Travers had the flushed face and wide body of a salesman. His forehead was shiny with perspiration. He drummed pudgy fingers against the polished surface of the lectern as he stared at the two men. "Doctor Connors was added to the team."

"He has no business here," Wilkinson thundered.

Connors raised his eyes and held the other man's angry gaze.

"Gentlemen, please," Travers appealed. He turned to Wilkinson. "Doctor Connors is a member of this team, and that comes from Houston. If you have a problem, we can discuss it later." Travers nodded cordially at Will, then introduced the others. Connors shook hands with Yanni Shimota, whom he recognized. There was someone named Tavey Bohanon from Paragon Security, who extended a callused hand across the table.

"We're missing somebody," Travers said, "but let's start anyway."

The pudgy man took a moment to regain his focus, then launched into his presentation.

"The age of genetic medicine has arrived," he announced, "and it's changing the nature of human existence. Science is altering the concept of life itself. Within the next decade, we will eradicate all human disease. Nobody will die of a heart attack, stroke or cancer. Doctors will be able to identify the genes that predispose us to disease and eliminate them before they occur. There'll be no more wheelchairs because geneticists will be able to repair or regrow a severed spinal cord by simple genomic programming. We'll live in a world without crutches or prosthetics because severed limbs can be regrown."

Travers paused for dramatic effect and shook his head in mock disbelief. "There will be no necessity to harvest human organs because we will grow them in the laboratory. You might receive a transplant from a genetically modified pig. A new heart or liver could be ordered online and implanted as easily as installing a new battery in your car.

Medications will be created specifically for patients based on their genetic profile."

The pudgy man flashed a photo of a human genome onto a screen. "As you all know, this microscopic piece of genetic material is the foundation of these miracles," he said. "The genome carries our biological inheritance and is the blueprint of human life. It was once considered fixed and unchangeable. That's old science, gentlemen. Now the human genome is as programmable as your computer."

Travers nodded respectfully at the small group of men. "You gentlemen are experts in your respective fields. You are intimately familiar with these scientific advances. So let me explain the reason we invited you here today." He punched a button and a wiring diagram appeared on a screen behind him.

"Nova Labs is a subsidiary of Steele Pharmaceuticals, and over the past ten years we've operated the Tikal Project in Central America. This project is the cutting edge of genetics research, and it involves developments so advanced they dwarf the miracles I've already described."

Travers' face grew serious and the pudgy man lowered his voice to a stage whisper. "Let me give you a taste of what the Tikal Project is about," he said. "What would you think of a drug that will stop you from growing old or even make you young again?" Travers quivered like a Springer Spaniel on point as he stared around the table.

"Elaborate, please," Shimota asked in a clipped voice.

"We've developed a drug that can slow the aging process, and eventually stop or reverse it." Travers said the words slowly and allowed his audience a moment to absorb them.

"Think of what this means. There's a single constant to nature and all human life. There's one experience that's immutable and unchangeable. *We die.* Every living creature has a shelf life. Every human on the planet worries about dying, and we fear this experience more than any other. For centuries people have searched for a way to extend life, but until today it was just a dream. Nova Labs has developed a drug that can keep you young. Maybe even restore youth. That's just the beginning. Our researchers have taken genetic manipulation to a level never before imagined. We can shape a living organism into anything we want. This isn't fantasy stuff, gentlemen. This isn't tomorrow's dream, it's today's research. The Tikal Project is like nothing else on Earth. We think it will transform human existence."

"How you make this breakthrough?" Yanni Shimota asked softly, affixing Travers with a somber stare.

Will Connors turned to gaze at Shimota. The old man's narrow face and guttural voice were familiar to public television watchers. The tiny man was the new Sagan of science. A renowned geneticist from Yale, Shimota was famous for conservative views and a prodigious output of publications. Shimota's brusque manner and stilted language made him a media darling, and he had become a reluctant celebrity. The man had long since celebrated his seventieth birthday, but his slender frame and full head of hair caused him to look younger. Only his translucent skin and a dusting of liver spots gave away Shimota's age. He had a serious manner and wore a muted three-piece suit perfectly reflecting his personality. He stared sternly at the fidgeting Travers, who grinned and continued his spiel.

"We've discovered something in the jungle," Travers said, "that's allowed us to make a quantum leap in genetic research."

"What you find in jungle?"

"We'll show you tomorrow." Travers' face was intense as he leaned against the lectern and spoke in a husky voice. "Nothing like it exists on earth. It's shown us the way to develop a drug that will change the world in ways you can't imagine."

"Have you given a thought to the problems this could cause?"

The clear feminine voice rose from the back of the room. The assemblage turned to look at the woman calling out the challenge. She was tall, middle-thirties, and stood provocatively in the doorway. She had an attractive, vibrant face highlighted by rouged cheeks and heavy red lipstick. Her frizzy brown hair and colorful appearance provided a distinct contrast to her severe business suit and Bally briefcase.

"Gentlemen, meet Dr. Tamara Rodgers," Travers smiled, "our remaining team member. Doctor Rodgers is our authority on cultural anthropology."

"More specifically," she announced, "I study the implications of technological advances on cultures. I'm interested in discoveries that artificially impact human health, like this new drug you're talking about."

"Come and join us." Travers paused to nervously re-knot his tie as the woman walked to the table.

"In answer to your question," Travers blustered, "we believe our products will affect human existence like no other in history. How could there be a problem with a technology that extends human lifespan and has the potential to eliminate the world's killer diseases?"

"That's the problem with scientists," she said. "You can't see the world outside the laboratory window. I can think of a thousand problems."

"Like what?"

"You mentioned extending human lifespan," she said. "If your company developed a miracle drug that added just a decade to human life expectancy, the consequences would be catastrophic. Add ten years to everybody's lifespan and the country's population would double in eight years. That's nearly seven hundred million people. Don't you think that kind of change would create social chaos? Or economic problems, Mr. Travers?" Her voice had risen an octave and her face was tight with intensity.

Travers threw up his hands, contorting his flushed face into a smile. "If we make no effort to improve the human condition, what's the good of science?"

"You're fooling with a delicately balanced planet. There are things to consider before you unleash your drugs on the world. Human lifespan's based on complex biological and evolutionary factors, and nature doesn't tolerate radical or artificial change."

Travers turned to address the table. "Gentlemen, this is precisely the reason we've added a cultural anthropologist to the team. It's Dr. Rodgers' job to ask these kinds of questions. In Tikal, we will give you some answers. Ma'am, please continue to raise questions every step of the way. We want to hear them."

"I'll bet you do," she muttered. She gave Travers a cynical smile, then she pulled out a bright red cell phone and began furiously texting.

"We depart at six-thirty tomorrow morning for Guatemala," Travers said. "Until then, enjoy the amenities of the hotel as guests of Steele Pharmaceuticals and Nova Labs."

———— ◆ ————

Will Connors found his waterside villa and unpacked. He hung the contents of the garment bag, then carried his shaving kit into the bathroom. He caught a glimpse of his gaunt, roughened face in the mirror. For a moment, he failed to recognize the image staring back at him.

He had once been a rising star in science, a contemporary of Shimota and the others. He was now an outsider, considered an eccentric and no longer a part of this fraternity of scientists. He absently rubbed a hand over his chin and considered shaving. Instead, he returned to the bedroom and opened the satchel, removing a small photograph.

He stared at the photo. Connors felt a tremor of emotion as he studied the face of his little girl. He whispered a promise and kissed the image of her face, then tucked the photo back in the satchel.

He rotated his neck and reached up a hand to massage it, trying to unknot the day's accumulated tension. He decided to find the hotel bar. Connors hiked across the lush grounds to the Barefoot Bar, locating an outdoor table with a view of the bay. Sipping scotch, he gazed across the emerald bay. There was a big city beyond the water, with a cluster of gleaming towers rising against a blue-sky backdrop. It was a peaceful scene, and Will absently stared while he chewed on ice.

Tamara Rodgers walked in, absorbed with her cell phone and punching furiously into it. He examined the woman as she moved towards him. She wasn't overly attractive if each physical part were studied. There was too much nose, and she had chosen to highlight her prominent cheekbones with rouge. Some might criticize her wide mouth and the generous lips she'd covered with heavy lipstick. She was too tall for most men's comfort. But put the package together and Tamara Rodgers was an eyeful. She spotted him and walked to his table, laying the phone in front of her. He ordered drinks, then waited as she checked her lipstick with a little compact.

"So where have you been hiding the past two years?"

Connors arched his brows and said nothing.

"I know who you are," she said. "Dr. Will Connors. For a while you were the hottest researcher in the world. Everything you touched was magic. You developed the inoculation against multiple sclerosis. A year later you figured out a way to put insulin into capsules. No more daily injections for people with diabetes. You were all over the internet. Ted Talks. Soundbites. Interviews. Biographies. Paparazzi chased you like a movie star after you made the cover of Newsweek, and you were short-listed for a Nobel." She paused for a breath, staring expectantly at him.

"Then you disappeared."

Connors picked up his glass and examined it, then dumped a piece of ice into his mouth and chewed. He resumed staring across the Bay at the skyline of San Diego. Tamara waited expectantly for his response.

"I took a sabbatical," he finally answered.

"You dropped off the planet," she said. "Once in a while, you'd be spotted in some oddball place like Timbuktu. Then you'd disappear again. The media went crazy speculating on what you were doing." Tamara thrust her face forward and put on a pretty smile. "So what's your story?"

"There's no story," Connors said curtly. His body grew tense with annoyance at her prying questions.

Tamara shrugged in surrender, then turned her attention to the glass of wine. Her phone buzzed. She picked it up and studied it, then punched in a lengthy text before launching into another subject.

"That was some show today." She pursed her lips and dabbed at something with her pinkie.

He nodded. "You rattled Travers' cage."

She shrugged and sipped at her wine. "It's why they hired me. To point out things they don't want to see."

"This research could change the world," Connors said.

"That's the problem," Tamara said. "We have no idea if the world's ready for it. Or whether those changes are good for the world. And Travers? He reminds me of a carnival barker or used car salesman."

Tamara leaned forward and batted emerald eyes.

"Are you attracted to me?"

Connors shifted irritably and picked up his drink, catching the sarcastic remark before it escaped his lips. *Like I'm attracted to a buzzing mosquito,* he was about to say. He stared at her earnest face, bright with makeup. He could see her become nervous at his scrutiny. She reached up to caress a cheekbone and pulled her mouth into a crooked smile that softened her features. She seemed fragile at that moment, like a delicate porcelain doll. He exhaled slowly as his irritation faded.

"Most men would be."

"Why?"

"Well, you're....."

"Pretty?" She waved a hand toward her face. "I wear lots of make-up? I smell good? That attracts you to me?"

Will compressed his lips and twisted the glass between his large hands. "I hadn't thought about it," he said softly. "I don't see what that has to do..."

"Sorry," she said more softly, reaching across to squeeze his hand. "I didn't mean to embarrass you, but I was trying to make a point. Things aren't always the way they seem at first glance. This research looks pretty from the outside. You can't let appearances fool you."

He was studying her face as she spoke. "You're young to be a cynic."

"I'm old enough to recognize snake oil." She brought the wine glass to her mouth and swirled the ruby liquid. She took a sip, then she picked up the phone and began jabbing at it with both thumbs.

"This isn't snake oil," he said patiently. "It's science. We're going to Guatemala to inspect the Tikal Project. If the research represents good science and the drug has potential, we'll recommend its approval for clinical testing."

Tamara compressed her lips, revealing her frustration. She raised a ruby nail and pointed it at him. "It's not that simple. The Tikal Project isn't about science. Or helping humanity. It's about business. They've got billions of dollars invested in this research. Don't buy their crap about helping society or changing the world."

"I'll keep it in mind," he said. He could see that her moment of vulnerability was gone. She was brassy and aggressive again. "You always this suspicious of people?"

"Usually," she said. "But I will say that I'm also curious."

"About what they found in the jungle?"

She nodded. "I want to see this big discovery that's supposed to change the world."

"Me, too," he said. "The world could use some changing."

CHAPTER TWO

Steele Pharmaceuticals
Houston, Texas

Andrew Glass stared out the window at the sprawling decay of Houston. Miles of ratty neighborhoods spread in all directions from the gleaming Steele Pharmaceuticals Building. Glass gazed at the vista and wrinkled his nose in distaste. For the thousandth time in the past five years, Glass felt the urge to locate Steele's corporate headquarters in a city with some energy. New York would be preferable. Someplace further West, like Phoenix, would be better. Those cities were vibrant and growing, not laying fallow like the decaying shithole of Houston. He consoled himself with the thought that things would soon be changing. Andrew Glass moved from the window and focused his attention on the pair of men who sat in front of his desk. They fidgeted nervously, eyes trained on him like bird dogs.

Andrew Glass was among the youngest corporate CEO's in America, thirty-five years old and running the country's third-largest pharmaceutical company. Glass was well-suited for the job. All hard edges and controlled energy,

Ivy League-educated and hardened by years of clawing his way to the top. He was a man described in media profiles as an aggressive young lion perfectly suited for the competitive wars of the pharmaceuticals industry.

Glass had hired on at Steele twelve years earlier, starting as a drug rep and moving to the top in record time. Promoted to regional manager after three straight years of record sales, eighteen months later he was running the company's enormous East Coast division. Glass made corporate vice-president before he reached thirty. From that point, the final step in his mercurial rise to the company's top job was accomplished in less than five years.

Andrew Glass wasn't satisfied with his success because he knew the true giants of business had staying power. He admired men like Rockefeller and Hearst, and more modern titans like Bezos and Gates. These men had risen to the top and stayed there. Glass knew that ascending the corporate mountain had been the easy part. To assume his place as a legitimate business icon, he had to stay on top. Glass was aware that the next few weeks would determine if he possessed the mettle to join the company of these giants of the business world.

"Okay, Barney, let's have it," he said.

Barney Fried held a bulky folder in his lap. "We've got twenty-nine million shares of common stock in the public sector, after the two-for-one reverse split last August. Share prices have dipped under thirty-five over the past two weeks," reported the company's Chief Financial Officer.

"Merrill Lynch changed its recommendation from Hold to Sell. They don't like our short-term debt picture. Same with Schwab and a couple of other big houses. That loudmouth on the business channel is telling everybody to sell. Also, the P-E Ratio's over twenty-five now, and that's caused some institutional shuffling. Otherwise, nothing on the public front's changed much."

Glass stared speculatively at Barney Fried, causing the man to shift nervously in his hard seat. "Do a mock-up of a buy-back," Glass said, "five hundred thousand shares at thirty-five. I'll personally cover the shares. Get with the advertising people and have them work up a press campaign. Spread the word that we're buying back our stock because it's undervalued or some bullshit like that."

Fried nodded and scribbled a note. "I'll work this up and get back to you. It might take a couple of days. You want the quarterly sales figures?"

Glass nodded.

"Pretty much the same as last quarter."

Glass already knew the numbers. He stifled a surge of irritation and gave the man a stony stare as he waited for Fried to continue.

"Domestic sales are flat as a pancake, the same as they've been the last couple of years. Gross revenues haven't changed, but there's been product fluctuation. We're holding our market share for Rejuvex, and there's been a nice uptick in Depcor, but everything else has continued to decline. We're still losing market share in over-the-counter products." Fried exhaled and raised his hands. "Of course, the biggest drain on revenue is increased costs in R & D over the past three years."

The chief executive officer of Steele Pharmaceuticals tilted his head skyward as he contemplated the information. The company had been built on its line of cardiac and blood pressure medicines and had been a world leader in that niche for decades. Things had changed. Cut-throat competition had forced Steele to broaden their product line. Antidepressants and anti-wrinkle ointments had carried them through the next decade. Now even those standard-bearers had begun to fade in the face of stiff competition.

"What about Nuvor?"

"Foreign sales are great, particularly in Europe," Fried said. "We'll probably gross a half billion this year from European revenues alone. The Asian market's ticking up. But until the FDA says we can sell the drug in the States, we won't make any real money."

Glass could feel his blood pressure rise at the mention of the Food And Drug Administration. The agency's ridiculous restrictions and byzantine procedures routinely cost his company billions of dollars and years of delays in getting products to market. He felt his face flush in irritation.

His company spent ten years developing Nuvor and two years earlier launched the drug with great fanfare. Europeans were gobbling it up by the ton, and Glass had anticipated capturing a big piece of the American antidepressant market. His company was touting Nuvor as more effective than anything currently being marketed, and Steele would sell it at half the price of its chief competitor. In one masterful stroke, the company would capture the multi-billion-dollar antidepressant market and return Steele to its accustomed place as the industry leader.

Then the FDA sucker punched him.

"Any action with those assholes?" He'd directed the question at the third person in the room. Elliot Masters was a tanned and trim gray-haired barrister who'd been staring indifferently at his Italian wing-tipped shoes as Fried had briefed on Steele's financial picture.

"Nope," Steele's corporate attorney shrugged. "They want two years of clinical trials under their direct supervision before they'll consider approving the drug for domestic sale. They won't budge."

Andrew Glass slapped a hand on the desktop and spun to look again at Houston's smoggy skyline. He hated the goddamned Food and Drug Administration. Thanks to that collection of asshole bureaucrats, drug companies were forced to spend billions developing any new drug. It took a minimum of seven years to develop and test a medication, then years more of wading through FDA bullshit for their stamp of approval to sell it. Patent laws allowed only seventeen years of exclusive ownership of a product. That meant drug companies had a five-to-seven year window to recoup their investment. Most companies had to hustle to squeeze out any profit before competitors started spitting out clones.

It was a constant battle with every new drug. Andrew Glass resented the fact that his company's profitability was dependent on such an inept and slow-moving government agency as the FDA.

He abruptly dismissed Fried, who quickly gathered his documents and left the room. Glass leaned back in his chair and stared at Elliott Masters. The attorney studied his manicured nails and waited for his boss to speak. Glass twisted at a big ring on his finger as he considered the next item on his agenda. "What's the status of our acquisition?"

"It won't be easy." Masters arched his brows and shrugged. "Dowd-LaPorte is a multi-generational, family operated business. Most of the corporate officers are related to one another. These people aren't going to hand over their company without a fight. But they're vulnerable, and it's there for the taking."

Glass was intent on a hostile takeover of the little company, which held a niche position in the prescription drug market. A fringe player for decades in dental medicine, Dowd-LaPorte had developed a mouthwash that screened for oral cancer. Overnight, every dentist in the world started using it. The company was suddenly hot and its market value increased tenfold. Some in leadership were pushing for a public offering, a move opposed by the founding families. The conflict had gotten vicious, and blood in the water invariably drew predators. Dowd-LaPorte was vulnerable to takeover. That was precisely Glass' intention.

"What's our horizon?" He asked, although he already knew the answer.

"Forty-five to sixty days. After that, the opportunity's gone. We have to be ready."

"We'll be ready." Glass smiled at his attorney.

Masters raised his brows. "Question?"

"Go ahead." Glass shrugged.

"Why this rinky-dink company? And why now? I don't see the play, Andrew."

"I know you don't," Glass said.

The exchange was interrupted by the intercom.

"What is it?"

"Mr. Travers calling from San Diego," his secretary informed him. "He said you'd take the call."

"Tell him to hold a sec." He jerked his head towards the door, prompting Elliot Masters to stand and move briskly from the room. Glass punched a button and activated the speakerphone.

"How's California, Bob?"

"Nice, Andy," Travers' voice boomed into the room. "Clean and sunny, with tons of half-naked women running around. We oughta get our asses outta Houston and move out here."

"We might do that if everything goes well the next ten days." Glass picked up the handset and disconnected the speakerphone, lowering his voice. "How'd the meeting go?"

"Smooth as baby shit. Everybody got the briefing. There were sparks between Connors and Wilkinson, but we expected that. We're taking off for Guatemala City in the morning and should arrive at Tikal tomorrow afternoon. I'll let you know when we get there."

"How's the site team look?"

"What we expected. Bunch of friggin' eggheads, bickering like kids." Travers paused, humming into the phone as he thought. "Bohanon's making the trip. He's bringing new cameras to install around the perimeter fence. Infrared. Body heat detectors. High-tech shit."

"What about Connors?"

"He won't cause trouble," Travers said. "You know that. Neither will Rodgers. Great ass, by the way. The wildcard is Shimota."

"Don't worry about him," Glass said. "This inspection needs to go right. You know what's at stake."

"A miracle drug that's gonna change the world," Travers intoned. "Billions in profits for Steele, a shitload of glory for you, and a fat bonus for me. It's under control, Boss."

"Just pass the goddamn inspection," Glass snapped.

CHAPTER THREE

Lindbergh Field,
San Diego, California

The aircraft rose above the San Diego Bay in a steep takeoff, and the passengers applauded. They were on their way to Guatemala. A huge plane had been chartered for the site team, and the accommodations were first-class. The group had spread itself out inside the spacious cabin, and a pair of attractive flight attendants moved among them and offered every amenity.

Will Connors sat alone in the back of the aircraft, eyes closed and breathing deeply. As the plane leveled out at cruising altitude, he opened his eyes and picked up a newspaper. He soon tossed it aside. Tamara Rodgers sat a dozen rows ahead, looking radiant and engrossed in a technical report. Headphones covered her ears, and she chewed earnestly at a fingernail. He watched her fiddle with the cell phone, then she impulsively threw it down and began rummaging through her purse.

Bob Travers came lurching down the aisle in a sailor's gait. He was waving something over his head. "This came for you this morning."

He tossed the email printout into Will's lap. Connors stared at it, and the world's molecules rearranged themselves. Time became frozen. He couldn't breathe. He became aware of the hissing white noise that filled the aircraft. He watched as Travers made a slow-motion retreat. *She's gone. My little girl's gone.* He unfolded the paper with wooden fingers. He scanned the document, and the world slowly rotated back into focus.

It was only a job offer.

Dowd-LaPorte, a middle-sized research outfit in Northern California, was offering him a position as director of research. They wanted him onboard by the end of the month and were offering an annual salary of two hundred and fifty thousand dollars. He was surprised by the offer. He had no idea why they wanted him, or what might cause them to think he was worth such a sizable salary.

He reached into his satchel for the dog-eared checkbook and leafed through it. The paltry balance reflected the ruin that was his life. His every material possession was held in his garment bag and the satchel. Will chewed a lip and gazed at the email before stuffing it into the satchel.

He noticed that Tavey Bohanon had settled into a seat across the aisle. He nodded, and Bohanon grinned broadly. Will recalled Travers had identified the man as security chief for the Tikal Project. Bohanon looked the part. He had a broad, flushed face and a beefy body that severely stretched the seams of his clothing. Bohanon wore the blue cotton garb of a rent-a-cop, and the black baseball cap perched on his head was adorned with a Paragon Security patch. Will also noticed the man was wearing a sidearm.

"Big news for ya?" Bohanon asked in a rolling brogue, nodding towards the message.

"It might be." Connors said nothing more, and Bohanon appeared to get the hint. The man smiled easily and changed the subject.

"So, yer goin' ta find tha Fountain 'a Youth?"

"The pharmaceutical version, I guess," Will shrugged.

"Well, ye'll be lookin' in tha right place. They say Ponce De Leon believed fer tha longest time tha Fountain A' Youth might be down thar in Central America, 'n he spent a fair amount 'a time lookin' fer it in tha area. Only it weren't youth he was seekin', ya know."

"It wasn't?"

"Lak most things men do, it had ta do with sex. He thought thar' was a magical fountain in tha New World that restored fertility. He was tryin' ta find a cure fer *enflaqeucimiento del sexo*," Bohanon grinned and leaned conspiratorially towards Will, "what the old men 'a Spain called 'tha debility of sex'. Meanin' ta me that they couldn't keep it up. Accordin' to tha legend, ya could fix all that if ya dipped yer wick in these magical springs."

"You're well informed on this stuff."

Bohanon shrugged. "Ponce De Leon was a fascinatin' man, tha's all, with his searching fer tha' fountain, 'n such. Ah got interested in 'im, 'n did a bit 'a readin'. Thar's a shitload 'a stuff on tha man down at Tikal."

"I didn't know he looked in Central America."

"After discoverin' Florida, tha bastard sailed 'cross the Gulf of Honduras 'n landed in Belize. Thrashed around tha jungle fer half a year lookin' fer those magical springs. His landin' point's only a couple hunnert miles from whar we're headed. A bit 'a irony, don't ya think?"

"He wasted his life looking for a miracle," Will said.

"Take a sip 'a tha' water and ya'd stay young forever," Bohanon said. The man chuckled. "Or ya'd keep yer weiner hard, Ah s'pose. Ah figure Ah'd go traipsin' half-way 'round the world searching fer tha Fountain 'a Youth if Ah thought it was real. Ya could make a pile of money sellin' drinks 'a the stuff."

"I imagine that's what Steele Pharmaceuticals figures."

"Wall, nobody wants ta' git old. Ah figger most people'd take pills made 'a undiluted cow dung if they believed it'd make 'em younger."

Connors gave Tavey Bohanon another glance. There was something mushy about the man's voice, a slight rolling of words that was more than a brogue. His eyes had a glassy look and his face was flushed with sweat. Connors realized the man had been drinking, although it was barely eleven o'clock. He returned his attention to the porthole, watching the endless green forests of Northeastern Mexico pass below. He turned back to Bohanon.

"Why the need for a security person on this trip?"

"Jest hitchin' a ride. My comp'ny, Paragon Security, installed tha original security system 'round tha research site. Thar's a' eight-foot perimeter fence wi' five thousand volts 'a electrifyin' capability, a battery of infrared sensors, 'n a ten-man team a' security guards. We also set up a video monitorin' system. It's fierce damp down thar, 'n it's bloody hell on electronics." Bohanon unwrapped a big cigar and sniffed at the thing, then laid it on the seat. "We periodically go down 'n inspect tha facility, takin' care 'a routine maintenance 'n repairs, changin' out personnel, 'n makin' sure everythin's runnin' smooth. Ah've got some new equipment ta install."

"Seems like a lot of security."

"Wall, they've got some amazin' things in tha place," Bohanon said. "Ya'll be seein' some stuff tha next few days that ya won' believe. Things tha don' exist anywhar else 'n tha warld."

"What kinds of things?"

"Ah'll let ya see fer yerself," Bohanon smiled mysteriously. "Anyways, security's important. Tha site's sittin' in a sod'n jungle. An' don't forget thar's a couple 'a billion dollars worth 'a technology inside tha place. All their secret formula's, 'n such. They warry 'bout thar stuff gittin' nicked. But really, Nova's not just warried about wha might git out, ya know."

Tavey Bohanon chuckled and leaned across the aisle, bringing his flushed face an inch from Will Connors' nose. A heavy booze smell enveloped Will as the man winked at him.

"They're warried 'bout wha' might git in."

Bohanon flashed a toothy smile and reclined his seat. A minute later he was snoring.

Connors studied cloud formations through the porthole and noticed the aircraft was dropping through them. He sensed the change in pressure, and a minute later the airliner made a broad banking turn. Through the porthole, he could see the sprawling outskirts of a huge city that appeared carved from the green jungle. Rising thermals caused a few bumps as the airliner rounded into its approach pattern, but the pilot had flown this route before and fifteen minutes later they were taxiing to the main terminal in Guatemala City.

———— • ————

The first strange thing happened inside La Aurora's northern concourse.

They passed without incident through customs, which consisted of a fat Guatemalan guard in soiled khakis showing more interest in Tamara's undergarments than contraband. The site team straggled into the terminal building, which appeared surprisingly modernized given its primitive location.

The place swirled with a colorful mass of brown-skinned humanity. Every traveler seemed laden with wailing children, overstuffed suitcases and shopping bags. A woman chased a squawking chicken through the terminal, while onlookers shouted encouragement. Will Connors took in the chaotic scene, wrinkling his nose at the smell of disinfectant. He glanced at Tamara, who was staring with suspicion at a uniformed soldier. The man was lounging near customs, eyeing their party. An automatic rifle was slung carelessly over his shoulder.

Bob Travers jogged up and began herding the group towards a distant gate. Through the windows, they could see a cluster of private planes sitting on the runway. Travers was chattering about the itinerary when something in the stream of dark faces caught his attention. A skinny white man, going the other way. Travers whirled around, peering into the departing crowd.

"Hold it!"

Travers jumped into the mass of people, scattering bodies like a bowling ball. He ran to the Guatemalan guard and shouted something in Spanish. The soldier unslung his rifle, and the pair went running through the terminal. They disappeared around a corner, and a moment later a burst of gunfire rattled through the terminal. Everyone dove for cover. The site team hunched behind a plywood ticket counter. A minute later Travers came huffing back, exchanging a look with Bohanon.

"LeDoux," Travers said.

Bohanon uttered an oath. The beefy Irishman activated a cell phone and punched in a number, then walked away as he began talking. The site team clustered around Travers, peppering him with questions. A minor revolt broke out, with Travers facing off against an angry Will Connors.

"You tear off after somebody and fire shots in an airport," Connors said, his voice rising in anger, "and you tell us not to worry?" Tamara stepped forward and stood beside him, hands on hips.

Travers compressed his lips and started to say something, but appeared to think better of it. "This has nothing to do with us or the inspection," he said. "You need to trust me."

"We don't know you," Tamara said. "Why should we trust you?"

A look of menace flashed across his face, instantly replaced by a salesman's smile. He raised conciliatory palms. "It *really* is no big deal. The man is a petty smuggler, a low-life wanted by the Guatemalan government. I recognized him and ran over to tell the soldier. They chased him outside and the dumb-ass fired a couple of rounds in the air. Nobody was hurt."

"Did they catch him?"

Travers shook his head. "They will. Now can we please move along?" Travers began pushing, and the group reluctantly moved. They filed from the terminal and onto the runway.

"Everybody climb aboard." Travers pointed with a flourish at the battered twin Otter that was taking on fuel. The aircraft's body was peeling yellow paint. A nearly-flat tire had it listing precariously. Adorning its side was a sloppy logo that read Air Guatemala.

"We take this to Sangrita, which is three hundred miles to the North. We'll put down on a dirt airstrip outside the village."

"We're flying in that thing?" Tamara gaped at the dilapidated aircraft.

"Don't be deceived by looks," Travers said. "This airplane's the pride of the Air Guatemala fleet. It's logged fifty thousand flying hours and the thing's still ticking like a Rolex."

They looked doubtfully at the aircraft, which looked like anything but a fine Swiss watch.

The Otter rose to altitude and started bouncing across the tops of a swirling cloud mass that had formed above the tropical flatlands. His third flight in two days was too much for Connors. He canted his head and began taking long measured breaths, pretending he was anywhere but strapped into a raggedy airplane stuttering four miles above the jungle. Tamara sat next to him, lost in something emanating from her headphones. After a while she glanced over and laid a hand on top of his.

"Talk to me," she said. "It'll help you relax."

He wanted to continue staring out the window. He preferred to remain isolated in his thoughts, thinking about the Tikal Project and what it might mean to a frail girl. He shifted in his seat so that he could see Tamara. She was wearing the crooked smile again, the one that made her appear soft and vulnerable. The sweet scent of her perfume encompassed him.

"Okay," he said. "What shall we talk about?"

"Well," she said, "you could tell me what you've been doing the past couple of years."

He stared at the dark clouds flowing beneath the aircraft, feeling his stomach undulate. He turned back to Tamara, who was waiting patiently.

"Attending to personal matters."

"Have you ever been told you're a scintillating conversationalist?"

"Have you ever been told….." He stopped himself but couldn't keep the irritation from creasing his face.

Connors watched the starburst of hurt flare in her eyes. Now it was her turn to stare out the window. They listened to airplane noise for several long minutes. Finally he rolled his head towards her and offered an apologetic smile. "Sorry," he said. "Can we try again?"

She stared deeply into his eyes, apparently satisfied with what she saw. "Okay," she said. "Here's something that's got me curious. I know your recent research involves cancer. Why are you interested in the Tikal Project?"

"Because curing cancer and perpetuating youth aren't as different as you might think."

"They're not?"

"There's a protein in the body that affects cellular growth. Healthy cells have it, and so do cancer cells. This protein's genetically programmed to last only so long. When it stops working, you begin to die. If you can modify the protein and make it work longer, you can extend human life. Make it stop working in cancer cells, and *they* die. The people at Tikal are claiming they've figured out the first part."

"You believe them?" Tamara chewed on a lip as she studied him.

"I want to."

Nothing more was said, so she returned the headphones to her ears. After a while, she yanked them off. "There's obviously more to your story. What are you really doing here?"

He sighed and leaned back, massaging the bridge of his nose. "It's a long story. I'd rather not….."

Tamara Rodgers grabbed his arm and screamed.

Because at that moment they were nearly jerked from their seats as the plane dropped through a cloud layer and plunged towards the ground. Will felt Tamara's nails dig into his arm. The jungle rushed towards them, and at the last possible moment a brown strip of dirt appeared through the cockpit window. The aircraft dropped onto it and skidded to a halt.

———◦———

Fifteen miles due North of the dirt airstrip, Joseph Hermann stepped into an animal enclosure. He felt a sour hiccup of bile rise in his throat, and he clenched his teeth as he forced it back down. Hermann paused inside the steel-reinforced gate and inhaled the fetid smell. The putrid scent aroused a primal tingle of fear. He dropped a hand and gripped his sidearm. He raised his other hand and wiped the sheen of perspiration from his forehead. He took a tentative step into the enclosure.

Three dozen primates resided in this facility. All were valuable research animals, imported from around the world at great expense. Lemurs and howlers. Four African chimps, and a chattering family of green baboons from Kenya. The enclosure even contained a pair of huge mountain gorillas, illegally imported from the Congo and purchased for a million dollars apiece.

All were dead.

The floor was scarlet with blood. Shredded bodies lay scattered about the enclosure. Limbs had been savagely torn off. All the smaller monkeys had been ripped in half, while the larger ones exhibited gaping wounds and exposed internal organs. Hermann knelt by the male gorilla and stared at its bloody head. The mountain gorilla is the most powerful primate on earth. Yet this animal had huddled in the corner of its cage and cowered in terror when death arrived. Its massive skull was crushed. Hermann shook his head in disbelief.

Rising from the carnage, the blocky scientist swayed and extended an arm to the wall for support. He removed the handkerchief from a pocket and mopped his brow. He backed carefully from the gorilla's cage. Hermann slowly walked through the rest of the enclosure, taking in the devastation. Cage doors had been ripped from hinges and flung aside. Animals had been yanked out and torn to pieces. Not a primate was spared. Hermann spun and walked briskly to the enclosure's entrance, where a nervous team of Paragon guards stood waiting.

"How'd it get in?"

"Up there." The guard pointed skyward. Hermann glanced at the retractable dome that housed the garden and animal enclosure. The domed roof was standing wide open.

"It breached perimeter security, scaled the outside wall, and climbed on top of the dome? Then it jumped in here?"

The guard nodded. "We slide back the dome every night at midnight. It stays open six hours and we close it at daybreak. We also open it up a few hours during the day."

Hermann's brows shot up in alarm at a sudden thought. "What about Sheila?"

"She doesn't stay in the enclosure. The orangutan's fine, too."

"Thank God." Hermann looked again at the dome. "Keep it closed until further notice. When's Bohanon due?"

"The inspection team's in the air now. Bohanon's with them. Should be here this evening."

Hermann jerked his head toward the animal enclosure. "Clean up this mess before they arrive," he said. "Tell your men to shut up about what happened here, or there's hell to pay."

"Looks like hell's already been paid," the guard murmured.

CHAPTER FOUR

The Tikal Research Center,
Guatemala

Will Connors stepped from the Otter and into the jungle. The rest of the site team clambered from the aircraft and stood bunched together, examining the lush and exotic landscape. The dirt runway was cut into a tangled forest that spread in all directions. Towering trees extended gigantic connecting branches to form a canopy of green, creating the suffocating humidity of a hothouse. Arboreal life grew in profusion. Exotic animal sounds echoed across the narrow clearing.

There was a roaring sound from the jungle. Bob Travers burst into view driving a Jeep, with two others following close behind. After everyone clambered aboard, the caravan lurched into the jungle. They drove fast through the fading daylight, jarring along a rutted road that seemed freshly carved from the wilderness. Tamara Rodgers rubbed at goosebumps as she peered into the shadowy forest.

"Anything dangerous out there?"

"Jaguar's tha only thin' ta worry 'bout." Tavey Bohanon drove with one hand and pulled a silver flask from his boot with the other. "Lots 'a jungle cats 'n this region. Thar tha nastiest creatures on this earth, lassie. I doubt ye'll ever see 'un, though." He grinned wickedly at the wide-eyed woman. "Ya never do, until it's got ya in its jaws. Then it's too late."

Tamara shivered, Bohanon chuckled, and the expedition jolted onward. Night dropped quickly onto the jungle. Soon after, the skies opened and gave the landscape its nightly deluge. Canvas tops were snapped into place, and the vehicles continued their spine-jarring journey through rain-filled ruts. A blinding flash of illumination caused a whoop to escape Tamara's lips. An ear-shattering peal of thunder followed the lightning burst.

A loud crackling noise caused Bohanon to slam on the Jeep's brakes. They skidded to a halt. There was a surge of movement ahead, and a shrieking, tearing sound rose above the din. A huge tree slammed across the trail in front of them. The blocky man leaped from the vehicle and ran forward. He returned a minute later, shaking his head.

"Lightnin' strike," he muttered. "Thar's no way we kin git 'round it." The security man stared at the sky. "Tha rain'll stop in a half-hour. We'll pull out tha tents 'n camp here tonight."

"How far to Tikal?" Tamara's teeth were chattering.

"Three 'r four miles. We'll hike in tamarra' mornin'."

Bohanon set up tents, then the Irishman walked into the jungle and found chunks of wood dry enough to burn. Everyone settled around a flickering fire. Yanni Shimota sat cross-legged staring at a magnetic chessboard. The old man wore starched khaki's and an oversized pith helmet and appeared unfazed by the stifling humidity. Shimota dabbed at his forehead with a folded handkerchief as he studied the board. Wayne Wilkinson tamped at a briar pipe and awaited his move. The FDA man had imperiously ignored Will Connors all day. Bob Travers was perched on a low-hanging tree limb, engaged in an animated debate with Tamara about gene splicing.

Will watched as Tavey Bohanon stood motionless at the jungle's edge. The man's head was cocked, and he held a hunting rifle at the ready. Will walked carefully towards him.

"Everything okay?"

Bohanon lowered the weapon and reached for his boot. "Jest bein' careful," he said, raising the flask and studying it before taking a measured swig. "Thought I heard somethin', but I s'pose not."

"What was that commotion in the airport?"

Bohanon studied the other man a moment, then shrugged. "Travers saw somebody, tha's all. Man named LeDoux. He's one 'a them.....how kin I say..... aw, bugger, LeDoux's a friggin thorn 'n Nova Labs' side. Fancies 'imself some kind 'a mercenary. He tries ta nick things, 'specially industrial secrets, 'n sells 'em ta whoever's buyin'. He's a bloody goddam snake, nothin' more. Everybody in tha pharmaceuticals industry despises Anton LeDoux."

"Is he dangerous?"

"Don't ya' worry, Doc. Thar's not a bunch 'a blood-thirsty mercenaries hidin' in tha jungle, getting ready ta slaughter us all. This ain't a Spielberg flick. LeDoux's a weasel who makes a livin' outta stealin' things. The location of tha research center's technically a secret, an' LeDoux could probably sell tha site coordinates ta somebody if he knew 'em. We get a wee bit worried if he's in tha area."

"What's with the shooting?"

"Guatemalan's are crazy. They'll shoot at a friggin' flea if it bites 'em in tha arse." Bohanon slapped Connors on the back and extended the flask. Will shook his head, so Bohanon grinned and brought the whiskey to his lips. Connors returned to camp, brow furrowed in thought.

Hours later, in the black deadness of night, the camp was startled awake by a series of percussive bangs. Connors jumped up and ran from the tent. The others were gathered around the fire's embers. Shimota flipped on a flashlight and aimed its beam towards the jungle. The light illuminated Tavey Bohanon, who was pointing his rifle into the darkness.

"What was it?"

"Not a thin'," Bohanon said, "wild pig…maybe a jaguar. Go on back ta sleep, folks. You're as safe as in yer bedrooms back home."

"Give me a break," Tamara muttered.

High morning sun streamed through the tents and the travelers emerged to a glorious tropical morning. Gone was last night's oppressive atmosphere, and a festive mood infected everyone. They broke camp and began the hike to the Tikal Research Center. Travers walked in front and played scout-leader, energetically pointing out wondrous sights.

Connors paid no attention to the clownish man or the exotic environment. He was thinking about his little girl, and the last time he saw her. The disease was relentlessly draining the life force from her body. Her skin had taken on the fragile look of fine parchment. Her body had shrunk into itself, causing her to appear wizened and ancient. She was dying before his eyes, and Connors could do nothing to stop it. He had that same sense of helplessness now, and he felt an urgency to run from this jungle and back to her side. He slowly exhaled and forced away the dread. He reminded himself of the reason he was here.

He put away thoughts of Mollie and concentrated on the trail. Tamara moved alongside him. She was wearing headphones, swaying her body in rhythm to the tune blasting in her ear. He pointed to the headphones, and she pulled them down around her neck.

"What's playing?"

"The Eagles. Hotel California. Oldie but goodie. Wanna listen?" She extended the headphones, and Will raised them to his ears. He winced and handed them back. Tamara laughed in delight.

"Too loud for ya'?"

"A bit."

Tamara turned off the music, and they walked together along the rutted jungle trail. He glanced at her. "So what's a cultural anthropologist?"

Tamara shrugged. "Anthropologists study human beings in their natural state. I study the development of cultures – how they organize their societies, their religious customs and generational dynamics. How people live, what they do for fun. That kind of stuff. A few years ago, I got interested in primitive societies and how modern technology impacts them."

"I'd imagine," he said, "the impact's pretty significant."

"'Remember that movie a while back, about a Coke bottle that fell from an airplane and landed near an African village? The villager who found it believed the bottle had spiritual significance. That Coke bottle changed the village's way of life." She rolled her head at Will, flashing him a smile.

"Why are you going to Tikal?"

"Nova Labs invited me to give my opinions about these new drugs. They want me to anticipate problems in lifespan extension. You've already heard some of my objections to that idea. But that's not my only reason for making the trip. There's a native village close to the research facility. The villagers are barely past the stone tool age. It's likely the construction crew who built the Tikal facility were the first non-natives to visit this region in a half-century. I want to see what effect the Tikal Center has had on the cultural dynamics of the Guyama tribe."

"Like the Coke bottle?"

"Exactly. If I'm lucky, these Guyama tribesmen will have a musical culture. They might sing for me. Or dance. It's fascinating to see how common music is to all societies. Besides, I think this trip's a blast. I'm getting a ten-day trip to Guatemala, all expenses paid by Nova Laboratories."

They stepped into a clearing and there stood the Tikal Research Center. A large rectangular brick building three stories high, it appeared out of place in the dense tropical jungle. An array of satellite dishes and antennae rose from the building's flat roof, and in the rear a towering dome could be seen. Heavy chain link fencing ringed the complex and rolls of glittering razor wire sat atop the barrier.

A pair of security guards rolled open a double gate as the site team approached. They were ushered through the building and into a plush conference room. Bohanon deposited the inspection team, then the Irishman disappeared. A moment later another door opened and a half-dozen smiling men filed into the room. A squat and craggy-faced man with a powerlifters body stepped forward. Connors recognized him as Joseph Hermann, the man running the Tikal Project.

Hermann introduced himself and announced he would provide a brief orientation, then he would lead the team on a tour of the research facility. He smiled at his audience. "I may as well start with the question you all want to be answered. What have we discovered down here?"

Hermann took a deep breath, somberly eyeing the site team. "We've found something here – a living entity that doesn't exist anywhere else on Earth. It has unique and amazing capabilities." Hermann stepped aside and pointed at a small shrouded object on the table.

"I'd like to show you the most important scientific discovery in human history."

With that, he whipped off the cover and stood aside. Hermann was silent as the assemblage stared at a scrubby green plant barely a foot high sitting in a brown ceramic pot. Small oval-shaped leaves covered its branches.

"I give up," Tamara finally said. "What is it?"

"The natives call it jobara." The squat scientist leaned against the table and gently caressed a silky leaf. "This particular specimen is estimated to be fifty thousand years old."

Everyone gaped at the little shrub. No living thing on earth could be that old, and they all knew it.

"We've discovered a living organism with an infinite lifespan," Hermann said. He clasped his hands worshipfully, and his voice took on the wondrous timber of a preacher about to reveal a miracle.

"Let me tell you the story of the jobara plant," he said. "Sixty years ago, this region was explored by a group of anthropologists, including a woman named Margaret Staley. She was quite young, although later she became well-known. Some of you may have heard of her." He glanced at Tamara Rodgers, who nodded vigorously.

"Margaret Staley was also a botanist," Hermann continued, "and she found the jobara plant during the expedition. When it blooms, the flower's an incredibly bright purple color. I imagine that's what caught her eye. Staley dug one up and put it in her bag." Hermann stretched a leg, then began pacing. "She went home to New York, stuck the plant in a window of her office at Syracuse, and forgot about it." The man paused and arched his brows. "For more than a half-century."

"Doctor Staley retired in the late nineties, and while cleaning out her office she found the jobara plant. I'm sure she would have tossed it, except for one thing. Fifty-some years earlier, she'd wrapped a label around the plant's trunk. It said, 'Jobara Plant, Tikal Region, Guatemala, July 1959'. She took a closer look at the thing and discovered something that astounded her."

"Plant still alive," Shimota said. The old man held the jobara close to his face as he studied its branch system.

"And healthy," Hermann said. "The plant sat untouched in her window for fifty years. It wasn't watered or fed, yet the plant looked the same as the day she'd put it there." Joseph Hermann smiled. "Let me get to the best part of the story. Because Margaret Staley was retiring, she gave the plant to a colleague in the botany department. That colleague was a scientist named Paul Swanson. A few months later Swanson left university life for a more lucrative career in the private sector. He threw the jobara plant into a box and brought it along with him."

"Paul Swanson," Hermann continued, "went to work for Steele Pharmaceuticals in September of two thousand and nine. He was hired to study lifespan and aging factors in plant life. The following year the plant was taken into the laboratory and seriously examined for the first time. It wasn't long before this little shrub became the focus of the most intensive research scrutiny in Steele Pharmaceuticals' history."

"We had stumbled across something unique. It didn't take long to realize we possessed a living organism genetically programmed to live forever. Steele Pharmaceuticals recognized the jobara's potential and funded a secret research program. They built this facility and brought down a team of top-notch scientists. Let me boil down ten years of intensive research to some findings so amazing that they defy belief."

The scientist picked up the jobara plant and handed it to Wayne Wilkinson. The crusty scientist sucked on an empty pipe as he glanced at the plant, then he passed it to Connors.

"This plant in front of you," Joseph Hermann said, "is estimated to be fifty thousand years old. It will never die unless deliberately destroyed. Our genetic botanists tell us it takes a thousand years to mature, and flowers once every five hundred years. It's the most efficient living organism on earth, having built-in safeguards against disease and predation. The species mortality rate is zero. We've yet to find any remnant of a dead jobara plant. It grows only in a five-mile radius of this spot, and in ten years we've found exactly twelve of them. We're in the process of cultivating the jobara in the lab, but it'll be decades before we'll learn if we've been successful."

"What's its secret?" Connors rotated the plant in his hands, staring at it in fascination.

"This plant possesses capabilities unlike any other living organism on Earth. Its immune system has a unique way of defending itself against any invading disease or virus. Also, it has no DNA trigger code for degeneration, and it can indefinitely produce its protein-repair enzyme."

"Similar to lotus seed, from China?" Shimota asked.

"Precisely," Hermann said. Several years previously, a plant physiologist at the University of California had grown a green shoot from a lotus seed estimated to be twelve hundred years old. The seed came from a dry bed in China that was once the site of an ancient lotus lake.

Hermann glanced at a large gold watch. "If you don't mind, allow me to continue discussing the jobara tomorrow. I can demonstrate its miracles better than I can explain them." The scientist raised his big head and smiled behind his gleaming steel-rimmed glasses.

"I want to show you something far more interesting."

Hermann led them from the conference room and down a long corridor towards the back of the facility. He paused at a set of double doors. The scientist turned and half-bowed, throwing open the doors and spreading his arms with a flourish.

"I'd like to show you our little garden," he smiled.

CHAPTER FIVE

Steele Pharmaceuticals,
Houston, Texas

There was a wet bar in the corner. Andrew Glass reached into a polished mahogany cabinet to remove a chunky bottle of Chivas Regal. He grimaced and twisted his neck, trying to release the accumulated tension. Glass was perpetually wired, routinely working sixteen-hour days and wearing down the sturdiest of assistants. His office was as cold and functional as the man himself, furnished in chrome and teak. This was purely a workplace, as lean and efficient as its occupant.

Glass poured a slug into a heavy tumbler, then took a pull of the strong booze. He fidgeted in the darkness, absently clicking the glass against the enamel of his teeth. He moved across the room and onto the balcony, where he stood gazing pensively into the darkness. Houston looked different at night, garish and festive with illumination. The city emanated primal energy that seemed a powerful distillation of the masses of people moving through its streets. The light from a distant street lamp extended to his tower suite and reflected off his brooding face. The lamp's fluorescent glow revealed tiny lines of age that eventually mark all men.

Glass stared at the city and felt its energy pull at him. He detested the place, but its streetlight-illuminated boulevards held an edge that attracted him. Danger and violence lurked in the darkness. There was action down below. People dying on the streets. Weapons fired with deadly intent. Hookers selling their bodies. Thieves creeping into homes. The strong taking from the weak. Glass was confident he could thrive on Houston's mean streets. He saw himself as the apex predator - the lion, not the deer.

He craved any adrenaline high. He loved to skydive and was an avid extreme skier. Each winter he went to British Colombia and choppered to the top of an ungroomed mountain peak, then he would traverse the dangerous slopes alone. He was a regular in Las Vegas and received VIP treatment at the big casinos. Glass played high stakes blackjack and knew every trick to shave the odds. He was a wealthy man, indifferent to the money he won. Glass savored the challenge of winning against odds stacked against him. He believed he was smarter than the casino bosses who catered to his every whim while trying to rip him off. He enjoyed proving his superiority by taking the house's money.

Is this the best you can do?

Glass fingered the massive ring on his right hand as the gruff voice swam into his consciousness, as intimidating as it had been twenty years earlier. The ring was his father's, one of two things Andrew Glass had wanted after the old man had toppled over in an Oklahoma City motel room five years earlier. Glass had gone there to bury him. He remembered sorting through the pathetic residue of his father's life. Everything had gone into the trash except the ring and a pair of reflective aviator's glasses. The ring was of the heavy military type with a dark ruby setting. It was encrusted with the logo of West Point.

Andrew Glass had been a military kid, growing up inside the wide perimeter fences of one Army base after another during a well-traveled childhood. It hadn't been a bad life, just an insecure and constantly changing one. His father had been a stiff-backed academy graduate, sharp enough to survive twenty years of up-or-out pressures of the officer corps, but lacking the leadership abilities required for ascension to the senior ranks. His father became an embittered, passed-over major called Hard-Ass Glass by his troops. He was called worse by his three sons, because the man ran his home like a platoon. He was the lean and hard-nosed company commander with the shiny glasses, his wife the hapless aide, and his boys were Major Glass' little outfit.

Another memory floated unbidden from somewhere, causing Andrew Glass' mouth to lift in a tight smile.

He was standing in some kid's version of parade rest, hands nervously twisting while his father looked over the report card. Everything was great except history. Glass didn't like the subject, even at that age considering the past to be a waste of time. But he knew what was coming. The shiny glasses would come off, his father would twist at the heavy ring, and finally a stiff finger would stab at the offending grade. No blows would be struck, but the words would sting like a bullwhip. There would be the hard stare, and then the tongue lashing.

"A goddam C? Is this what you are? Average? Are you an average person? You're either going up or down, boy. You're

promoted or passed over. Is this the best you can do?" The
boy would stand trembling, saying nothing, feeling the warm
stream of urine insinuating itself down his leg.

What had happened was predictable. Andrew Glass
grew up and became precisely what his father had wanted,
a perfectionistic and brutal competitor who clawed straight
to the top. Glass set impossible standards for himself and
everyone around him, and his achievements never satisfied.

He sighed heavily and pushed the neurotic ideas from
his mind, then he abruptly turned and strode to his desk
as the phone rang. The shrill sound caused the other man
in the room to jump like a startled jackrabbit. Glass stared
at the phone until the ringing stopped, paying the man
no mind. Whoever was calling gave up, and for a minute
the only sound was Glass' clacking with the whiskey glass.
Barney Fried sat stiffly in a straight-backed chrome chair,
watching as Glass picked up the two-page document and
scanned it for the third time.

"When did this arrive?"

"Three-thirty this afternoon, hand-delivered by a
courier from New York."

"Has Masters seen it yet?"

"I took it straight to him and asked his opinion
concerning legality." Fried shrugged. "He says they're within
their rights. He's prepped a brief requesting a temporary
restraining order, and said he could file it tomorrow morning
in federal court. Said Judge Mullaney owes him a favor and
would grant the motion. But Masters doesn't think he can
do more than delay things for a week or two. And he figures
that'll make us look worse."

"Shit," Glass swore, and sipped nervously at the scotch. He picked up the letter and stared at it. "Cut through the bullshit, Barney," he said, tossing the document across the desk. "What's this goddam thing mean?"

Fried laid it out for him. The Securities and Exchange Commission was formally notifying Andrew Glass of their intention to invade his company. They demanded access to all financial documents relevant to the company's operations, including gross sales and revenues over the past ten years. They wanted production figures, purchase orders, shipping documents, sales invoices, personnel records. They intended to verify corporate cash surpluses by inspecting banking records covering the past decade. In a final slap, they demanded to interview all of Steele's senior officers including Andrew Glass himself.

"Fucking bastards," Glass suddenly raged, whirling and throwing the whiskey glass against the picture window. It bounced off the reinforced pane and shattered on the floor, splashing whiskey and crystal shards across the polished floor. "Mother fucking assholes. Nobody fucking tells me....."

Glass stopped abruptly and took a couple of breaths. He paced across the room and back, like a powerful caged animal. "Why, Barney?" he demanded. "Tell me why the fuck they're doing this to my company. Why me? And why right now, of all fucking times?"

"They're suspicious of our business practices," the accountant answered in a shaky voice. "There could be something wrong with our financial reports or tax returns. Maybe they suspect trading irregularities. Our stock's been falling, and I've been doing the buybacks like you ordered.

Maybe they're looking for insider stuff. Somebody could have filed a complaint. Or maybe they think we're cooking our books, to inflate Steele's financial picture artificially."

"What if we refuse?"

Fried raised his hands helplessly. "We can't do that. If we don't open up our books, the SEC can halt trading of our stock. And they'll do it if we're crazy enough to resist them. Believe me, this kind of thing's happened dozens of times. You can't strong-arm these SEC people – they'll take our stock off the board."

"And if our stock stops trading, then what?"

"That would be a disaster. It would be the end of Steele Pharmaceuticals as a publicly traded company. We'd be discredited in the financial world, and the public would lose faith in our products. Every share of preferred and common stock would be recalled, and we'd immediately lose every dime of working capital. This company would be bankrupt in sixty days."

The accountant wiped a sheen of sweat from his forehead. "If we're not able to keep a lid on this, major stockholders and institutional buyers will stampede. Just the whisper of an SEC inquiry could trigger a sell-off, and that would drive share prices into the ground overnight. And if these people come in here and find a serious problem, well, sir....." Fried shrugged grimly at his boss.

"Who's in charge?"

Fried scanned the document. "Raymond Towles."

"You know him?" Glass asked.

"I know of him," Fried shrugged. "He's supposed to be tough. Not somebody we want examining our books."

"Can you get us through this, Barney?"

"It won't be easy. This is a complicated situation – we're a huge corporation, with facilities and records spread around the world. It won't be like doing fancy bookkeeping for the IRS. These SEC people are sharp, and you can't mess with them. They'll come in here with the best forensic accountants and tax lawyers."

"You've got to find a way, Barney," Glass appealed in a fervent voice. "Put your staff to work around the clock. You've got an unlimited budget. Talk to Masters and have him bring in the best securities attorneys in the country. Hire the top consultants. Anybody you want. You've got to make this goddam SEC team go away." He leaned into Fried's ear and lowered his voice to a raspy whisper. "We're so goddam close, Barney."

Glass abruptly opened a desk drawer and rummaged through it. He pulled out a big corporate checkbook and scribbled a check. He tore it from the book and pushed the check across the desk. Fried picked it up. It was for two million dollars, post-dated to the end of the month.

It was made out to Barney Fried.

"Get us through this," Glass said, "and you can cash it."

He watched as Fried held the check in a trembling hand. Glass knew what was running through his corporate accountant's mind. Thoughts of retirement and a lifetime of financial security. Fried was imagining how his sons would look in Princeton blazers. Glass figured the little rabbit was fantasizing about walking away from the pressure cooker of Steele Pharmaceuticals, never having to count another bean. Fried appeared dazed as his boss walked around the desk and grabbed him by the arms.

"We're so close," Andrew Glass whispered. "Can you make it go away, Barney?"

Barney Fried looked at the two million dollars in his hand. He let out a shaky breath and nodded. "I'll make it go away."

He waved a hand and the accountant scurried from the office.

Glass flipped off the lights and sat in the darkness, sipping warm whiskey and clicking the glass against his teeth. He picked up the phone and dialed Elliot Masters' extension. The corporate attorney picked up on the first ring.

"This is fucked, Elliot," Glass said without preamble.

"It's a problem," Masters soothed, "nothing we can't handle."

"Our future's in Barney Fried's hands," Glass rasped. "Doesn't that concern you?"

"Our future's in your hands, Andrew."

"Let's push back the timetable."

"You know we can't do that," Masters said firmly. "We solve these problems now, or everything goes to shit. You have to pass the inspection in Guatemala. You have to get the SEC off your ass. And you have to buy your little company. That's all that's left, Andrew. Those three things. Get past them, and you'll be king of the world."

"Alright," Glass said. "I'll figure something out."

"Did you motivate Fried?"

"Post-dated a check for two million."

Masters chuckled. "That should light a fire under his ass. But you can't go up against Raymond Towles and his bulldogs with Barney Fried as your point man. They'll eat him alive."

"I know," Glass sighed. "You have a better plan?"

"How about Midlands Investigations?"

"We don't have much time," Glass said. "Take care of it, Elliot."

"I'll put Midlands on Towles' trail. Let's see if that old fucker's got any skeletons in his closet."

"Everybody does," Glass said. "Trick is to find them."

CHAPTER SIX

Renewal Gardens,
Tikal Research Center

They stepped through the doorway and into the Garden of Eden.

A lush park stretched before them. It lay beneath the high dome they'd glimpsed earlier, and the structure seemed vast from the inside. The dome's ceiling was holographically configured to reflect a brilliant blue sky. A smattering of clouds was included in the mosaic, and they appeared to float across the dome's azure backdrop. The ceiling was climatically controlled and electronically synchronized to precisely duplicate the weather and skies outside.

Joseph Hermann led the team towards the glass-enclosed control room built into the facility's North wall. He stopped them at an ornate fountain in the park's center. A circle of cerulean blue tile enclosed an emerald pool of sparkling water. A powerful column of water rose majestically from the fountain's center, gushing fifty feet before dropping to earth in a glittering cascade. Ponce De Leon Fountain was an amazing sight designed to impress.

Hermann motioned for the team to follow as he led them through the garden. The place had the misty, ethereal appearance of another planet. A profusion of unusual greenery grew in abundance, and good-sized fish splashed at the pond's surface. In another section, rows of domestic crops flourished. Bright beds of flowers grew everywhere. In a far corner of the garden was a wire mesh enclosure that sat dark and shrouded.

Hermann led the site team into the antiseptic control room. A wide panel of glass provided a panoramic view of the garden, and a bank of overhead monitors allowed for close-up viewing of each section. Teams of white-clad scientists sat at computer consoles, monitoring the garden's activity.

"Renewal Gardens," Hermann said, "is an incredible feat of genetic agriculture. The costs and challenges of building this place in the jungle were enormous. Suffice it to say you are standing in the world's most expensive indoor garden. Every plant, shrub, and tree in this park is genetically grown in our laboratories and transplanted into this garden. Each one has special and unique qualities. Let me start with the simplest elements and work up to the more complicated stuff."

A camera zoomed to provide a close-up of a lush lawn growing in front of the control room. "This is a common variation of Bermuda grass, but the seed that grew it was genetically developed at Tikal," he said. "Once planted, this particular strain will grow to a height of precisely two inches. Then it'll stop growing. It'll live forever, and will never need mowing. It's immune to all known parasites. This grass will only need occasional nutritional supplements that can be applied with a lawn spreader. If a section gets torn up, like on a golf course, you re-seed and regrow it. We call it Living Astroturf."

The man nodded at a technician, and the camera panned the profusion of plant life beneath the dome. The team watched in fascination as Hermann explained that the plants in Renewal Gardens existed nowhere else in the world and possessed unique capabilities. Each plant would develop to precise maturity, then level off and grow no further. Nutrients were added until a plant reached maturity, at which point it became self-sufficient. These plants would have an unlimited lifespan unless genetically triggered to die.

A young woman in a lab coat walked through the room, passing out firm tomatoes. "Those are domestic tomatoes," Hermann announced, "indistinguishable from ones grown in gardens around the world. Go ahead and take a bite."

Will Connors bit into the tomato and chewed impassively, then carefully laid it down. He looked at Tamara, who had a smear of juice on her chin. She gave him an enthusiastic nod.

"Good?" Hermann inquired, smiling benignly. "Those tomatoes were grown in Renewal Gardens. Believe it or not, they're five years old. They matured in less than a week on our genetically-produced vines. They've been unrefrigerated since two thousand and thirteen. They taste as fresh as the day they were picked. These tomatoes are designed to remain edible indefinitely, as will every crop grown in our garden."

"How'd you do this?" Tamara had taken another tomato from the basket and was studying it intently.

Hermann explained the process, which involved simple genetic programming. The DNA of a tomato plant contains a chemical code that triggers the production of a certain enzyme, called PGT in genetic shorthand. The PGT enzyme activates when the tomato is separated from the plant, and its function is to cause the tomato to decay. An ordinary tomato loses its starch and juices after seven days and becomes inedible.

The scientist held a large tomato aloft. "Normal tomatoes decay, but not this one. Our scientists have developed a strand of antisense RNA that blocks the translation of the trigger code for deterioration. The PGT enzyme is cut out of the plant's genome, and we splice in the new RNA strand. Our tomato never decays. The result is a fruit that never goes bad."

"So, everything in this place," Tamara called out, sweeping her hand towards Renewal Gardens, "is genetically grown, can live forever and needs no tending? These plants will produce fruits and vegetables that never spoil?"

"That's exactly what they do."

Tamara gazed raptly across the lush garden. "This kind of agricultural technology would ensure the world an endless supply of food. Famine, starvation, malnutrition—they'd disappear from the planet. It would alter the world."

"That would be correct," Hermann said.

"But the world doesn't tolerate radical change," she said. "This would result in unintended consequences. It could create chaos."

"You are again correct," Herman said. "We plan to integrate this genetic technology into society slowly. It will take years, maybe decades, before our products reach the market. We estimate five years to market for Living Astroturf and other agricultural products. Foods like the tomato will take longer, maybe twenty years." He shrugged. "People are funny about genetically altered food."

Yanni Shimota raised a hand and waited until Hermann nodded. "All very interesting," he said in a soft voice. "Park impressive, tomato fascinating and delicious. But what of Storsky's research, please? Was not his finding that genetically altered RNA trigger uncontrollable cell growth or mutation in host organism? How you fix this problem?"

A shadow of irritation crossed Hermann's craggy face. "With due respect to your colleague, Doctor Shimota, that's old research. Storsky published his studies a decade ago, and our current methods of genetic manipulation are vastly different. We've developed advanced protocols to guard against unprogrammed cell growth and genetic mutation."

Hermann watched as Shimota held a tomato to the light and scratched at its skin with a fingernail. The old man scribbled down a note, then stuck the tomato into a coat pocket.

Hermann waved a wide hand towards a large monitor. "Let me show you something that makes these advances in plant genetics seem like small potatoes, no pun intended." Hermann chuckled at his little joke as he nodded towards the monitor.

The camera swiveled towards the animal enclosure, which appeared deserted. Three figures emerged from a large gate and began walking across the park. One was a man who appeared ready for a lunar landing. He wore a bulky sterile suit and headgear. Strapped to his back was an oxygen tank. Two primates flanked the man. As the trio approached, it became apparent the spaceman was holding hands with an orangutan and a chimpanzee. Hermann motioned the team forward and led them to a wide Plexiglass window. The site team watched as the two primates cavorted around the spaceman, begging for the banana he held aloft.

"First let me tell you about Gus," Hermann said. He pointed at the orangutan.

They stared through the window at Gus. The animal moved in lazy response to his trainer's commands, shuffling languidly on knuckles and stubby legs as he participated in a sign language exchange. Gus had the typical elongated moon face and long red fur of the *Pongo pygmaeus* species, and he reacted with elegant indifference as the chattering chimp danced around him.

"He's a fifteen-year-old orangutan from Malaysia. We acquired him as a research animal three years ago. Gus is quite special. Watch the overhead monitor, please."

A video clip began running. It showed a medical vehicle drive through the gates of Tikal. A close-up shot revealed the young orangutan on a stretcher, lying motionless as it was carried into the facility. The scene faded to an operating room where men in surgical gowns clustered around the motionless animal. The men stepped aside as the camera zoomed onto an ugly puncture wound on Gus' hairy back. One of the surgeons reached forward with a scalpel and made an incision, and Hermann mercifully cut off the video at that point.

Then he told them the story of Gus.

Three years earlier, the orangutan was living a mundane life at the Lower Kinabatangan Wildlife Sanctuary in Malaysia. The orangutan is an intelligent and sociable creature with few natural predators, but it is vulnerable to poachers who harvest and sell its skull and penis. A poacher shot Gus in the back, then ran off when the game warden came to investigate. The orangutan was still alive, so the warden carried the poor fellow to the park office. A staff vet determined the bullet had shattered his spine, a complete C7 separation. Gus was paralyzed, and there was nothing anyone could do for him.

But fortune smiled on Gus that day. The morning he was shot, Nova Labs had messaged every game preserve and zoo in the world, asking to be informed about severe spinal trauma in primates. The vet at the preserve happened to see the message, and eight hours later a team of specialists was on the scene. Gus was stabilized and brought to the Tikal Research Center.

"That orangutan suffered a complete spinal separation?" Wayne Wilkinson seemed dubious. The crusty FDA representative walked to the window, watching as Gus shuffled sleepily on the grass. Wilkinson ran a hand through his thatch of white hair, then pulled the pipe from his jacket. He fiddled with it as he watched Gus. There were no observable limitations to the animal's movements or motor coordination.

"That's correct," Hermann said.

"You mean, you've.....?" Wilkinson turned to stare at the scientist.

".....found a way to regenerate spinal nerve tissue?" Hermann beamed. "Indeed we have, and Gus is living proof. We completely restored his spinal cord nearly three years ago, and he's regained his full range of motion. Gus has recovered all his physical abilities and suffers no adverse consequences of his bullet wound. It's as if he were never injured."

Hermann gazed out at the orangutan. "Scientists have been trying for a hundred years to find a way to reattach severed nerve cells, but until now it was considered impossible."

"How you do this?" Shimota asked politely.

"The human spinal cord grows during fetal development," Hermann said. "The trick was to find the code among the hundred thousand genes contained in the body. A decade ago the Human Genome Project did just that, identifying the specific gene in a human embryo. After that, it was simple to locate the marker in embryonic primates. Our researchers developed a synthetic analog and introduced it into the orangutan's spinal cord. It's a complex process, but look at Gus and you'll see our progress. Within three years this technology should be perfected, and in ten years you'll never see another wheelchair."

"And the chimp," Will asked. "Was it paralyzed, too?"

"No, she wasn't," Hermann said. "That's Sheila, and she represents something completely different."

Hermann nodded towards the chimpanzee, who was bouncing on all fours and screeching for a banana. Sheila had the brown mug face and lean body of an adolescent chimp. Hermann thumped the heavy glass with a thick knuckle as he continued. "Sheila represents a huge leap in biogenetic research. She's the culmination of ten years of intensive research and biological engineering by Nova Labs. She's the most unique creature on earth."

"If we measured her in human terms," Joseph Hermann said, "Sheila would be a hundred and thirty years old."

CHAPTER SEVEN

Renewal Gardens,
Tikal Research Center

Pan troglodyte is a single species in the family of Pongidae, of the mammalian order of primates. It's known by the more familiar name of chimpanzee. The most intelligent of the apes, their genetic design is remarkably close to homo sapiens. The species' cell structure and DNA configuration are nearly identical to humans, with a compatibility factor of ninety-eight percent. Because of their biogenetic compatibility, chimps are widely used in human research. So closely related are the two species that the concept of chimp to human organ transplants is under serious study. Chimpanzees are also being studied for the warehousing of human organs. A donor's heart or liver might be implanted into a chimp and kept there until needed.

Humans and chimps are extraordinarily similar in other ways. Chimpanzees have opposable thumbs, make and use tools, and are capable of walking upright. They possess complex language abilities and sufficient intelligence to learn and use sign language. Chimps in the wild organize themselves into sophisticated social systems that include family units and large communities.

The chimpanzee is a physical freak of nature, six times stronger than any human. A mature male can reach a weight of one hundred and fifty pounds and stand five and a half feet tall. They are intelligent and effective hunters, organizing into packs and utilizing coordinated stalking tactics. Chimps also possess human-like emotions. They kiss, hug and fall in love. Males are invariably promiscuous and are by nature jealous and possessive. A chimp can erupt into sudden rage and unprovoked violence, and inflict devastating damage. They form gangs, wage war, and ambush and kill one another.

Everyone stared through the window, watching Sheila in fascination as Hermann expounded on chimpanzees. Sheila had moved close to the reflective glass, attempting to see her audience. The chimp had an intelligent face and expressive eyes, and her coat had the glossy sheen of good health. She began chattering and pounding on the glass, then scampered over to the door and vigorously tried the handle. She wanted to come inside and meet her visitors.

"Despite their innate aggressiveness, most chimps are easy to work with in the lab," Hermann was saying, "because their learning curve is impressive, much greater than previously thought. They catch on easily and love to work for rewards. The species has a gestation period of eight months, achieves sexual maturity at age twelve or thirteen, and their lifespan in the wild can reach fifty years. They don't live nearly that long in captivity. Chimps used for research rarely live past thirty."

"Why the space suit?" Connors nodded in the direction of the primate's trainer.

"Routine precaution," Hermann said. "We're in new research territory down here, working with laboratory-bred plants and genetically-altered animals, and we want to be careful. There's a lot of time and effort tied up in Sheila. We want to protect our primates from human viruses and infections, and vice versa, so we use a sterile environment whenever possible."

"Can we see her up close?" Tamara Rodgers moved to the window and was waving and making faces at the chimp. This caused Sheila to jump and shriek with excitement.

"Not this morning," Hermann said. "Perhaps later in your visit."

Captivated by Sheila's antics, they continued to watch her cavort in the garden. The chimp was scampering back and forth across the grass, performing various tasks assigned through hand gestures by her trainer. It was apparent that she was going through the paces of a well-rehearsed routine. Finally she came and sat by the man, bouncing restlessly as she held her palm upward. The trainer smiled and reached into a bag, handing her another banana. Sheila expertly peeled the fruit with hands and feet, relishing her reward.

"Sheila may look like a normal chimp," Hermann said, "but she's far from ordinary. She's nothing less than a research miracle and represents the future of Steele Pharmaceuticals. We estimate there's close to a billion research dollars tied up in that ape, and she reflects the leading edge of Nova Labs' research program. We asked you all to come to Tikal for the express purpose of showing you Sheila. Now let me ask one of you a question."

He nodded at Yanni Shimota. "Doctor Shimota, based on Sheila's physical appearance, what would you guess her age to be?" Hermann watched as the diminutive scientist moved close to the window and observed the chimp, scratching his chin in concentration.

"Must consider fur coloration, muscle tone, and general behavior within species context," Shimota said. "This chimp in good health, and very active. She appear in late juvenile stage, perhaps nine or ten. Twelve to fifteen years at oldest."

"In many ways, that's absolutely correct," Hermann nodded. "But Sheila was born in nineteen-seventy, in the St. Louis zoo. Nova Labs bought her seven years ago, and we've had her ever since. Last month we had a little birthday party for Sheila. That chimp's forty-eight years old. That makes her the oldest captive chimp on record, a fact we'd be happy to irrefutably prove. We have her birth records, chronological history, ID tattoo, and DNA samples drawn every month for the past ten years."

Connors moved closer to the glass. He stared speculatively at the cavorting chimp and wondered if what he came here to find might be circulating inside this animal's body. He gave it considerable thought before returning his attention to Joseph Hermann.

".....thus far she's been immune to biological disease, and her heart and vital organs are completely healthy," the man was saying, in response to a question from Shimota. "About a year ago she lost her gray muzzle and her muscle tone began firming. She's gradually taken on the appearance of the young chimp you see dancing around out there."

"Excuse me," Connors called out, "are you talking about cellular immortality, Doctor Hermann?"

Joseph Hermann smiled indulgently.

"I can't believe you've solved it," Connors murmured. Cellular immortality was hallowed ground to genetic theorists, a nirvana-like concept endlessly debated but considered impossible to create. Will stared transfixed as Sheila tugged impatiently at the trainer's hand. The chimp was making a series of exaggerated hand gestures, demanding to be held.

"The technology's far from perfect," Hermann said. "We've got bugs to work out, but you'll have to agree our progress is spectacular. We've taken an ancient primate and made her young. When you begin your facility inspection tomorrow, I'll bring you up to speed on problems we're still trying to solve."

Connors stared again at the chimp and felt a tremor of excitement. He reached into his pocket and ran his fingers around the outline of Mollie's photograph. He absently rubbed a hand over his unshaven chin and recalled the events of the past year. The worst of his life, a jumble of bleak diagnoses and failed treatments. And now, emotions he hadn't felt in a long time - a faint plume of hope and possibility.

"I have a question," Tamara broke in. She was staring speculatively at Sheila. "You said somebody's doing chimp-to-human organ transplants. Are you doing anything like that on a genetic level? You know, injecting chimp DNA in humans, or the other way around?"

"No," Herman said flatly. "That would be unethical."

"What about cloning?"

"That's not our research objective."

"I have another question," Tamara plowed on. "Have any of your animals ever escaped from this facility? Out into the jungle, I mean?"

"Absolutely not," Joseph Hermann assured her. "We've never lost a laboratory animal in the ten years I've been here. We have fail-safe inventory procedures, and Mr. Bohanon has installed strong security measures to ensure nothing like that could happen." He smiled and held Tamara Rodgers' gaze.

It wasn't the first time that morning that Joseph Hermann told a lie.

———————

Two miles due East of the Tikal Research Center, a bright midday sun illuminated the vast greenery of the rainforest. A fine mist rose swirling from the dense jungle floor. Although most of the world's rainforests are located in Africa and South America, a slender finger extends northwards into the *Peten Itza* area of Guatemala and results in a far different topography than is found in the country's southern region. Not a bare patch of ground exists anywhere. Thick vegetation of all kind grows in profusion, crowded together in intense competition for precious root space and access to sunlight. Gigantic kapok trees tower two hundred feet overhead, their vast canopies shading acres of earth beneath them, while thick *liana* vines crisscross the ground and twist themselves around every available tree-trunk. So varied is the landscape that a single square mile of rainforest contains more varieties of plant and arboreal life than the entire continent of North America. Thousands of animal species exist within the rich panorama of the rainforest, and all occupy a specific position along the jungle's remorseless food chain. Every creature feeds on other living things, and each is prey to something stronger or faster.

In a tiny forest clearing that somehow existed among the towering greenery and relentlessly spreading undergrowth, the atmosphere was dead calm and heavy with humidity. Nothing stirred in the jungle heat, and even the incessant buzzing of insects seemed to have abruptly stopped. Some natural dynamic was occurring, and a rapidly accumulating tension hung in the hot air like an approaching thunderstorm. It had taken a few moments for the jungle to assume the crouched and silent atmosphere that signaled a pending confrontation. Things remained this way for another ten minutes, with nothing moving and not a sound being made.

Finally, a tiny rustling disturbed the heavy foliage bordering the far side of the clearing as something shifted and rose stealthily from hiding. The animal stood on two legs and scanned the area with cold, unblinking eyes as its sensitive nose carefully tested the air.

Satisfied, it stepped cautiously into the clearing.

The Guyama warrior stood like a statue in the shadow of a towering kapok tree. His ebony eyes were riveted on the quarry he'd been hunting for days. Every muscle in the warrior's lean body was tense as he observed the animal move from concealment and expose itself in the clearing. The man's copper face was painted blood-red with river mud, and the lone eagle's feather braided into his hair signaled his readiness for a battle to the death. His hands gripped a small bow and quiver of arrows. Each triangular tip had been dipped into a deadly paralytic drug made from the skin secretions of the bright orange tree frog native to this region. The slightest penetration of skin would instantly bring down any creature in the Guyama warrior's world.

The warrior had tested his arrow earlier in the morning, shooting it into the shoulder of a black monkey he spotted high in the branches of a *Ceiba* tree. The animal had instantly fallen to the ground, paralyzed and suffocating. But despite his formidable armament, the man felt a shiver of fear course through him as he stared across the clearing at the animal he planned to kill.

The warrior's nostrils flared as he remembered his wife and infant son, and the horrific things done to them. Hatred encompassed his heart as the images flashed in his head. Bubbles of blood on her lips as his dying wife gasped a description of the animal. This creature standing in the clearing forty feet away.

This was the thing that had killed his family.

The man felt revulsion in his stomach as he stared at the animal. He didn't know what it was. Part of it looked like one thing, and the rest like something else. He'd never seen anything like it. He didn't care what kind of creature this might be. In a minute the thing would be dead.

He carefully notched an arrow into the bowstring, and slowly raised it to his shoulder. The creature sensed the movement and turned towards him, giving the warrior a perfect frontal target. The man drew the bow so deeply that a thumb touched his copper shoulder, then he exhaled softly and released the bowstring.

The arrow made a whisper as it flew across the clearing and embedded itself in the creature's chest. The warrior felt a shiver of anticipation as he realized his aim had been true. In an instant, the animal would fall paralyzed to the ground, then the warrior would take his knife and do to it what the thing had done to his family.

But the animal didn't fall.

Instead, it looked dumbly at the feathered shaft protruding from its chest, then raised its black eyes to the Guyama warrior. A low rumbling arose in its chest. The man's resolve turned to terror as the creature began to move towards him. The warrior dropped his bow and ran in panic through the thick jungle, nearly hysterical as he heard the beast crashing behind him.

One thought penetrated his petrified mind as the man ran for his life. He was sure he had prepared his arrows properly, his draw had been strong, and his aim perfect. The animal should be dead, suffocated by paralysis and cut to pieces by the warrior's angry knife. But it hadn't died. It was alive and chasing him through the jungle. This was the single thought that formed itself in the Guyama warrior's mind as he heard it draw nearer.

Why hadn't it died?

CHAPTER EIGHT

**Midlands Investigations,
Chicago, Illinois**

Scottie Bowers wasted no time in starting the excavation.

Although he was planning to dig up some dirt, Bowers wasn't in the construction trades. He was the head of Midlands Investigations, a small security outfit with a select client list that included Steele Pharmaceuticals. Bowers was paid a hefty annual retainer by the drug company for his services, and he wasn't perturbed that Elliot Masters' call roused him from a solid sleep. After-dark urgency was the norm in his profession. Everybody who called wanted some kind of information, and they always wanted it immediately. Bowers had listened patiently to Masters' request for a background investigation of Raymond Towles. He barely grunted at the two-day turnaround. Scottie Bowers hung up the phone, then sat on the edge of the bed and smoked a Marlboro.

Midlands Investigations was located on the third floor of a towering reflective-glass skyscraper in midtown Chicago. The office had been professionally decorated and the atmosphere inside was muted and professional. High-grade prints of various military aircraft covered the walls. Bowers strode briskly through the deserted office, flipping on lights and equipment along the way. Jockey-sized and crew-cut, he had the hard and triangular frame of a gymnast. Only the lines in his face and a sprinkling of gray above the temples gave a hint that he was approaching sixty.

Scottie Bowers was not the typical private investigator. He'd logged twenty-one years in Air Force intelligence, retiring as a full colonel with a chest full of medals and a pack a day habit. Bowers had spent his military career ferreting out the secrets of others, so was natural that he continued along these lines in the civilian world. But Bowers was the antithesis of the stereotyped private eye squeezing out a living by peeping through windows at philandering spouses. Bowers was a different breed. He was a serious investigator, trained in espionage and adept at uncovering the secrets of nations. He was well-versed in the use of technology. His military intelligence tools had included satellite imaging, covert surveillance, and computer stealth. Bowers applied these levels of sophistication to his current occupation.

He had chosen the fertile field of industrial espionage as the target market for his services, establishing Midlands Investigations as an elite and unusual investigative agency. Scottie Bowers charged outrageous retainers and accepted only a single client from any particular area of business. This practice ensured confidentiality and eliminated conflicts of interest. Steele Pharmaceuticals was his sole customer from the drug industry.

Bowers had established a reputation for discretion and efficiency, and his services were in high demand in the cutthroat world of industrial spying. Midlands was a one-person shop. Bowers handled every investigation, utilizing a nationwide network of trusted contacts. Over the years, Bowers had cultivated relationships with operatives in various law enforcement and intelligence agencies. He paid his connections huge under-the-table sums for information and never exposed a source.

Bowers lit a cigarette and watched curling smoke drift to the ceiling as the computer booted up. He pondered Elliot Masters' request. The man had asked for a rapid and thorough investigation of Raymond Towles. Masters hadn't minced words. He wanted Bowers to dig up something negative on the man. Bowers had asked no questions. Whatever Steele Pharmaceuticals was doing, it wasn't his concern. Masters had provided Towles' full name and told him the man worked for the Securities and Exchange Commission. It was all Bowers needed.

He opened his computer and accessed the website for the Federal Census Bureau. He entered a screen name and twelve-digit password, and a second later was granted access to the agency's data banks. He requested a search for all available information on Raymond Towles. Bowers watched as a stream of data scrolled across the screen. He ordered the info printed out, and a minute later signed off the system.

Bowers leaned back and examined what the data banks had yielded. A single page, it contained Towles' home address, birthplace, family composition, work and business phone numbers, income bracket, and social security number. Scottie Bowers nodded in satisfaction. Armed with this information, he could unearth anything about Raymond Towles. Bowers picked up the phone and began calling his contacts, starting with an FBI agent who worked at the Hoover Building in Washington.

An hour later the fax machine came to life and information began flowing. Bowers enlisted three investigators in Washington and a couple of others in Towles' home state of Louisiana. He studied each individual report as it arrived, then began building a profile on his quarry.

Raymond Towles was sixty-two years old, and a legendary SEC asshole. He had worked thirty years for the Securities and Exchange Commission and was roundly disliked. Towles was a career investigator who bragged openly about the big companies he had brought to their knees. The man had made a career of chewing up companies like Steele Pharmaceuticals. Wall Street scuttlebutt was that Raymond Towles constituted the worst nightmare for any company with something to hide.

Bowers perused a news story that appeared in last week's Journal. The article trumpeted Towles' brilliance in uncovering research shenanigans at Decker-Brown Pharmaceuticals, a major Steele competitor. Thanks to Raymond Towles, a pattern of fraud had been uncovered, resulting in a billion-dollar fine. The company had been forced to pull an entire line of anti-hypertensive medications from pharmacy shelves around the world. Not only were the company's financial losses monumental, the Decker-Brown CEO was summarily fired in the aftermath of Towles' investigation. Raymond Towles was often described as looking like a mournful basset hound, but it was obvious the man was no dumbass. Scottie Bowers studied Towles' profile and knew that Steele Pharmaceuticals was in very deep shit.

By noon most of the reports had arrived, and Bowers chain-smoked as he perused each one. Nothing about Raymond Towles jumped off the page. Towles had been married forty years and lived in a modest Georgetown suburb. Four grown children. Didn't drink or smoke. He had no criminal record. Towles had served two years in the Army, earning an honorable discharge. The man made two hundred and eighty-five thousand dollars a year and appeared to live within his means. According to Bowers' FBI contact, the Bureau's folder on Towles was empty.

This paltry information didn't faze Bowers. He knew secrets were always well hidden. Scottie Bowers possessed a disciplined military mind, and his investigations were systematic. This initial gathering of information was merely a high-altitude flyover, a general reconnaissance to determine the lay of the land. Bowers knew he wasn't going to find dirt on Raymond Towles through a simple background search. He'd have to dig deeper to find anything interesting. The fax whirred again, and Bowers walked over to grab the latest intel. An itemized list of Towles' checking transactions the past two years. A decade of income tax returns and a copy of the man's stock portfolio. Bowers pulled out a cigarette and tamped it against his watch face as he considered his next move. He decided to spend a couple of hours going over Towles' financial documents.

Then he'd fly to Washington.

CHAPTER NINE

Tikal Research Center,
Guatemala

"You go in jungle?" Yanni Shimota asked.

Tamara nodded vigorously. She was sitting cross-legged on the floor, fiddling with a digital recorder. She planned to hike into the jungle in the morning to visit the Guyama village and wanted to make sure her equipment was in working order. The old Oriental was sitting on the edge of the bed, squinting at a spiral-bound notebook. They were in Tamara's room. One wing of the research facility was set up dormitory-style, with team members assigned to small windowless rooms.

Tamara had already unpacked her suitcase, stuffing her belongings haphazardly into drawers. She quickly became bored with the Spartan setup, so like a dorm rat she propped open her door and waited for someone to wander past. When Shimota emerged from his room, Tamara collared the academic and pulled him in for a chat. She soon had the old man blushing with her flirtatious behavior. They were an odd pair, Shimota the grumpy stone-face and Tamara a teasing adolescent, but she was relentless and endearing. Not long afterward Shimota was showing her pictures of his kids.

"Careful out there," the old man cautioned. "Dangerous in jungle."

She smiled and gave him an exaggerated bow.

Shimota studied her. "You like garden?"

"I can't believe I'm saying this," she chewed on a lower lip, "but I'm impressed. What they're doing is like something from the Sci-Fi channel. They're growing crops that could solve world hunger, and the plant life in Renewal Gardens will put every landscaper in the world out of business. They've figured out a way to re-connect spinal cords, and that means paralysis might be eliminated. According to Hermann, they've developed a medicine that made an old monkey young. For me, it's magical. Almost unbelievable."

"Is hard to believe," Shimota agreed.

The old Oriental flipped shut his notebook and stood. "Thank you for visit," he gravely bowed before Tamara. "Must prepare for inspection tomorrow." Shimota moved stiffly out the door, nearly bumping into an incoming Will Connors. The startled academic bowed and muttered an embarrassed apology, then scurried down the hall. Connors stood in the doorway, watching Shimota's hasty departure with bemusement. He cocked an eye at Tamara as he moved into the room.

"I like him," she announced saucily, "he's a nice man. Not nearly as stuffy as you might think."

"Oh, really," Will said, stifling an irrational surge of jealousy.

"Yes really." She intently studied a fingernail. She grabbed her cell phone and studied the little screen, then threw it down. "Can you believe he's been married forty-six years? He's got seven kids, two in medical school at Harvard. Says his kids run all over him. Not only that," she chattered, "he's department chair at Yale and a world authority on genetic engineering."

"I knew the last part. He hasn't deemed it necessary to tell me anything personal about himself."

"Maybe you don't know the right way to ask," Tamara said, raising her brows flirtatiously and flashing him a smile. Her face was made up, although they were three thousand miles from civilization. Bands of glittering mascara highlighted her eyes, and her generous mouth was smeared with ruby lipstick. She was wearing multi-hued tights and a designer sweatshirt. Her sneakers had purple tassels that matched her eyeliner. Will Connors was fascinated by the getup, and couldn't stop himself from giving her the once-over. Tamara boldly returned his stare, and he dropped his eyes in embarrassment.

"Maybe I don't," he shrugged. "Whatcha doin?"

"Getting ready to go to the village," she said. "Talking with Yanni about the stuff we saw today. What'd you think, Will?"

"Impressive," he enthused. "These genetic advances will change the world. And I can't believe *I'm* inspecting the research of Joseph Hermann."

"Is he big?"

"Hermann held a department chair at Harvard for years, doing serious research. His name's everywhere in the genetics literature. His books were required reading in my undergraduate program. A few years ago he resigned his tenured chair – something rarely done at Harvard – and dropped out of sight. I guess Nova Labs dangled some big dollars under his nose, and now he's in Guatemala."

"Anyway," Will dropped onto the floor and stared at Tamara, "what do you think about Renewal Gardens?"

"I came down here with an agenda," she admitted. "My concerns are about the social costs of extending lifespan. Scientists should be careful about what they unleash on the world. I'm not convinced anyone's really thinking about the consequences. But now that I'm down here, seeing all this….." She shook her head in wonder.

"What about Shimota?"

Tamara grinned. "He's Asian. Inscrutable. But he thinks the makeup of the inspection team's unusual."

The team was preparing to investigate the most significant scientific development in human history. This genetic technology held the potential to change the world – on the level of a moon landing or discovering the cure for AIDS. The secret to immortality might be found in these laboratories. The implications were enormous. Shimota had pointed out that no team member had any significant experience conducting FDA inspections. It was the first one for Connors. Wayne Wilkinson was the team's nominal chief, yet the perpetually irritated man was a relative unknown, a department chair at a small university in Montana. Only Shimota's appointment to the team made sense, as he was a respected authority on genetics.

"Yanni thought the FDA could have assembled a more experienced team," Tamara said. "Maybe included an expert on age reversal. Don't you think it's a little odd?"

Connors shrugged. "I don't know," he said. "I hadn't given it much thought."

—————◆—————

The next morning they gathered in a staff dining room and ate a cafeteria-style breakfast. Will settled for strong black coffee, sipping the stuff as he watched the early-morning activities. A flush-faced Bob Travers was making his rounds, doing a pitchman's routine as he back-slapped and pep talked like a wired-up coach preparing his team to take the field.

Tamara, resplendent in a khaki ensemble and Aussie bush hat, breezed in and announced she was going into the jungle to find the Guyama village. After turning up her nose at breakfast, she grabbed a piece of fruit and sat down across from Yanni Shimota. She started chattering, and the impassive man immediately broke into a shy grin.

Joseph Hermann entered the dining room and announced the morning would begin with a tour and a short briefing. The team would then be free to start inspecting. The blocky scientist led everyone down a wide hallway and into the research center's west wing, where the lab was located. Shimota and Connors exchanged puzzled glances. They had expected a large and centralized facility, but Nova's arrangement was quite different.

A series of small rooms had been set up, each one accessed from the central corridor. Each lab contained identical equipment. A long stainless-steel laboratory table with a row of high-tech magnifying instruments, including an atomic force microscope. Above the table, arranged in a uniform line, were flasks of rose-colored liquid. These contained human cells suspended in a nutrient solution of amino acids and vitamins. A pair of steel vats were located in the corner, all filled with liquid nitrogen and assorted cells in long-term frozen storage.

A parallel table held a variety of specialized devices, including a Gilson micropipettor and a 96-well microtitre plate. Will paused to stare at the gleaming Eppendorf, a high-speed centrifuge the size of a portable radio, and a pair of bioreactors. He whistled appreciatively. He'd only seen equipment like this in vendor booths at conventions and was amazed at the Nova Labs' set-up.

He noticed a Novell server on a corner table. Each workstation had a computer terminal and monitor. At the far end of the room a segmenter and a DuPont biolistics unit were hard-wired into the computer. Will Connors stopped to admire the biolistics machine, which genetics researchers called a "particle gun." He gazed through the double eyepiece, then wrinkled his brow as examined the complex control panel.

"What do one of these babies go for?"

"Two million a copy," Hermann said proudly, "but the technology is incredible. This machine can embed a tiny piece of genetic material into a particle of tungsten, then fire the particle into a cell nucleus with perfect accuracy. An electrical charge vaporizes a water droplet, which explodes like a cartridge and transfects the genetic material into the cell body. With computer-aided optics and targeting, there's no error tolerance. It makes gene splicing a piece of cake."

The scientist nodded towards the segmenter. "'Course, we still use restriction enzymes and electron beams to cut and section DNA molecules, but the biolistic unit's faster and more accurate."

"I assume these facilities meet federal standards for clean rooms." Wayne Wilkinson frowned and ran an index finger along a table top. He studied his finger as if expecting to see dirt.

Hermann nodded in affirmation. He explained the facility was a Level Four containment structure and carefully controlled for contaminants. Every laboratory was equipped with particulate filters, walls were painted with dust-resistant materials, and lab stations equipped with laminar flow hoods. Federal inspectors visited twice yearly and had never written up a violation. Hermann offered to provide the team chief a notebook containing years of inspection results. The crusty Wilkinson declined with a shake of his head and ran his finger along another tabletop.

"Excuse, please," Yanni Shimota said. "Forgive silly observation. Your laboratory very fine, and equipment first-rate. Best I have seen anywhere. But layout unusual. Small rooms do not inhibit communication among scientists?"

"Not at all," Herman responded. "We have daily staffings, and all research data is fed into a common data bank. This environment allows our people the isolation and freedom from distraction to do their work. As you know, Doctor Shimota, geneticists work in a sub-cellular world. Much of their research is done individually, and the slightest distraction can cause problems. Besides," he nodded towards a trio of men clustered around an electron microscope, "we operate on the work team theory. Each team owns a piece of research, and this arrangement increases intrinsic reward. We've found this setup works quite well."

Will leaned in towards Shimota. "It also ensures nobody knows the whole picture."

The team was taken into the conference room. Hermann advised them that he would provide a research overview. The team would then be free to begin their inspection.

"Yesterday in Renewal Gardens," Hermann said, "you saw a few of the amazing genetic advances we've made here at Tikal. This morning I'd like to tell you how we've done it. A bit of background might provide perspective for what's to come." He punched a clicker, and a slide appeared on a screen behind him. It was a grainy black and white photo, obviously decades old.

Will recognized the man in the ancient photo as Wilhelm Johanson, the Danish scientist who first identified the gene and created the field of genetics. Hermann spoke in an interesting, authoritative voice as he ran through slides and reviewed the brief history of genetic science. Mendel's groundbreaking research on pea plants in the mid-1800's, de Vries' genetic breeding experiments, and Morgan's work with fruit flies at Colombia. Early in the twentieth century, Johanson coined the terms gene and genotype. There were few advances until the early fifties, when biologist James Watson unveiled the molecular structure of DNA. In collaboration with the British scientists Crick and Wilkins, he constructed a molecular model of DNA, identifying its now classic double-helix configuration. This event signaled the beginning of modern genetic research.

"Steele Pharmaceuticals is interested in advancing genetic research, particularly in the area of aging," Hermann said. "They've had a working alliance with Nova Labs for two decades. To be honest, we were just part of the research pack for the longest time. Ten years ago," Joseph Hermann paused and smiled at the thought, "Doctor Paul Swanson left Syracuse University and went to work for Steele Pharmaceuticals. He brought along that funny looking plant you saw yesterday."

Hermann brought on-screen a picture of the jobara plant. "We began making real progress when we combined what we learned from the jobara with new genetic technology. Now, to help you a little," he paused and smiled at Tamara Rodgers, "let me give you two minutes' worth of cellular biology."

He punched a button, and an animated sequence began. A human outline appeared on the screen, and a single cell emerged from the figure. The picture was magnified thousands of times, and a cell body took shape. "If you remember your high-school biology, you'll recall that genes are nothing more than specific segments of DNA. Genes are the blueprints of human existence. They dictate the function of every living cell. A gene is the basic unit of existence – controller and shaper of all forms of life, including human beings."

Although this was kindergarten material for everyone except Tamara, they all listened attentively. Everybody knew he was leading up to the "big reveal," Nova Labs' major breakthrough in genetic research.

"What causes us to grow old and die?" Hermann asked the question rhetorically. "We've been researching the question for ten years. We know human lifespan is programmed in our genetic makeup. We had to first develop an understanding of where that programming is located in the human DNA sequence before we could develop a direction for our research. In the past decade, science has provided the answer." Hermann rapidly ran through slides until he got to the one he wanted.

"The answer can be found in telomeres," the scientist continued, nodding towards the depiction of a twisted rope ladder with golden tips on each end. "As I'm sure you all know, a telomere is a sequence of repetitive nucleotides that prevents a chromosome from deterioration."

"Huh?" Tamara whispered to Will. He could feel her warm breath on his ear as she leaned close.

"Those little tips at the end of the sequence," he said. "I'll explain later." He returned his attention to Joseph Hermann. He thought he knew where the man was going and was eager to find out.

Hermann was explaining that all living creatures are born with a finite number of telomeres. Humans lose the capability to generate them during the embryonic stage, and over time telomeres gradually shorten or become damaged. New telomeres can't be created, but old ones can be repaired by an enzyme called telomerase. Human aging is caused by gradual shrinkage or damage to telomeres, and death becomes inevitable when the body can no longer repair them. If the human body could endlessly produce or repair telomeres, a person could theoretically live forever. Because of this tantalizing potential, science refers to the telomere as the immortal enzyme. For decades, the challenge for genetic science had been maddeningly simple. Find a way to infinitely repair or regenerate telomeres, and you unlock the genetic code of human aging.

"This jobara plant has shown you the way to do it?" Connors asked.

Hermann nodded. "The jobara has a protein-repair chemical similar to telomerase. It never runs out of this enzyme, which it uses to repair its own DNA strands. That's the secret to the jobara's immortality. We've broken its code and used synthetic technology to create a drug that will do the same thing in humans."

This last statement triggered a hundred questions. They remained in the conference room another hour before Hermann stopped and suggested the team begin inspecting. Tamara departed for the Guyama village, accompanied by a pair of smitten security guards. The remaining team members were assigned a biotechnologist, and at shortly past noon the group broke up. They were on their own to begin their inspection of the Tikal Project.

Concealed behind a ventilation grill mounted in the laboratory ceiling, a high-resolution camera and omnidirectional microphone recorded every movement of the site team. Other cameras were strategically deployed to allow direct observation of every laboratory workstation and computer monitor in the facility. The images were transmitted to a bank of monitors in the basement of the building, where a cluster of men in lab coats watched the activity with interest.

The fact that a basement existed in the facility was a closely guarded secret. Only a few people were aware of this particular room's existence. The place was filled with an array of high-tech imaging equipment, data transmitting devices, and a complete photo lab. Mainframe computers were spaced around the room, with thick cables running from each unit and joining at a coupling device on the wall. One end of the room contained a fully equipped genetics lab, identical to the ones upstairs. The group of men crowded around the monitors, watching as Hermann finished his briefing.

Bob Travers picked up a telephone and punched the speed-dialer. The man continued to closely watch the bank of video monitors as the satellite connection to Steele Pharmaceuticals was completed. Travers spoke into the phone, then listened impassively before acknowledging his instructions. Then he hung up the phone and nodded at the group of men.

"Showtime, everybody," Travers declared, pasting a confident smile on his face. "Are you ready to boogie?" The men nodded, and Travers slapped a stocky man named Johnson on the back.

"Do this right and you'll be rich," he said. "You sure you can pull this off?"

"Not a doubt in my military mind," Johnson said.

CHAPTER TEN

Guyama Village,
Guatemala

Tamara barged clumsily through the thick rainforest, cursing as a thorny bush grabbed at her bare leg. The stinging nettle left a fat welt on her tanned calf. She winced and slapped irritably at the offending vegetation before moving onward. Exhausted, sweaty and disheveled, she was ready to turn back after fighting her way through a mile of dense jungle. She'd spent an hour carefully applying makeup to her face, and now it was shiny with sweat and a runny mess of jungle dirt. The Aussie headgear she'd thought so cute had been swept from her head by a springy tree branch and went flying into an overgrown ravine. Tamara gazed into the deep depression and decided she was too fatigued to retrieve the thing.

This wasn't what she had expected.

Two hours earlier she'd left the facility in high spirits, excited by the jungle trek and swaying to rock tunes blasting through her headphones. This was the adventure she'd come to Guatemala to experience. She couldn't wait to get to the primitive Guyama village. As far as she knew, no anthropologist had visited the place in a half-century.

Tamara was eager to begin her study of the tribe. If she could document the tribe's musical culture and record their songs, she was guaranteed a half-dozen papers and a year's worth of conference presentations. But the little expedition hadn't pushed two hundred yards into the jungle before the going got rough. The heat became sauna-like the instant she stepped into the dense bush, and the heavy backpack straps were soon digging into her shoulders.

She was tired and exasperated.

She found herself thinking of Yanni Shimota as she pushed wearily forward. She was drawn to the old man. She liked his polite and deferential manner. She also respected his complexity. Shimota was obviously wise. But Tamara had also detected steel in the old man, a toughness and independence she admired. She wished she were more like him. She stumbled over a tangled vine and wondered how Shimota would find his way through this mess. He'd probably study the terrain and vegetation, then uncover an easier path. Shimota took a cautious approach to life, waiting until he gathered enough information before making a decision. This was a quality the impulsive Tamara found lacking in herself. She pushed through the thorny undergrowth and thought of the conversation she'd had with the old man last night.

"Are you afraid of getting old?"

"Am old," he said.

"You know what I mean." She gave him a stern schoolmarm look, and this caused the old man to grin mischievously.

Shimota shrugged. "For Oriental, old is good. Reward for hard life. Accumulate wisdom, avoid mistakes of youth."

"What if you could have youth and wisdom?" She held a hand aloft and inspected it, then frowned and wiped the red nail polish from an offending index finger. She bit her lip in concentration and started over.

"Don't know," Shimota responded, then in a softer voice asked, "you happy?"

"I've had better years," she sighed and arched her dark brows at him.

The old man nodded sympathetically. "You young, not happy. I old, happy. I take old."

She showed him her nails and the old man grunted in approval.

"You be careful here," he said softly.

"About what?"

"Danger here. In jungle. In this place, too. You be careful. Okay?"

"Okay," she said, dabbing at her toes with a cotton ball. "I will."

She tripped again, this time falling hard to the spongy ground. The two Paragon guards dropped back to help her regain her footing. Both were blocky and crew cut, and they moved confidently in the tangled jungle. They'd worked hard to ease the journey, hacking through the tangled brush and treating Tamara like precious cargo. Still, it was a tough and exhausting hike through the dense jungle and Tamara felt energy draining with each step.

The sun rose higher as they moved slowly towards the village. The day was wet and humid. Waves of steam rose from the ground. Tamara had the sensation of walking through a hothouse, and her clothes were soon soaked. She continued onward and was clambering over a gigantic rotting carcass of a kapok tree when she felt a painful spasm in her calf. Tamara cursed, then sat heavily on the toppled tree to try and rub out the cramp.

"Not much farther, ma'am." The guard was a burly twenty-year-old named Brunson who spoke in a soft southern drawl. He nodded at the dead tree. "Ah'll cut a path around this thing if ya'd like."

"No," she said, shaking her head. "I can handle it. Give me a minute to get rid of this cramp."

The man nodded respectfully and stepped away. Tamara continued to work at her calf. Finally the locked-up muscle released and she was able to scramble across the tree trunk. The guards resumed their hacking, with Tamara limping behind. They'd gone another hundred yards when the other leg gave out and she fell to the ground. Tamara cursed and tried to continue, but she was nearly finished. She was ready to call a halt and head back for Tikal.

Brunson spun and motioned for her to stop. The man raised a finger to his lips as he listened to the jungle. Finally, he signaled her to move forward. She stumbled again, drawing a warning glance from the wary guard. The man's Paragon uniform was soaked with sweat and he continued to stare intently into the jungle. She slowly moved to crouch beside him. Brunson pulled aside the branch of a thick bush. Tamara glimpsed the Guyama village.

"This is weird," the man muttered.

The village was quiet. Tamara wondered if the villagers might be sleeping or the men hunting in the jungle. She watched as the guard studied the scene and quizzically canted his head. He instructed her to stay put while he and his partner stepped cautiously into the open.

Tamara hunched to the ground, watching nervously as the pair of guards moved down a path separating two uneven lines of ramshackle huts. She recognized the dwellings as classic pre-Mayan, arranged in parallel rows with a centralized fire pit. This would be the center of the community's activities. The social structure would be communal, primitive and male-dominated. This culture would likely have a tradition of music, probably involving chanting and drumbeats. This village was likely undisturbed and unrecorded by anthropologists. She felt a shiver of excitement at the thought of a new discovery.

Her attention was drawn to the charred remnants of a hut at the far end of the village at the jungle's edge. It had burned to the ground, and the smoky odor suggested the event had happened recently.

The guards completed their reconnaissance and moved down the path more easily, talking quietly and motioning for Tamara to come towards them. She slung the backpack over her shoulder and stepped from her hiding place. They slowly moved into the deserted Guyama village.

"What's going on?"

"Don' know, ma'am," Brunson drawled. The husky man lowered his rifle and glanced around the village. "They don't let us come over here anymore. But we used to visit this village all the time. These people are shy as can be, but they've been friendly enough. It takes 'em a while, but the whole damn' village usually comes out 'n looks us over. We used to bring 'em things – food and trinkets, stuff like that. This here," he motioned at the deserted village, "is downright strange."

Tamara's stared in puzzlement down the rows of huts. "Where are they?"

"No idea, ma'am." Brunson nodded towards a hut. "Wanna go inside?"

"I don't think so," Tamara frowned, "I doubt they'd like it."

"Suit yourself," the man said, raising his rifle with a confident smile, "but ah don't think they'd mind if you looked around."

"Okay," she said, impulsively changing her mind. "Let's do it. Keep your eyes open for anything that might be a musical instrument. They might have drums or reed flutes. I wouldn't mind photographing one."

Tamara heard a little whisper. The security man's face was transformed into a wide-eyed look of pain and surprise. The weapon fell from his nerveless hands as he pitched forward into Tamara's arms. She couldn't hold his weight, and they both slumped to the ground. It was then that Tamara spotted the arrow protruding from his back. The other Paragon guard spun into a crouch and raised his rifle. Another arrow arrived and embedded itself into the fleshy part of his arm. The man uttered a gasp and his eyes fluttered. He fell over, still clutching his weapon.

Tamara stifled a scream and looked wildly around the village. It remained deserted. There was no sound. Struggling to control a surge of terror, she followed the instinctive urging of her panicked mind. She threw herself face-first onto the ground and stretched her trembling arms upward.

"*S-S-Soy amiga,*" she called in a hysterical voice. "*No mal.....no mal.....Por favor.....soy un amiga.....no me matan..... Por favor.....Por favor.....no me matan.....Soy amiga.....no me matan!*"

Fighting off convulsions of fear, she remained motionless on the ground. She darted her eyes left and right, and she saw only the lifeless bodies of the security guards. She could stand the suspense no longer. She slowly raised her head, and the terror engulfed her anew.

A dozen warriors surrounded her, painted for battle and pointing drawn bows. The frightened woman began to swoon as she saw their painted faces and angry eyes. Then a realization struck her, one her terrorized mind could not rationally comprehend.

"My God," she whispered. "You're children."

CHAPTER ELEVEN

The Watergate Hotel,
Washington, D.C.

Scottie Bowers always stayed at the Watergate when he came to Washington.

It was a sort of professional homage. Bowers' credo was that all is fair in war, politics, and business. Even today he was incredulous that the event had stripped Richard Nixon of his Presidency. A national crisis over a nickel-and-dime break-in by a couple of "plumbers?" To his way of thinking, it was routine politics, a couple of small-time snoops doing a simple excavation.

Dirty tricks were a way of life in Washington, and he had done far worse than a petty break-in during his years in military intelligence. For two decades Bowers had lied, cheated and stolen in the name of his country. Because he was good at his work, and because it was done against his nation's enemies, he had been amply rewarded for his labors. He'd risen through the ranks to bird colonel, then he'd retired with full military honors and a decent pension.

Bowers was contemptuous of high-minded moralists who ignored real issues to vent their spleens on hard-working investigators. In his view, the nation's fury should be reserved for the people with nasty secrets. If Washington scumbags didn't want their dirty laundry exposed, they shouldn't have affairs or flaunt the law in the first place. It all came down to who signs your paycheck. A police detective was treated with respect, an investigative reporter admired, and an intelligence agent turned into a movie hero. But a private detective was treated like dog shit. All were doing the same job - uncovering the crap that people wanted to hide.

So he had no problem with Watergate.

Bowers spent the afternoon at an uncomfortable French desk, chain-smoking and wading through the mountain of information that represented Raymond Towles' life. Everything was here. Birth certificate, baby footprints, parochial school records, high school and college transcripts. His military record and documents of his Peace Corps duty. Bowers had hacked into a D.C medical clinic and stolen Towles' electronic records. One of his leg men had dug out the man's credit history, civil service records, and fifteen years of credit card receipts. Other operatives had searched the digital world and forwarded links to articles and profiles. Social media had been scoured for information on Towles and his family.

The amount of dirt he found could fit under Scottie Bowers' fingernail. Towles was a Boy Scout, literally and figuratively. He had grown up in rural Louisiana. He had been an eagle scout, high school wrestler, and president of his senior class at Princeton. He was a solid citizen, dedicated public servant, and devoted family man. He went to church on Sundays, sat on the school board, and paid his taxes on time. His financial picture was stable, and his modest mutual fund portfolio was managed through a blind trust. There were no unusual expenditures, no sudden infusions of capital.

The man was damned close to being a candidate for sainthood. Oh, Towles had once received three whacks with a ruler from Sister Mary for pitching a spitball across his third-grade classroom at Thibodaux's Saint Elizabeth Catholic School. In 1992 Towles was issued a parking ticket at the Lincoln Memorial, and just last year he'd had the gall to abruptly resign as a church elder. This scandalous act had garnered a headline in the church newsletter. That was the extent of the dirt Bowers could dig up on Raymond Towles. A spitball and a traffic ticket were the sum total of two days of investigative work.

Bowers was frustrated. It was growing dark outside, and tomorrow morning at 0800 sharp Raymond Towles and his SEC crew would descend on Steele Pharmaceuticals. Bowers needed to put something in Elliot Masters' hands before then. The wiry Bowers stretched his shoulders, threw his legs over the desk, and lit another Marlboro. Blowing smoke rings, he watched them waft upward as he ruminated on Raymond Towles.

Sex or money? These were always the secrets people wanted to hide. He'd ruled out sex in Raymond Towles' case. There was nothing even hinting at extramarital shenanigans. Was Towles was a rare man of morals among the horny and predatory citizens of the nation's capital city?

If the man *was* screwing around, Bowers wasn't going to find it, at least not before tomorrow morning.

That left money. He pulled the laptop across the desk and began punching in commands. Few data files were safe from Bowers. He had been trained by the military in electronic snooping, and he knew that nearly any database could be accessed with a minimum of effort. After spending thirty minutes digging through Raymond Towles' electronic financial records, Bowers was rewarded for his efforts.

He earmarked two items for closer investigation. A monthly check drawn for twelve hundred dollars made out to an entity called Evergreen. This entry appeared two years ago and reoccurred monthly. The second item that caught Bowers' attention was another check written every two weeks. The draft was always for three hundred dollars and made out to M. Lomas.

Both leads held promise. Bowers resumed his electronic snooping. The Evergreen Nursing Home was located in Lafayette, Louisiana. Bowers hacked the facility's computers and located their database. He scanned Evergreen's patient census, then moved to the accounts receivable files. Bowers discovered that Towles' ninety-year-old mother had resided at Evergreen for the past twenty-three years. The first twenty-one of those years, her stay had been covered by Medicaid. Two years ago, Towles began picking up the tab.

Bowers pondered the information. Why was Raymond Towles now paying for his mother's nursing home care? It was an intriguing question, but it was the other item that quickened his pulse.

The "M. Lomas" in Towles' checkbook turned out to be Doctor Martha Lomas, a prominent Arlington psychologist.

Raymond Towles had been writing this woman checks for two years. Bowers put fire to another Marlboro, feeling the little trill he got when he was on to something. It was a familiar sensation harkening back to his Air Force days. The same exquisite rush of adrenaline he'd felt studying a satellite photo and spotting secret troop movements or a hidden military installation. After two days of excavating, Bowers was about to strike pay dirt.

Raymond Towles was seeing a shrink.

Bowers spent a fruitless hour searching for an electronic footprint for Dr. Lomas. He located her website and scanned a brief biography. She was a solo practitioner. No electronic records. Patient files would be kept in her office. He would have to go old school.

At just past midnight, Bowers took the Roosevelt Bridge across the Potomac into Arlington. The streets were empty, and it didn't take long to find the office of Doctor Lomas. Her suite occupied the third story of a renovated brownstone, and the place conveniently had a back alley. Standing in the darkness, Bowers surveyed the balcony twenty feet overhead. The wiry man stepped to the brick wall, checked it for handholds, then climbed the wall like a monkey. He pulled himself over the ornate wrought iron and onto the balcony. He studied the lock securing the French doors, then sorted through the ring of bump keys until he found the one he needed. In less than a minute, he stepped inside the doctor's office.

The beam of his flashlight illuminated metal file cabinets containing patient records. It was secured by a small cam lock. Bowers went to the receptionist's desk and rifled through the drawers. It didn't take long to find the key and unlock the file cabinet. He sorted through case files until he located the one belonging to Towles. Bowers moved his flashlight around the room until he spotted the copier. He waited while the machine warmed up.

Walking down the hallway, he pushed open a door. He shined his beam into the doctor's office. A feminine space, furnished with soft chairs and abstract art. A comfortable room for therapy. Bowers felt a certain kinship with shrinks. They both dug up the crap of people's lives and exposed what was carefully hidden. He returned to the receptionist's office and copied Towles' chart, then replaced it in the file cabinet. A minute later he was scrambling down the wall. Doctor Lomas would never know her private sanctuary had been violated.

Back at the Watergate, he returned to the curved desk and lit a cigarette. He studied his booty. Raymond Towles had a personal problem, and he'd been seeing a psychologist for two years. His file was thick, and Dr. Lomas was a meticulous record-keeper. She wrote in a strong hand and kept copious notes of each therapy session. Towles had seen the therapist nearly a hundred times over the past two years. His childhood and life history had been well documented, and Lomas recorded the man's mental state during each visit. She made observations concerning Towles' problem, and after each session she summarized his progress.

Bowers read every entry in Towles' psychological record, scribbling notes on a legal pad. The process took several hours, and he felt himself growing drowsy. After calling down for a pot of coffee, he chain-smoked as he methodically sifted through the records. The morning sun brightened the room and he looked at his watch. Six-thirty.

Two hours earlier in Texas. Elevating his legs on the French desk, he lit a cigarette and reviewed his notes.

He had found something, but it wasn't much. Nothing that could be used for coercion or blackmail. Masters had instructed him only to find out whatever he could. Bowers didn't know what was going on between Steele Pharmaceuticals and Raymond Towles. He wondered if there was a connection to the Tikal Project in Guatemala. Bowers had run background investigations on the site team members and uncovered good information on all of them. The intel he produced regarding Tamara Rodgers had resulted in a fat bonus. He wasn't confident what he'd discovered on Raymond Towles would be useful to his client.

He picked up the phone and called Elliot Masters.

PART TWO

The Third Messenger

CHAPTER TWELVE

Tikal Research Center,
Guatemala

"It's amazing."

Will Connors stared at the activity taking place on the color monitor. A young biotechnologist was synthetically altering the nucleotide base sequence of a human RNA strand. A pinhead camera mounted inside the electron microscope magnified the process ten thousand times and transmitted the images to the computer, which added enhancements and color before relaying the picture to a twenty-seven-inch monitor.

The result was surreal.

Microscopic bodies were transformed into great red planets that swirled on-screen against a midnight-blue backdrop of cellular materials resembling the vast Milky Way. The narrow stalks and ganglia of synaptic fibers took on the appearance of dancing purple octopi with clutching tentacles that stretched towards neighboring cells. Molecules of serotonin and other neurotransmitters shuttled back and forth across synaptic regions like streams of multi-hued ants.

The whole scene represented a fantastic transformation of actual cellular activity into a computer-aided visual display of stunning detail.

Connors watched in fascination as a nuclease resembling an oblong bubble slowly encased a human genome. Within the nucleic orb, an RNA strand snaked towards a DNA chain that resembled a corkscrewed railroad track. The RNA strand began to insinuate itself inside the helix, sinuously dancing through the genome until it stopped at a programmed target location.

An enzyme separated from the strand and bound itself to a precise location on the genome, and Connors watched spellbound as two protein molecules acted as chemical scissors cutting out a piece of genetic material. The strand of RNA shifted microscopically, then it loaded a replacement gene into the now-vacant space on the DNA strand. The video image spasmed for an eye blink. This caused a frown to crease the biotechnologist's face. Then perfect resolution returned and Connors watched as the RNA strand began to separate itself from the genome.

"Incredible," he said. His voice was hoarse with excitement. "I knew this technology existed, but I've never actually seen it."

"You're watching genetic microsurgery," said the eager young biotechnologist, a Harvard graduate named Russell. "We can locate any genome in the human body, cut out a specific gene, and plug in a new one. We can program the RNA to do anything. Remove or disable defective genes. Implant onto the genome any genetic coding we load onto it. It's easy as editing and replacing text in a word processing program."

"Is this first or second messenger RNA?"

"Third," Russell said, grinning at the blank expression on Connors' face.

"I've never heard of third messenger RNA."

"It's synthetic," Russell said. "It never existed until Dr. Hermann created it, and it's the key to this project. This technology came straight from the jobara plant."

Connors continued to stare at the monitor. "How did he do it?"

Russell explained that several years earlier primitive bacteria with a unique capability had been discovered. The bacteria's immune system possessed the ability to identify and destroy any invading virus. This capability made the microorganism invulnerable to any form of predation. It accomplished this feat by harvesting a DNA sample from viral invaders and creating a defender enzyme from the invader's own genetic material. When the virus returned, the defender enzyme recognized and bound itself to it, destroying the invader's genome. The invader was rendered incapable of replicating itself and quickly died. It was a fantastic discovery that rocked the world of science, although it was universally accepted that only primitive bacteria could create such immunity to invasion.

"Then we found the jobara plant," Russell said, "and we realized that little shrub uses an identical process. Obviously, the jobara isn't a bacterium. It's a highly complex organism that can also immunize itself against anything that tries to invade it. This is the jobara's secret to immortality. Dr. Hermann realized its potential and started adapting the capability for broader genetic applications. This led to the development of the synthetic RNA strand you see on the screen. It's the key to the drug we've created to stop the aging process."

Connors shook his head in wonder. "I can't believe you've created a third kind of RNA."

"The development of third messenger RNA is huge. It's made genetic manipulation a simple process and led to the miracles you've seen here. There's talk about a Nobel for Dr. Hermann."

"Did you know him from Harvard?"

"He was gone before I got there. I guess he resigned a good ten years ago. Joseph Hermann's legendary in the genetics department. I guess it was a blow when he resigned and took the job with Nova, although his image was tarnished at the time."

"Really?" Connors responded, curious. "There was a scandal?"

"Rumors and whispers mostly," Russell shrugged, "long before my time." He lowered his voice and glanced around the room. "According to the rumor mill, he might have been doing unethical research and his resignation wasn't voluntary."

"Any idea what got him in trouble?"

"Nope," Russell said, "and I don't care. The man's brilliant. He personally recruited me to work here. You wouldn't believe what they pay us. It's triple what I could get in the States. This lab's state of the art and we're doing cutting-edge research. I've got no problems with Hermann."

"Thanks for the gossip." Connors chewed a lip. "You think this genetic technology could apply to cancer treatment?"

Russell shrugged. "Don't see why not."

The biotechnologist pulled a lab culture from cold storage and placed it under the microscope. He punched more commands into the computer, and Connors returned his attention to the monitor. He watched genetic strands corkscrew across the screen, his mind racing with permutations and calculations. He felt things begin to click into place. He had the sense that he was nearing the end of a long journey. He stared into the computer monitor and wondered if he had stumbled onto the miracle he had traveled so far to find.

———◆———

One floor below, Gene Johnson took a drag from the stub of a cigarette and watched the identical images Connors was observing. The man exhaled a plume of smoke and crushed the butt into an ashtray, then raised his right finger to signal a pending command.

"Okay, patch Thirteen to Monitor Two on my command," he said, "and three.....two..... one.....now."

Johnson slashed downward with his hand.

A technician operating a sixty-four channel video mixer punched a sequence of buttons. A tiny signal interruption caused the monitor to blink, then the process of embedding a synthetic RNA strand into a virus continued as before. But the demonstration was no longer live. One floor above, Connors was now watching a pre-recorded sequence.

"Fuck," Johnson muttered, giving the technician an angry glance.

"It wasn't that bad," the man whined, "we're talking a millisecond interruption that looks exactly like a power fluctuation."

"I want a goddam seamless intercept," Johnson growled. "You've got to activate both switches at the same time. Goddamit, get this shit right." Johnson glared at the technician, who nodded nervously and returned his eyes to the panel. Johnson bit a lip in frustration and ran a hand through his crew cut. It probably didn't matter, but Johnson wanted things perfect.

Johnson didn't fully understand what was going on upstairs. From what he'd been told, the geeks up there were doing legitimate research. The problem apparently was timing. The drug company had to get its new drug to market fast. It couldn't take the chance of failing the FDA inspection. Delays could cost the company billions. Hermann had hired him to choreograph the video sequences. The men had spent weeks pre-recording the images they wanted the site team to see.

The stakes were high for Johnson as well. If he could off carry this scam, he'd receive a flat fee of one million dollars. In cash. He'd never been in sniffing distance of that much money. Johnson leaned back in his chair and watched the proceedings upstairs, imagining how he'd set himself up when this was over.

He lit another cigarette and allowed his mind to drift. He studied the plume of smoke and thought about his future. He was fifty and planned to retire after this job. The minute this team of FDA birdbrains was off-site, Bob Travers was going to hand him a million dollars. That like a billion in Guatemala, and Johnson had decided he would stay here when this shit was done. He'd buy a house down on the South Coast, a big-ass place on the beach, and hire local women to keep it clean. Get a stable of whores, maybe seven of them, and screw a different one every day. He'd drink good whiskey, smoke righteous weed, and fuck dark-skinned women.

He allowed the tiniest twitch of a smile cross his tight lips as he daydreamed. It wouldn't be long before he'd be lying on the beach. All he had to do was fake out a bunch of dumb ass academics for three days. He gazed through the surveillance monitor at the scientist upstairs, going nuts over fake video images. Johnson allowed his smile to broaden into a contemptuous laugh.

CHAPTER THIRTEEN

Nova Labs began its animal experiments a decade ago. They started with smaller primates such as lemurs and howlers, and worked their way up to chimps. Sheila was being treated with the latest generation of experimental drugs, and Connors observed the chimp with great interest when she was brought into the lab. Russell led her to a glassed enclosure, insisting Connors don a mask and surgical gloves before approaching the chimp.

Sheila gazed at him with curiosity and Connors glimpsed the intelligence in her wise brown eyes. She shook his hand at Russell's prompt, then obediently held out a hairy arm when the young scientist approached. The chimp sat passively as a dose of Novix, the anti-aging medicine, was injected into her body.

The scientist prepped one of Sheila's tissue samples and allowed Connors to examine it under the microscope. Computer enhancements allowed him to observe how the drug was functioning in the chimp's body. Sheila's DNA had been modified, and now it contained a telomerase activation gene. Connors stared into the scope as Russell pointed out how this gene repaired telomeres on DNA strands in the chimp's body. This was the magic of Novix – the drug ensured Sheila's cell bodies would remain healthy indefinitely. Connors glanced at Sheila, who was now pounding restlessly at her glassed-in enclosure and chattering for the men's attention.

The chimp would never get old.

Before this moment, he hadn't thought seriously of what this research might mean to the world. He caught his reflection in the glass. His hair was streaking with gray, and tiny lines were clustering around his eyes. Youth faded fast, and he hadn't seen it happen. Things would get worse from here. Connors thought about the last twenty years of his life. What if he could get them back? What if he grew no older? As he studied Sheila, he understood it might actually be possible.

Novix would transform human existence like no other development in history. It would alter the definition of life. Age would become irrelevant. An ideal age could be established, and Novix would halt aging at that point. You hit twenty-five and stay there. Russell had said that achieving immortality was unlikely, but lifespan might be extended two hundred years.

Will pondered the implications of such a dramatic development. Every aspect of existence would shift exponentially, in directions he couldn't imagine. He began to understand Tamara's concerns about the social consequences of extending lifespan. She had also reminded him of the purpose of this research. Money. Profit. Steele Pharmaceuticals stood to make millions from Novix, perhaps billions, because everybody would want it.

Who wouldn't want a drug that would make you young?

He stared at the adolescent chimp and realized she carried in her body the ability to change the world.

Over the next several hours Russell worked earnestly to explain the research, patiently going over protocols, setting up tissue studies, and demonstrating techniques with the computer. It was late in the day when he made a tiny mistake, and this was the opportunity Connors needed.

———•—•———

"Caught the mother fucker," Johnson exclaimed. "Did you see that?"

A technician named Woody looked up from his monitor. "See what?"

"Up in the lab. Run back the surveillance feed about a minute."

Woody rewound the video and ran it in slow motion. Russell was prepping a slide with Connors looking over his shoulder. Russell used a micropipette to place a droplet of fluid on the slide. As he reached to return pipette to its place in a sterilized rack, Connors nudged him and few droplets of liquid spilled onto the table.

"Shit," they heard Russell say. He turned to reach for a sanitary wipe. As he did so, Connors ran his finger through liquid. Then he wiped it on his pants.

"Motherfucker just stole the messenger strand," Johnson said. "Fucking Russell never noticed."

Woody stared at the screen, then at Johnson.

"A fuckin' drop of that liquid's got a million RNA strands in it," Johnson said. "Connors just wiped it on the front of his pants."

———◆———

Will returned to his room, removed his pants, and carefully snipped a one-inch square from the pocket. He held the fabric to the light, then tucked the snippet into a pocket of the leather valise. An effervescence filled his chest. He felt his spirits grow buoyant, freed for the moment from their tether of despair. His face creased into a grin as he pumped his fist in triumph. He'd traveled three thousand miles to bet on a long shot, and it had just paid off.

He stretched out on the bed and closed his eyes. His body hummed as if energized by an electric current. His mind was running at warp speed as he savored his accomplishment. With the swipe of a finger, he had obtained the key to fighting Mollie's disease. Images from the morning's presentation rushed through his head. Corkscrewing DNA strands. Dancing synapses. The messenger strand floating through it all like a silent starship.

He took several deep breaths and forced his mind to slow down. One problem was solved and there was reason to feel good. But more significant challenges lay ahead. He was broke. He had no job, although there was the promise of one. He lacked access to a laboratory or equipment. He needed computers powerful enough to run the biogenetic software necessary for gene splicing.

These were formidable problems, and he had no idea how he would overcome them. Connors stretched his neck and focused on breathing, still trying to slow his busy mind. *One step at a time.* He had just made a giant leap. He possessed the third messenger strand. He considered the next step. Could the strand be programmed to attack cancer?

There was a genetic relationship between extending human life and killing cancer. They were opposite ends of the same conundrum. Nova's researchers had discovered the means of directing the human body to repair telomeres, those golden tips at the end of the genome, by using the jobara plant's secrets and the third messenger strand. Cancer cells innately possessed this capability, essentially allowing them to live indefinitely. Cancer never died until it killed the body it inhabited. So powerful was this capability that science referred to it as "malignant immortality." Connors was convinced he could reverse engineer the process by programming the third messenger strand to destroy cancer cells. All he needed was a lab. A mainframe computer. A thousand other things. And enough time.

He stretched and looked at his watch, realizing it was time for dinner. He stopped to tap on Tamara's door before moving on the dining hall. A full buffet had been set up. Will loaded his plate and spotted Yanni Shimota sitting with Hermann. He moved to sit next to them, but the two men barely gave him a glance. Sensing the tension, he kept his mouth shut as he studied the unfolding conflict.

Shimota was angry and was directing his bile squarely at Joseph Hermann. The research director shifted uncomfortably as Shimota laid into him, then Hermann attempted a response. This brought on another staccato outburst from the angry Shimota. It was a dramatic departure in demeanor for the stoic man, and Will could see the surprise on Hermann's face.

Will soon understood the problem.

Shimota was unhappy with the restrictiveness of the inspection. He complained that he was being shown only what the Nova scientists wanted him to see, not the studies he was requesting. The lab's biotechnologists had little autonomy, and everything Shimota wanted had to be 'authorized' before it could be done. He didn't like seeing results on a computer monitor. He wanted to look into the microscope and replicate with his own hands what he was seeing on the screen. Shimota demanded that things be structured differently tomorrow.

"Okay, Doctor Shimota, I hear you," Herman said, raising his palms in supplication. "I'll see what I can do. But you've got to understand this is the way our inspection protocols are set up. We do our research using computer models and want to show you our results in the same way." Hermann sighed and rose from the table. "I'll have to call Houston, but I'll see if we can meet your requests."

Shimota glared at Hermann's departing backside, then shook his head in frustration. The man looked at his plate of food and emitted a disgusted grunt, pushing it away with another shake of his head.

"I take it your afternoon didn't go well," Will ventured. This resulted in another snort from Shimota.

"Too restrictive," Shimota complained. "Only see what they want me to see. Everything I ask gotta be 'cleared' – even simple things – looking in electron microscope or cloning DNA myself. Worst, they not use lab notes. All records on computer. Procedure very poor." He paused to take a cautious sip of hot tea, then made a face and slammed the cup to the table.

"Food stink, too," he muttered.

"What do you think's going on?"

"Not good procedure to limit access to data," Shimota said. "They should let inspector see what is requested. Should let me replicate procedures." Shimota looked up at Will as if realizing for the first time who was sitting there. "How you day go?"

"Not bad. They let me see whatever I wanted."

"You do hands-on?"

Will shrugged. "I didn't really ask to do anything myself. Still, I'm pretty impressed with what they're doing. Sheila's an amazing monkey."

Shimota grumbled something that Will didn't catch, and the conversation drifted into silence. Will focused on his food while Shimota fussed with his tea and began scribbling notes on a yellow pad.

"By the way, have you seen Tamara?"

"Not since morning," Shimota said. "She go in jungle – to village. Not back yet."

Nor was she back three hours later.

Will gave in to his growing anxiety and went searching for Tavey Bohanon. Paragon Security had a suite in the back of the facility, and Will found the Irishman staring at a bank of security monitors. Bohanon drummed his fingers as he scanned the screens. He was focused on the front gate of the Tikal Research Center, which appeared ominous in the nighttime glare of flood lamps. Will tapped on the door.

Bohanon startled and looked up, and then motioned him into the room.

"Where is she, Tavey?"

"Ah wish Ah knew, ta' be sure," the security man sighed. "They should'a bin back. Tha' guards had specific orders ta get Doctor Rodgers ta tha village 'n back by six p.m. Ah canna imagine wha could'a gone wrong out there. Hell, tha sod'n village is jest a mile away."

"Weren't they carrying commo gear?"

"Yah, two-way radios. We've been tryin' ta raise 'em, but....." Bohanon shrugged and bit the end from a long cigar, then stuck it in his mouth. "Ah'm sartain there's nothin' wrong wi' tha lass. My lads're competent, believe me, 'n they're both armed. They probably decided ta spend the night at tha village. Maybe their radio's 'r turned off 'n they don't know it. We'll go to tha village 'n find them in tha morning, 'n get it all sorted out."

"Not tonight?"

"Nay, not tonight, Doc," Tavey Bohanon said. "Like Ah said, we don' go inta tha jungle at night."

"You mind if I look for them?"

"Ya dinna wan' ta' do that, Doc," Bohanon said gravely.

"You said the village was a mile from here. Give me a flashlight and some kind of weapon, and I'll be fine. I'm capable of taking care of myself."

"Mebbe in yer suburbs, ya can, but not out thar," Tavey Bohanon said, nodding towards the monitor. "Tha's a vary bad place, tha jungle. Take my word fer it, Doctor Connors. Ya canna take care'a yerself out thar."

"Then neither can Tamara."

"Tha lass is tougher than ya might think," Bohanon said. "It won' help 'er if ya go stumblin' around in tha dark. Ah'll go 'n find her at first light."

"Is there anything I can do?"

"Ah'd take a swig 'a this," Bohanon extended the silver flask, "'n then ya might cross yer fingers 'n pray, lad."

CHAPTER FOURTEEN

They maintained a vigil in the cafeteria. There was strong coffee in a big aluminum urn, and Connors poured cups of the stuff into a churning stomach. He sat apart from the others, choosing not to participate in worried discussions about their missing colleague.

Connors watched as Shimota and Wilkinson engaged in an indifferent game of chess. The men sat stiffly, talking in esoteric terms about genetic theory while absently moving pieces across the board. Connors studied the two men. They couldn't have been more different. Shimota was a humble man of stature whom Connors respected. They had been colleagues during Connors' glory days. When Mollie was healthy and he was rocketing to success. When everything he touched was magic. When he couldn't have imagined a better life. Connors indulged in a moment of melancholy, wishing for days forever gone.

He was pleased Shimota was on the team. The shy and deferential man was a genius and a pioneer in genetics. Through public television appearances and grandfatherly lectures on genetics, Shimota had introduced millions to the wonders of genetics and inspired the creation of an industry. The world had developed a fascination with DNA and tracking genetic lineage. Billions of ancestral records were now available online, and websites were reaping huge profits developing DNA profiles. Entrepreneurs had advanced the science to the edge of silliness, even creating a dating website based on DNA compatibility. Shimota was unfailingly modest in acknowledging his contributions to this burgeoning field. Will admired the old man, who had always shown him courtesy and deference.

Wilkinson was a different matter. Connors didn't know the man but had met many like him. Stiff-necked academics who measured themselves and others by the volume of published papers. Such men rarely ventured into a laboratory and contributed little to science. Wilkinson had made clear his displeasure at Connors' last-minute addition to the team. He watched as the white-haired man pointed his ever-present pipe at Shimota and pompously lectured him on gene splicing. Connors wondered if Wilkinson had ever spliced a gene in his life. Shimota listened attentively, then bowed his head respectfully and returned his attention to the board.

Connors glanced at his watch. Past midnight and still no sign of Tamara. Her image filled his head. A wistful smile creased his face. She was as exotic and colorful as a jungle bird. She dressed too young, favoring short skirts and dangling costume jewelry. Her makeup looked as if it had been applied with a paintbrush. A cloud of exotic perfume invariably accompanied her.

She was a paradox. Highly educated and accomplished, yet a free spirit living on her terms. Tamara was unconcerned with what the world thought of her. She was as impulsive as a hyperactive child. Last night, she'd burst into his room carrying her phone. She played him a song about a sailing ship making a voyage to the South Seas. Tamara patiently explained that the song was a metaphor. About recognizing things that can't be changed. About accepting truth and sailing on.

The memory of a long-ago marriage edged into his consciousness. Mary Beth. He hadn't thought of her in years. Connors had been thirty when they'd impetuously married, and the flimsy union fell apart after three years. She'd been a graduate biology student with big glasses and glossy black hair. They'd enjoyed a few rowdy jousts in his bed, and there was no logic to their decision to marry. He wasn't sure they even loved one another.

Mary Beth proved to be a dour and passionless partner who demonstrated little interest in anything beyond what she could see through a microscope. They remained together three contentious and unhappy years. Inexplicably, in the final year she became pregnant. The last thing either of them wanted, the arrival of Mollie didn't save the marriage. Mary Beth was an indifferent mother, and she'd been happy to relinquish custody to him.

Energized by his freedom, Connors had thrown his life into Mollie and his work. He had settled into a happy life built around the laboratory and his daughter. She was an amazing child, bright and charismatic. Impossibly beautiful, with dark radiant hair and perpetually flushed face. The picture of health. He parented in a tolerant, permissive manner. His brilliance as a researcher emerged, and his career spiraled upward in a succession of discoveries and acclaim. He was gaining a reputation as one of the young lions of research. To his great surprise, he became famous. His world was perfect.

It fell apart two years ago with the ring of a telephone.

A late-night call from his mother. It's colon cancer, she informed him in a calm voice. Advanced and terminal. Connors dropped everything and threw himself into studying his mother's disease. Searching for anything that might slow down the cancer's progression. It was all for nothing, because six months later she was dead. He had been grieving her loss barely a month when Mollie began losing weight. After multiple exams and an extended hospital stay, doctors informed him that Mollie was suffering from acute lymphoblastic leukemia, an incurable child-killing cancer. Still reeling from the loss of his mother, Connors' world collapsed.

The disease began a relentless march through Mollie's body and lit a fire within him. Cancer had taken his mother. He wouldn't allow it to take his child. He resumed the battle. Sleepless weeks were spent in the laboratory. He ignored his appearance, rarely taking the time to shower or shave. He searched for answers outside conventional science, consulting with naturalists, psychics, and charlatans. Connors rarely showed up for classes and ignored his research. He defaulted on a million-dollar grant, an act that embarrassed his university and ultimately cost him his job. Few colleagues were aware of his circumstances, and his reputation for brilliance plummeted. Others began to see him as an oddball, and he became an outcast in the scientific community. He was barely aware of it.

His quest grew more desperate as Mollie drew closer to death. The journey finally brought him to Guatemala. The last thing he wanted was romance or adventure. He was perplexed by the schoolboy emotions rumbling through him. Tamara ignited something that had lain dormant for years. How could he be interested in this woman? Why now, of all times? Connors buried a weary head in his hands. The song floated into his head. About the ship sailing towards the Marquesas, and the South Seas. He wondered what truth he needed to accept.

———◆———

At first light Bohanon and a half-dozen guards trudged into the jungle. When they didn't return after two hours, Wilkinson brusquely suggested the site team continue their inspection.

The morning passed slowly, but the day was far from uneventful. Shimota continued to fuss about the conditions of the inspection. He insisted on being allowed to replicate studies and draw his own samples. Hermann continued dragging his feet, insisting replication studies follow the original research protocols. Shimota balked at the intrusion of computers during every phase of research. The old Oriental erupted in contempt when he learned that the Nova scientists had bypassed intermediate cell studies in favor of simulations.

Shimota was an old-timer, steeped in scientific tradition and insistent that time-honored procedures be followed. The issue of lab notes was a perfect example. For centuries, scientists had utilized notebooks to chronologically record laboratory procedures and findings. Errors or nonsignificant findings were duly recorded, often lined out in red ink to help subsequent researchers avoid the same dead ends. Shimota had little regard for recording data in computers or iPads. The usually stoic man sat red-faced and angry during an uncomfortable lunch with Will, muttering darkly about "bad science." Hermann relented in the afternoon and allowed Shimota to draw tissue samples, but this did little to mollify the man.

Will spent the day staring blankly into a monitor, trying to sort through the emotions reverberating through his body. Thinking of Tamara. And Mollie. Wondering if he was wasting precious time. Trying to understand how he could become infatuated with a woman he barely knew. He paid scant attention to the research wonders demonstrated by young Russell.

Bohanon and his squad returned as dusk was falling. They'd traveled to the village without incident and found it deserted. They spent the day hacking through dense jungle until fading light forced them back to the facility. There was no sign of Tamara or the guards. Bohanon had no answers for the stream of worried questions from the inspection team. Finally, he raised a thick hand to stop them and announced he would resume the search tomorrow.

Will spent the evening in Bohanon's office, staring at security monitors. A camera was trained on each section of the perimeter fence, and he watched the screens until his chin dropped onto his chest. He fell into an exhausted sleep, finally startling awake six hours later. He glanced at his watch. It was nearly four a.m. He rotated his neck and decided on a hot shower. He had nearly reached the door when a flash of movement on a monitor caught his eye. Connors turned and stared into the screen.

Tamara was at the front gate, shouting for someone to let her in.

———— ❖ ————

"It was horrible," she said, "I knew they were going to kill me."

Tamara sat pale and shaky on the bed. Trembling knees were drawn beneath her chin. Her hands clutched a cup of hot tea. Oversized hospital scrubs gave her the appearance of a child. Her face was scrubbed clean of makeup and her normally electrified hair hung straight down. Dark circles under her eyes gave testament to her hellish experience.

After Connors raised the alarm, security opened the gates and the exhausted woman walked stiffly into the compound before collapsing into Bohanon's arms. The rough-hewn security chief tenderly carried her into the back of the building. Bohanon refused to allow Connors see her, brusquely informing him that Tamara was receiving medical attention. Three hours later, Tamara was escorted to her room. She'd started bawling when she saw him.

"What happened, Tamara?"

"I'm not supposed to say anything," she muttered. A flush of color rose in her cheeks. "That asshole Travers came damned close to threatening me."

"Two people get killed and you're kidnapped by savages, and they don't want you to talk about it?"

"Travers doesn't want the rest of you to feel like you're in danger."

Connors shook his head in irritation. "Screw him. Tell me what happened out there."

She looked as if she might cry again. "They killed those guards, right in front of me. No sound, no warning. We were standing there talking, and the next instant those two guys were laying on the ground. They were just boys, and all of a sudden they're dead. Shot with tiny arrows. I've never seen....." She paused and gulped air, then took a sip of the tea.

"I figured they'd kill me too. I was lying on the ground screaming that I meant no harm. They dragged me into the jungle."

"They have a little camp miles from here," she continued. "Just a fire pit in a clearing. They've abandoned their village. They left me lying there all day. Last night they danced and chanted. It was ritual stuff, shuffling around the fire and beating a drum."

"You speak their language?"

"They use a dialect. I spoke Spanish and they understood."

"How did you get away?"

"I didn't. I figured I'd die out there. This morning they tried to give me food and water. I wouldn't take it. They got me to my feet and led me through the jungle. Brought me close to this place and let me go. I have no idea why."

Tamara sniffled and took another sip of tea. "They're terrified of this place."

"I can see that. All the lights and fencing. It's alien to them."

"It's more than that," Tamara said. She looked at him with wide eyes. "I'm not supposed to tell you this, but fuck Travers. Will, they're children."

Connors canted his head in puzzlement. "They had children with them?"

"No," she said. "The warriors. They look like they're ten years old, but they act like men. I don't know how to explain it."

"Are you sure?" He asked gently. "You were pretty scared."

"That's not the worst of it. They say an animal is hunting them."

"Jaguar?" Will's brow was furrowed.

"No," Tamara said. "They couldn't describe the thing. But they're terrified of it. And there's something else. Something weird."

"What's that?"

"They say this animal came from inside this building."

CHAPTER FIFTEEN

Steele Pharmaceuticals,
Houston, Texas

Early Monday morning, Raymond Towles and his team of Securities and Exchange investigators rolled into Steele Pharmaceuticals' corporate tower. Towles charged in like an invading Southern general, commandeering the company's executive offices and barking commands at scurrying subordinates in a crisp drawl. He was a scowling bear of a man with baggy eyes and the leathery face of age. Towles emanated authority and moved with an energy that belied his sixty-two years.

Andrew Glass greeted the man with a confident smile and extended hand, which Towles ignored. A six-man team of investigators trailed in his wake. All wore thin ties and carried laptop computers. Glass knew what was coming. Corporate colleagues had advised him that Towles and his high-tech soldier ants operated on one simple assumption: every large corporation engaged in financial mismanagement. If they didn't expose it, they weren't doing their job.

Towles wasted no time on niceties. He provided Glass a terse briefing, then put his team to work. They spread through the building and demanded to see everything. Inventories. Production costs. Sales figures. Research and development costs. Profit margins. Corporate tax returns. Price-earnings ratios. Salaries and bonus plans. Every entry was questioned. The most minor expense challenged. Each explanation treated with skepticism. Hours were spent grilling Barney Fried, challenging him to prove the company wasn't manipulating stock prices.

Glass chose to stay out of the fray, tending to routine business and paying little mind to the massacre taking place on Steele's corporate floors. He understood what was happening to his company. Towles was a baying bloodhound eagerly following the hot scent of corruption. The man had appropriated a large conference room to serve as operations center. Subordinates streamed through like a busy line of ants. Towles examined their reports and issued crisp directions, sending his minions scurrying after more damning evidence he knew was buried in corporate books. A mountain of it soon grew high on the long rosewood table. Towles ignored company executives. He didn't engage in small talk. He curtly refused to partake in a catered lunch. It was the order of business for two days.

By Wednesday, Towles called a halt to the proceedings and spent the morning huddled with his staff in the conference room. Glass returned to his office and waited. At noon he poured a tumbler of whiskey and clicked the glass against his teeth as he stared out at Houston. He opened a slender folder and re-read the report from Midlands Investigations. He stared out the window in contemplation.

This would be a gamble of gigantic proportions.

Towles held all the cards, with nothing less than the survival of Steele Pharmaceuticals at stake. Barney Fried had been a joke, a trembling rabbit who melted like grease in the heat thrown off by Towles. Thanks to Fried, the list of violations would probably include charges of stock manipulation and fraud. Glass was sure Fried was no longer thinking about cashing the two million dollar bonus check. His only concern would be keeping his ass out of jail.

Glass glanced one last time at the Midlands report and calculated the odds. If he used this material, he risked making things immeasurably worse. The stakes were enormous. But Glass was not inclined to fold his hand. He would shove his company to the middle of the table and play his only remaining card. *All in.*

Towles called for him at one-thirty.

Glass marched into the room and scanned the somber faces ringing the conference table. He felt the pulse of adrenaline reverberate through his body, causing a physical rush almost sexual in power and intensity. He'd felt the sensation only a few times in his life, and he took a moment to savor it. An image flashed into his head. Three years earlier, he'd choppered to an off-limits peak on Whistler Mountain. He had plunged down a slope far steeper than any groomed run in the world. Halfway down he'd felt the planet shake as a thousand-ton slab of snow separated from the earth and roared down the mountain behind him. Glass felt the adrenaline blast as he turned his skis straight downhill and tucked into form. Racing ahead of certain death and laughing aloud as clouds of billowing snow enveloped him. The sound of snapping trees felled by the awesome power of the avalanche unleashed another stream of adrenaline and further intensified the thrill.

Glass returned his focus to the serious men at the conference table. He nodded and smiled at Towles. He was neither worried nor intimidated. He was supremely confident. Adrenaline was pumping and he savored the rush. He was confident he would outrun whatever avalanche Towles might unleash. Even if this gambit failed, he'd find another way to outwit the asshole.

Towles rolled a Mont Blanc pen between his fingers and pulled his face into a knowing smile as he nodded towards the mountain of documents arrayed on the table. Without preamble, he tore into Andrew Glass.

"Mr. Glass, your company is a disaster. We've discovered undeniable proof that you're inflating sales figures and over-reporting corporate income. You've lied on your last four company reports. You've borrowed against capital to pay stock dividends the past two quarters. That's blatantly illegal, no matter how you want to explain it. You'll face major sanctions for deceiving your board and stockholders. Additionally, we've uncovered your efforts to artificially manipulate Steele's share prices through buy-backs and media manipulation." Towles pulled a thick report from his satchel and tossed it towards Glass.

"We're advising that you amend corporate earnings reports for the past four years to reflect Steele's actual financial status. You are required to file a public disclosure notice reflecting these adjustments. You will take this action in the next thirty days. Your company will be fined twenty-five million dollars for these blatant violations of policy, and you, Mr. Glass, will personally face a ten million dollar fine for your role in engineering the deception."

Towles seemed disappointed at Glass' relaxed demeanor and apparent lack of concern. He raised the pen and jabbed it at the other man. "We're recommending that your board of directors review the quality of your corporate leadership. Furthermore, unless you can provide convincing evidence of your company's present and future solvency, we'll have no choice but to recommend suspension of Steele's public trading privileges. Effective in forty-eight hours."

There it was. The kick in the teeth, administered with vindictive pleasure by Raymond Towles, the corporate giant-killer. Glass knew the man was envisioning the reverberations of his actions in the financial world and the headlines in next week's Wall Street Journal.

Glass was fully aware that he was perilously close to losing everything he'd worked a lifetime to achieve. His next action would represent his only chance to avert a disaster of Biblical proportions. The adrenaline still coursed through his body, and he took this last moment to relish the racing of his pulse. Then he took a calming breath. Towles had played his hand. Now Glass would play the one he held.

"Fair enough," he said evenly, "We'll issue the revised financial reports, and correct the other errors. I don't think we should be fined, and would ask you to reconsider that action. You know that suspending our trading privileges would destroy this company. Would you give me a chance to reassure you about this company's direction? I'm positive I can convince you that Steele Pharmaceuticals is close to financial recovery, and with the introduction of our new drug we'll enjoy unprecedented profitability well into the next century." Glass waved a hand at a large electronic screen, which illuminated to reveal a single glittering phrase.

Novix. Drink From The Fountain of Youth.

"Novix," Glass somberly proclaimed, "is Steele's newest product, and it's going to change the world. This is a drug that will restore youth, Mister Towles, and I don't mean clearing up wrinkles or restoring hair. Novix will make people young again. We're in the final stages of gaining FDA approval for human subjects testing of the drug. We expect to be test-marketing Novix in less than two years."

"And what exactly is this drug supposed to do?" Towles squinted dubiously at the screen.

"It stops the process of aging, at the biocellular level. Novix may even be able to reverse it. Laboratory animals have demonstrated actual growth regression. If that's not enough, there's the real possibility this technology will produce cures for cancer and AIDS within the next three years. This isn't speculation or rhetoric. Novix is the biggest research breakthrough in pharmaceutical history. Even if you're not concerned about Steele Pharmaceuticals and our stockholders, think of the implications of this drug for society."

"What's the market potential?"

"Billions," Glass enthused, "trillions. It's unlimited. The target population for this drug would be everybody in the world. Face it, Mr. Towles, everyone's obsessed with youth – looking young, feeling young, staying young. The anti-aging market's already huge. Think about wrinkle cremes and fillers, cosmetics, and hair replacements. Half the nonfiction best-sellers are about staying young. Con artists rake in billions selling products that are supposed to revitalize people or restore potency. Throw in the fitness boom, health foods and vitamins, and the worldwide marketing of youth is in the trillions right now. Imagine a medication that would actually restore youth. Wouldn't everybody in the world want that pill?" Glass moved across the room and laid a hand softly on the older man's shoulder.

"Think of the implications, Mr. Towles."

Glass nodded at the screen. A collage of images moved slowly across. Pictures of young people playing in parks. Throwing footballs. Running races. Driving convertibles. Dancing and laughing. Playing with children. The scenes gradually transitioned. Nursing homes. Shriveled old people in wheelchairs, staring at nothing. Nurses spooning Pablum and tending to bedsores. Vacant-eyed men moving checkers with trembling hands. Old women lying on beds, gaunt and resembling concentration camp victims. Dozens of images panned slowly across the screen.

Buried in the middle of the slideshow were pictures of the Evergreen Nursing Home in Lafayette, Louisiana. The scenes of Raymond Towles' mother lingered longer than the others. The woman stared blankly at the camera, a blind and pathetic skeleton reaching out with a clawed hand.

"The first patients to receive Novix will be the elderly," Glass said softly. "Those confined to nursing homes. We've selected some facilities to serve as test markets. The most severely deteriorated patients at these nursing homes will be given the chance to take Novix free of charge."

Towles fixed a gleaming eye on Glass.

This was the critical moment. If he had guessed wrong, Towles would explode in fury, call a halt to the proceedings, and add attempted bribery to the long list of charges. Glass' career would be dead and buried. But if Towles didn't act right now, there was a chance. The older man held Glass' gaze for a long moment, his wrinkled face set in stone.

Glass knew precisely what was going through Towles' mind in that instant, because Scottie Bowers had uncovered the man's secret. It didn't involve murder, abuse, or scandal. It had everything to do with shame. Raymond Towles grew up in a family that had been pitifully poor and among the most wretched in Thibodaux, Louisiana. Abandoned by a shiftless husband, Ada May Towles had raised five children on the pathetic income she received from cleaning houses. The Towles children had gone barefoot and wore rags to school. Food was little more than hog scraps. Raymond was the oldest, and he'd slipped away early. He left Thibodaux at seventeen and never looked back. He abandoned his miserable roots. He told his wife he had no family. He carried on this way for nearly a half-century.

Then shame caught up with him. According to his therapy notes, Towles began experiencing overwhelming guilt and sought counseling to absolve his pain. Tortured by the years he had thrown away, he struggled to come to grips with the self-loathing he felt for abandoning his family. The same thing his father had done. Towles had lived seventeen years of Hell before fleeing Louisiana. His mother was ninety and never escaped.

The gentle Doctor Lomas helped him recover, suggesting he make amends. Towles returned to Thibodaux and attempted to re-establish family ties. He provided financial help to relatives still living in the squalid conditions he'd left behind so long ago. As a further act of contrition, he began paying his mother's nursing home bills.

Glass intently watched as the man stared at his mother's image. This was the critical moment. The presentation carefully orchestrated to exploit Towles' guilt and shame. Glass wanted the man to remember his mother's impoverished life. But more importantly, to believe Novix would give her a new one.

"What's the status of FDA approval on Novix?" Towles spoke for the first time in several minutes.

"There's an FDA inspection team at our research facility in Guatemala right now," Glass said. "I've arranged a satellite link-up with my top assistant to give you an up-to-the-minute report."

Glass nodded towards the back of the room, where another huge monitor hung on the wall. A nervous Barney Fried punched in keystrokes, and a moment later Bob Travers' smiling face appeared. The chunky man wore a wrinkled khaki outfit and a rakish safari hat. He'd intentionally neglected to spruce up, preferring to give the impression that his appearance was unplanned. Glass called out a greeting, and asked Travers to provide an update.

"Gentlemen," Travers began in his confident voice, "the FDA site team has been on-site for three days, and things are proceeding without a hitch. The inspection's halfway done, and not a single problem has been found. To provide confirmation, I've asked the head of the team to address you." Travers stepped aside and Wayne Wilkinson's face appeared on the screen.

"Good afternoon," the man said, nervously pulling the ever-present pipe from his mouth. "We're a long way from completing our inspection, but things are proceeding well. Novix has tremendous potential. At this point, I can see no barriers to a successful outcome. We've had only one minor problem, and that's been....."

Static interrupted the transmission. The screen went black, and Glass quickly stood. "Must be a satellite problem," he said, "but I think you've heard enough to conclude that the site team likes what it's seeing. We're a lock to advance Novix for human subjects' testing. We've requested accelerated approval. We can start testing Novix on the elderly in less than six months."

Glass stood beside Raymond Towles. "We have a drug that will restore youth. I don't think Steele's stockholders will complain if their share values quadruple in the next two years. And I don't think we should prolong the suffering of our elderly because of a few minor infractions."

Towles gazed into the other man's sincere brown eyes, then sighed and pulled a gold watch from his vest pocket. He stared at it and flipped the thing shut, then ordered Glass from the office. Towles wanted to consult privately with his staff. Glass returned to his office and sat calmly in his leather chair for thirty minutes. He was confident the ploy would work. If not, he'd think of something else. He wasn't about to allow this dinosaur to bring him down. The intercom interrupted his reverie. Glass returned to the conference room. Towles' pained expression hadn't changed, but his tone was a millimeter more positive. The man picked up the massive report and weighed it a moment, then dropped it into his briefcase.

"Consider yourself on probationary status, Mr. Glass. File your amended financial statements, and issue a public disclosure statement acknowledging your dividend shenanigans. The twenty-five million dollar levy against the company will stand, although I'll suspend your personal fine. If you pass this FDA inspection, and if you're approved to begin human subjects testing, I'll grant you a twenty-four-month deferment on the suspension of your trading privileges. You'll have that period of time to get your company into the black. If you continue to violate regulations, I'll come back and shut you down, Mr. Glass. And I'll do it in a heartbeat."

Glass resisted the urge to thrust his arms high in victory. He didn't allow the smug grin to form. He put a humble look on his face and gave Towles a respectful nod. He trembled with the effort of concealing the adrenaline rush buzz-sawing through his body. He allowed himself to enjoy the intoxicating sensation of victory. With Towles out of the way, his vision would be realized. They would pass the inspection in Guatemala. Novix would proceed to human subjects testing. The hostile takeover of Dowd-LaPorte, the little company he coveted, was all but done. It was all clicking into place. Steele would soon rule the pharmaceutical world, and he would ascend to the pinnacle of the business world.

CHAPTER SIXTEEN

Tikal Research Center,
Guatemala

A soft vibration pulsed against his wrist, causing the wiry man to sit up in bed. He terminated the silent alarm and remained motionless until his eyes adjusted to the darkness. He focused on the watch's fluorescent sweep hand, slender body rigid as he carefully counted off sixty seconds. He cocked an ear and heard only the distant hum of an air conditioner. The man arose and pulled on his shoes, then activated a penlight. He shined it under the bed and located the canvas bag. He moved across the room and stood in the darkness, directing the light towards the ventilation grill. Earlier in the day he had stood on a chair and peered into it. He discovered the tiny camera concealed behind the grill.

Now he would disable it.

He unplugged the desk lamp and focused the penlight's narrow beam on the cord. Earlier in the day he had spotted a dissecting knife on a lab table and slipped the instrument into his pocket. He used it to saw the cord in half, pulling apart the pair of wires and stripping away rubber insulation.

He twisted the bare wires together and dropped it to the floor. He picked up the plugged end, took a deep breath, and inserted it into the wall receptacle.

Downstairs in the control room of Paragon Security, a young guard named Eugene Robinson was watching porn on his phone when he heard a loud click and the building was plunged into darkness. The man nearly swallowed the enormous wad of Red Man stuck in his cheek. He unclipped the flashlight from his belt and directed it towards the blue Folgers can at his feet. Robinson spat out the plug, then moved across the room to the electrical panel.

Every breaker in the box had been thrown. Robinson swore softly and returned to the security board, locating the switch that activated the emergency power system. He heard a loud hum from the next room as the 240-volt generator came to life. The room was bathed in dim yellow light as the generator began feeding juice to the network of emergency lights.

Robinson returned his attention to the bank of security monitors. All screens were black. The backup system lacked power to run the surveillance cameras or electrify the fence. The compound would be without security until an electrician could be flown in from Guatemala City. Robinson knew from experience it would take eight hours to get someone out here, and it might take days to repair whatever was wrong. Guatemalans weren't known for electrical wizardry, tending to intersperse brief periods of work with frequent breaks and interminable lunches.

The door swung open and a sleepy Tavey Bohanon walked into the room. He raised his brows as he saw the thrown breakers. Bohanon turned to the guard with a question in his eye.

"Don't know," Robinson said in a flat Texas twang. "Everything just went boom 'bout five minutes ago. No sparks. No warnin'. Nothin' unusual on the monitors. Somethin' shorted and threw the main breakers. The whole goddam building's shut down."

"Bugger," Bohanon said, giving the breaker board a thump with thick knuckles. "Get yer arse upstairs 'n rouse me a security detail. Ah wan' four men walkin' tha perimeter fence, 'n guards posted at tha front 'n back entrances to tha buildin'. Keep 'em thar twenty-four 'n seven 'til tha problem gits fixed."

"I haven't called this in," Robinson said.

"Ah'll take care 'a that, lad, soon 's we get tha goddam place secured. Ya get tha detail up 'n stationed 'round tha perimeter of tha soddin' buildin'. Tha's tha goddam priority righ' now. Ah'll take care 'a tha notifications."

Bohanon waited until the man was gone, then took another look at the security panel. What the hell it was now? Something was always going wrong with this fucked up building. Wiring corroded and shorted out in the humid climate, and daily tropical rains played havoc with anything electronic. The facility's computers seemed to fail more easily down here.

Last year, a big water rat chewed through thick conduit and shut down the electrical system for three days. Then there was the time somebody plugged in a toaster and blew out the entire panel, halting operations until a repairman could be shuttled in from Guatemala City to rewire the place. Bohanon had repeatedly requested an electrician be assigned full-time to the research facility, but Joseph Hermann turned him down flat.

Bohanon sat down at the control panel, nervously drumming his fingers and staring at the bank of yellow emergency lights. The facility was in darkness. Security cameras were down. A splendid idea came into his head and he cast his eyes upwards as he chewed on it. Bohanon reached into his boot and brought out the flask, indulging in a thoughtful sip. Then a few more slugs of the sour mash as he considered the risks and rewards.

Bohanon nodded his head as he made his decision. He took one last nip before returning the flask to his boot. He rummaged through the desk and found a flashlight, then Nova Labs' chief of security rose and walked out of the room, moving in the direction of the clinical laboratories.

———•———

Shimota stood in the darkness and listened. He heard only creaks and ticks as the facility's interior temperature began to rise and the concrete and metal structure began to infinitesimally expand. Shimota laid two fingers across his wrist, assessing the rapid pumping of his radial artery. The old man took several deep breaths, then set off down the long hallway. He crept furtively along until he reached Tamara Rodgers' door. He turned the knob and stepped into the room.

She lay curled in a fetal position, clutching a pillow in a tight lover's embrace. Shimota crept across the room and stared at the sleeping woman, noticing the gracefully exposed bare leg. He dropped his eyes and nodded respectfully before moving away from her bed. He scanned the room until he located her briefcase on a corner desk. He quietly opened it, placed an envelope inside, and re-latched the case. Then he slipped from Tamara's room.

He continued his stealthy journey down the dark hallway towards the center of the building. He passed Nova Labs' administrative offices and cafeteria, then entered another corridor and walked towards the facility's west wing. Shimota halted and cocked his head as the sound of approaching footsteps echoed down the hallway. He moved to an unlocked door and slipped through it, leaving the door cracked open.

Bohanon went striding past, flashlight bouncing off the shiny floor as he headed in the direction of Renewal Gardens. Shimota waited until the footsteps faded, then flipped on the penlight and continued his furtive journey through the halls of the Tikal Research Center. He shined the light's beam on each door until finding the one he sought.

Shimota took out a key ring filched earlier that day from an inattentive biotechnologist. He selected a key and unlocked the metal door. He gazed around the room before moving to the row of magnifying instruments. He flipped the power switch on an electron microscope. As he'd anticipated, the building's emergency system was set up to power the laboratories.

From a chilled storage locker he removed a container of tissue samples, then returned to the microscope. He prepared the first sample and placed it under the scope, then he bent over the eyepiece. Yanni Shimota began his private investigation of the Tikal Research Center.

He had no idea of the peril he risked, but it would have made no difference to Shimota. Despite being long past seventy years old, Shimota allowed nothing to intimidate him. It had been more than six decades since he'd felt anything approaching fear.

Shimota had been six when his universe exploded in a blinding flash of white-hot light, and a horrible gray-white cloud rained death. He'd been trapped for days in a tiny space beneath the ton of debris that dropped when the apartment building collapsed. Alone in the blackness, he stoically endured a severely burned leg and fractured pelvis. He didn't cry, and after the first twenty-four hours stopped calling for help. He eventually began to tear desperately at the rubble, moaning piteously as he dug at the huge pile of dirt and rocks with bare and bloody hands. His churning hands forced the debris away and he pushed into a tiny opening. When he pulled his hands away, a shaft of sunlight illuminated the boy's prison. Hours later he crawled into the devastated streets of Nagasaki.

He remained on those streets for two years, a skeletal waif who did what was necessary to survive. Eating from the trash bins of military posts. Stealing precious soap, shoe polish and chocolate candy from GI's and selling them in a booming black market. Shivering at night in the rubble of the building that entombed his family, watching the endless dirty rain that would leave an eternal legacy for his nation.

That was the last time Shimota had been afraid. He had survived an atomic bomb. He had crawled from the rubble. Every day of his life represented a bonus, each sunrise a promise, every breath a gift. Shimota felt no fear now, as he sat in the dark laboratory and studied one slide series after another.

The old man was unaware that his activities were being monitored by surveillance cameras beaming signals to a room a floor below him. Fortunately for Shimota, no one had raised their eyes to look at the monitors, which were powered by their own electrical circuitry. It was two o'clock in the morning, and Gene Johnson paid the surveillance monitors no mind. Johnson and his assistant were busy studying tomorrow's inspection schedule and ensuring pre-recorded video segments were perfectly sequenced and prepped.

Johnson was unhappy with yesterday's performance, finding a dozen flaws and problems. He demanded the video segments be spliced into real-time activity without interruption, an accomplishment his nervous assistant insisted was impossible. The film editor, an intense and sallow man named Woody, had been able to cut the transition time down to a few milliseconds. The switchover occurred in the blink of a gnat's eye. It was apparent nobody upstairs had the slightest idea what was happening, but this wasn't good enough for the perfectionistic Johnson.

He'd decided to replace conventional switching devices with electronic relays and had underestimated how long this would take. He'd been working at the swap-out for six hours, leaving Woody to number the video segments and assign each to a video port. Putting fire to another cigarette, Johnson glanced at his watch and silently swore. Replacing the relays turned out to be exhausting work and the sweating man chain-smoked one Camel after another as the night dragged on. He wondered if all this goddam extra effort was worth it. Then he recalled the big payoff. The beach house. Cases of good whiskey and dark-skinned whores.

Johnson mentally counted his million in cash. He fantasized chasing a whore through the house. She was buck naked, running, squealing, giggling, tits bouncing. He was just about to grab her when his reverie was interrupted by a soft call from Woody, who was standing in front of the video monitor.

"Come here," Woody said, "take a look at this shit."

Johnson walked over and looked up at the monitor. Shimota was in Laboratory Five, sitting in a ring of light and studying something beneath the electron microscope.

"Fuck," Johnson shouted, and ran for the phone.

CHAPTER SEVENTEEN

Shimota removed a half-dozen cases of DNA samples from cold storage. He placed each sample under the electron microscope, ignoring the computer and its fancy enhancements. Shimota first examined the studies relating to Gus, the orangutan whose severed spinal cord was miraculously reattached. The scientist carefully examined the animal's genetic history. He moved on to tissue samples identified as Sheila's, the chimpanzee receiving injections of Novix. A notebook lay open on the laboratory table, and as he worked Shimota occasionally paused to enter notations.

Turning on the computer, he scrolled through a sequence of menus. He opened files containing lab studies he'd been shown the past two days. He compared them to the notations he'd made in his notebook, occasionally shaking his head in puzzlement.

The tiniest noise, a little bump and a whisper of movement. He startled and raised his head, glancing around the room. He remained motionless, barely breathing and hearing only the bass-drum thump of pulse pounding against tympanic membrane. Finally he shrugged and went back to his work. He picked up his notes and returned to the electron microscope, where he again examined Sheila's lab studies.

"Sooo," he murmured softly, and scribbled a long entry in the book.

Shimota turned off the equipment and left the room, moving down the dark hallway and entering the next laboratory. He went through a similar routine, comparing DNA samples to computer entries. He worked more quickly through the next three labs, duly making notations in his book. As he powered up the last computer, he leafed through the notebook and reviewed his entries.

"Make no sense," he muttered.

"Now, what on earth are you doing, Doctor Shimota?" Joseph Hermann stood in the doorway.

Shimota whirled around with an embarrassed look. Hermann stalked into the room and moved in close. He wore a blue Polo shirt and tan slacks. Light from the table lamp glinted on his steel-rimmed glasses. He appeared angry and rumpled.

"You invite to inspect any way we choose," Shimota said softly. He held the other man's gaze. "This way I want inspect."

"By sneaking into the lab after hours? Examining experimental materials that have nothing to with your inspection? Looking at lab studies outside their research context? Exactly what do you hope to accomplish?"

"Find truth," Shimota responded, the anger raising his voice. "You hide truth in daytime."

"Well then," Hermann said in sotto voce, "tell me the 'truth' you've found. "I'm sure it's nothing more than a misunderstanding. Let's clear it up and go to bed."

"Where missing research? Invertebrate studies? Why orang studies incomplete? Computer files show you making progress each step of way, experimental foundation solid. But you skip critical steps. Go from cell studies to reattaching spine of monkey. Where intermediate work?"

"We did the appropriate studies, on a variety of animals leading up to primates. The computer models helped us....."

"Bull." Shimota's voice trembled with anger. "Computer studies fake. Data not consistent. All results perfect – no nonsignificant outcomes. No failed experiments. No iterations. Not possible in biological research. Science advance on trial and error. Make hypothesis, then test. Accept or reject, then make new hypothesis. Where null hypotheses? Where lab animals? Where other primates you worked on?"

"Dead and destroyed," Herman responded. "This is a remote research site, Doctor Shimota, not some goddam university center where you can obsess on the irrelevant. You surely don't expect us to keep ten years of dead animals."

"Where photos or documentation? Where outcomes and cell studies on failed experiments?"

"Okay," Hermann said, raising his hands in supplication and moving closer. "We took a few shortcuts. Perhaps we should have better documented our failures, and kept the research animals. Or used fucking handwritten lab notes. But you can't argue with results. Can't you agree that the incredible things we've accomplished are more important than methods?"

"No," Shimota said shortly, "can't agree. This bad science. Methods important. Bad procedures contaminate findings. Invalidate outcomes. Just like when you at Harvard."

Hermann blinked behind the glasses. "What's that supposed to mean?"

"I know about you. Why you leave university job. Ten years ago, Harvard president get suspicious about you research. Suspect cheating. Ask committee of academics to review. You fired from Harvard for same thing you do here. Take shortcuts, cheat on research, and change results to support hypothesis."

"That's rubbish," Hermann sputtered, "I left because Nova Labs offered me a million dollars a year. Even if what you're saying is true, it has nothing to do with the work we're doing here."

"Has all to do, because you doing same thing. You cheat, change outcomes. All research here invalid."

"What about our request for human subjects testing?"

"Cannot support." Shimota shook his head firmly.

"It's a damned shame," Herman said, also shaking his head, "that you just can't reason with some people."

Shimota saw cold eyes behind the shiny glasses. The door swung open and Bob Travers walked into the room. For the first time, Shimota realized he might be in danger. Travers roughly grabbed him and pushed him onto a chair.

"Well if it isn't Charlie Chan," Travers said, "the famous fucking detective." He grabbed Shimota by the face and viciously twisted his head, glaring into the man's eyes. "You should remember what curiosity did to the cat, Dr. Shimota."

Hermann stepped in close and grabbed Shimota by the hair, yanking his head to one side and exposing the neck.

Travers moved forward and drove a hypodermic needle into the man's carotid artery. They held the struggling Shimota until he fell unconscious to the floor.

"Fuck," Hermann said.

Travers shrugged. "The asshole brought it on himself."

"It's a complication we don't need," Hermann sighed wearily. "Grab his legs, and let's get him out of here. I'll call Houston."

—————◆—————

Four hours later the two men filed somberly into the cafeteria, where everyone had gathered for breakfast. Hermann raised his arms and called for their attention. "I'm terribly sorry to bring you this news," he said, "but Doctor Shimota has suffered a stroke."

Tamara gasped and swayed against Will. He felt a concussive wave of disbelief.

"How.....How b-bad is it?" Tamara stammered.

"Our staff physician's stabilized him, but we're not sure he'll pull through. We're arranging transport, and Doctor Shimota will be taken to Guatemala City as soon as possible. Unfortunately, the plane won't be here for two days."

"Does anybody know what happened?" Will asked.

"We found him in Laboratory Five," Hermann said. "He apparently went there this morning to look at lab studies. We found him unconscious on the floor." The scientist raised his hands. "There's nothing we can do except stabilize his heart and wait for the plane."

"I want to see him," Tamara said in a voice shaky with emotion.

Hermann led them down the hall to the clinic, standing aside as the others filed inside. Shimota lay motionless on a narrow cot while a technician pumped a blood pressure cuff.

"Oh God," Tamara moaned. She ran to kneel by the man. Shimota looked frail and ancient, his breath coming in rapid pants. She leaned close and grasped his hand. "Yanni," she whispered, "can you hear me?"

Shimota opened his eyes and looked around the room. He raised his head and tried to say something, struggling to open his mouth. He emitted a soft groan and collapsed onto the bed.

"Better not stress him," Hermann advised, "he's in critical condition." He nodded at the staff physician. The man moved to Shimota's side and began checking his vitals. "Try not to worry," Hermann soothed, placing a hand on Tamara's shoulder. "We'll keep him stable until the plane arrives."

Tamara continued to kneel by Shimota, still holding his limp hand. Travers pulled Connors and Wilkinson aside, raising his hands in a placating manner.

"Gentlemen, this is a tragedy," he said. "But this inspection is the most crucial event in our company's history. Can we can continue without Doctor Shimota?"

"I don't see why not," Wilkinson said. He glanced at Connors, then began searching coat pockets for his pipe.

Will gave the man a look of disbelief.

"Doctor Shimota's briefed me nightly," Wilkinson said. "He's satisfied the research is clean. He was impressed with the clinical trials and said as much to me last night."

"That's not the impression I got," Will said. "Besides, who'll take over his responsibilities?"

Wilkinson tamped tobacco into the briar bowl, and this time he lit it before pointing the thing at Connors. "You will."

"Great," Travers enthused. "We'll resume after lunch." The man turned to leave, then turned back.

"By the way, has anyone seen Bohanon this morning?"

CHAPTER EIGHTEEN

Site Coordinates 125, 22 W; 047 S-SE;
Grid Map 12,
Republic of Guatemala

Twin helicopters slanted towards the jungle with tandem thumping compressions, blowing foliage wildly as they dropped into the tiny jungle clearing. Painted drab military green with cloudy camouflaged underbellies, the choppers displayed neither insignia nor tail numbers. The pilots, dark-skinned young Hispanics wearing reflective aviator glasses, simultaneously powered down engines amid shrieking whines and bumped to the ground. Seconds later, squads of Guatemalan soldiers jumped to the ground and fanned out to form a loose perimeter. The troops formed an edgy defensive circle, peering into the dense terrain with assault rifles at the ready.

Anton LeDoux sat inside a chopper, clenching the heavy blue gym bag against his scrawny chest. He glanced around and saw that nobody was paying him any mind. He unzipped the bag and peered inside. The quarter-million was still there, neatly stacked in dozens of bundles of crisp green hundreds. LeDoux stared at the money, nearly as green as the cash with envy.

It pissed him off.

He had done all the goddam work, putting his ass squarely on the firing line. Meanwhile, the jerkoff he was meeting today was getting the big payday. He reached a grubby hand inside the bag and lovingly fingered a stack of hundreds, feeling his resentment swell.

He set up this goddam deal. He had thrown thousands of dollars around Guatemala City, most aimed squarely at the man he was greasing. After six months of coddling the jerkoff, LeDoux won the man over and brought him into the scheme. But not until after the asshole had milked LeDoux for everything he could get, and the fucker wouldn't budge from the quarter-million dollar price tag. With his supplier finally in place, LeDoux brought the principals together, negotiated the sale price, and arranged for the product's transfer. He was taking every goddam risk, even getting his ass chased through the Guatemala City airport by that prick Bob Travers. Yet everyone but LeDoux was getting the big money.

Despite all the bullshit, LeDoux was proud of himself. A year of hard work was finally coming together, here in the middle of the goddam Guatemalan rain forest. Pretty soon the deal would be finished, and he could get the hell out of this sweatbox of a fucking jungle. In less than an hour, his man would meet him at the designated spot and hand over the product. LeDoux would fork over the obscene amount of cash stacked in the blue bag.

"Mother fucker," he swore, nervously zipping the bag closed and hefting it off his lap. The goddam thing had to weigh thirty pounds, all of it hard U.S. currency. For the umpteenth time, LeDoux calculated his piece of the action, and for the umpteenth time he decided it wasn't enough. LeDoux would be paid four hundred thousand upon delivery of the product, less the quarter million owed his supplier. Lieutenant Villareal and his storm troopers had cost him another fifty. That left barely a hundred thousand in profit. LeDoux had sunk twenty large of his own money into this goddam project, meaning he'd clear eighty thousand when this shit was over. Meanwhile, the asshole who stole the product would waltz away with a quarter million dollars for a motherfucking morning of work.

It wasn't right.

LeDoux hugged the blue bag to his chest and as he peered from the chopper. He hopped gingerly to the ground with a distasteful look. That was another thing that pissed him off about the deal. He hated the goddam jungle with its incessant heat and swarming insects, yet it seemed he spent half his life tromping around one shithole place or another. He hated the entirety of Central America, with its blistering sun and never-ending fucking rain forest.

Of course, he spent the other half of his life in Saint Croix, lounging on the balcony of his waterside condo watching tanned and naked ladies stroll past on the boardwalk down below. On occasion, LeDoux bought a piece of pussy from the passing smorgasbord of brown Caribbean flesh. He couldn't bitch too much. But the good life was expensive. It wasn't going to last if he didn't start clearing more profit from these transactions.

Lieutenant Villareal hopped from the other chopper and jogged towards LeDoux. The sight of Villareal caused another round of disgust to fire up from LeDoux's gut and stick itself in his craw. The little Guatemalan was dressed in a stiff Cammy outfit two sizes too large and wore shiny leather combat boots so new they squeaked. Villareal wore a matching camouflage helmet that kept slipping forward on his head, and he carried a leather riding crop. The entire ensemble looked idiotic to LeDoux, and he chuckled derisively as Villareal approached. The man was a goddam Latin Barney Fife, a pathetic stickman stumbling around the fucking jungle. LeDoux wondered what the fuck the problem was now.

Lieutenant Villareal was a so-called officer in the Guatemalan army, a shrimpy Latino with a scraggly mustache which he pulled at constantly. Like everyone else in this fucked up South American shithole, Villareal was a corrupt little weasel. He'd demanded fifty thousand dollars to round up a squad of troops and a couple of choppers, a sum LeDoux considered highway robbery. Christ, LeDoux thought with disgust, that little bastard's getting nearly as much I am, for a fucking afternoon ride in the country.

"What's the problem?"

Lieutenant Villareal moved to stand nervously beside him. "Ees closest we can lan' to place you wanna go," he said, "chopper pilots say no other landin' spots. So we gotta hike into jungle from here. Ees veery dangerous aroun' here, Senor LeDoux. Many bad things happen een thees area. My soldiers don' wanna be here."

"Right," LeDoux snickered. "Veery fucking dangerous out here. You got your vicious swarming insects, your killer parakeets, and we can't forget your ferocious goddam ground squirrels. They're probably making up their battle plan, getting ready to swoop down on our asses." LeDoux shook his head in disgust. "How far we gotta hike through this shit?"

Villareal pulled out a topographical map and pulled at his mustache as he consulted it. "Tres kilometers, possible' quatro."

"Which way?" LeDoux felt a shiver as he looked around the jungle.

"Thees one," Villareal nodded towards the North. The little man looked speculatively at the gym bag, then tapped it with the riding crop. "Wha 'chu got een thees bag, she's muy importante, eh?"

LeDoux jerked the gym bag away, causing Villareal to give him a squirrelly grin. "It's none of your fucking business, is what it is. Now let's fucking vamanos."

Villareal grinned at the man's Spanish, then shouted something at his soldiers. The troops jogged over and lined up in a loose formation, and the lieutenant pointed the crop towards a narrow game trail. Weapons at the ready, the column of soldiers plunged into the jungle.

LeDoux walked in the middle of the pack, clutching the bag in a death grip. The string of men wound deeper into the thick foliage, occasionally stopping while a couple of soldiers with machetes hacked at the dense undergrowth and cleared the overgrown path.

Anton LeDoux was a tall man, thin to the point of emaciation. He carried his scrawny shoulders in a habitual stoop. He wore a linen leisure suit that had begun its life a pale ivory color, but the outfit was now turning chocolate brown from the incessant jungle dirt. A wide Panama hat shaded the man's angular face from the baking sun. LeDoux thought the ensemble gave him a rakish Peter O'Toole look, but he bore a closer resemblance to a grubby and sunburned Ichabod Crane.

Despite his distinctively Gallic name, Anton LeDoux was anything but a Frenchman, although he occasionally affected an accent and tried to pass himself off as a mercenary. The name change had come later in his life.

He'd been born Anthony Ludinski. He had grown up amidst the sour cabbage smell of a ratty three-room flat in a low-income Polish neighborhood in South Chicago, raised by a pair of indifferent alcoholic parents who seemed barely aware of his existence. Young Anthony had been a painfully thin and vacant-eyed kid who realized early on that no parental interest would be forthcoming. His parents were old when he was born, and so lost in their boozy existence that they barely exchanged words with the somber boy. Anthony learned to take care of himself.

By his fifteenth birthday he had been busted a dozen times. Nearly all of his offenses involved shoplifting, petty theft, or grab and dashes from the little corner stores that infected his neighborhood. He rarely stole toys or candy. Anthony focused on objects of value. Things like money, clothes, or jewelry. He was a natural-born thief and stealing became his sole activity. He would ultimately utilize this singular talent to devise an effective strategy to acquire the things he wanted from life.

He'd just take them.

Anthony seemed to bypass his teen years. He quit school during seventh grade. He had no social life. When he wanted something, he stole it. He became a regular at juvenile hall, and at age seventeen he was transferred to adult court and faced a jail term for armed robbery. Early one spring morning in 1990, Anthony impulsively ran down to Lexington Avenue and signed up for the Marine Corps.

He'd been in boot camp three days when subjected to a vicious GI party thrown by bunkmates who didn't approve of his disdain for basic hygiene. Anthony stoically endured the painful process of having his skin rubbed raw by rough scrub brushes, although he continued to ignore the shower. It didn't matter, because barely a week later he was caught pilfering a footlocker. After less than a month of military service, young Anthony Ludinski was booted out on his ass, although he bragged the rest of his life about his deadly Marine Corps training and the dangerous undercover missions he'd accomplished.

It was shortly after he walked out of Camp Lejeune, dishonorable discharge in hand, that Anthony discovered his true calling. In many ways, it was little more than a return to nature.

Anthony hitchhiked to California and took a job as a janitor at a defense plant in Santa Ana. While emptying trash cans from the research labs, Anthony found something that would change the course of his life. He was about to toss a load into a dumpster when something shiny caught his eye. A tiny microchip. Anthony impulsively stuck it in his pocket.

That evening he was sitting at a seedy bar a mile from the plant, sucking down fifty-cent drafts and absently toying with the thing, when a man walked up and offered Anthony a hundred dollars for the chip. He shrugged and took the sucker's money, and a few beers later the man offered to pay Anthony for the company's trash.

Anthony embarked on his career in industrial espionage. It was a perfect job match. He was a natural-born thief, and there was a ready market for anything he could steal. Anthony developed a routine. He'd hire on at some big defense company as a maintenance man, pilfer everything he could lay his hands on, then move on before anybody caught him. During his first year, he made twelve thousand dollars as a janitor and another thirty-five thousand selling stolen technology. He sold everything – blueprints, broken or discarded parts, old computers, memo's and letters from company executives, even discarded printers. He'd been nailed a few times but never convicted of anything more serious than petty theft.

He spent the next twenty years refining his skills and broadening his repertoire of thievery. Along the way, he began fabricating stories about his past. He'd sit in one seedy bar or another and brag about his training as an elite Marine killer or his adventures as a mercenary. Other times he'd refer to tours in the Middle East, and the top-secret missions he'd carried out. One year he impulsively changed his name to Anton LeDoux, faking an accent and bragging about the Foreign Legion. He hinted at contacts in the illegal arms trade and carried a little pistol he liked to flash around.

Anton wanted to be a player in the world of industrial thievery and wanted others to fear him as a dangerous man. He yearned to see the look of respect in their eyes, so his stories grew wilder each time he repeated them. He rarely fooled anybody. Anton LeDoux would forever be what he was and nothing more. A petty thief. A tadpole darting around in a tankful of gliding sharks.

Still, his career as a thief wasn't a complete failure.

When the defense industry fell into recession, LeDoux made the transition to pharmaceuticals, a field with considerably more upside. LeDoux made a few good scores, but nothing that would put him in the big leagues. The deal he was about to consummate would yield his biggest payday, but the eighty thousand paled when he thought of the quarter million he was carrying in the gym bag.

LeDoux felt the heavy weight of the cash as he trudged through the steaming jungle. Every step jarred at his burning resentment. He thought about the fucking stumblebum he was meeting. LeDoux burned with contempt for the man. It wasn't right that this asshole should get such a huge payout when Anton had done all the work. The idea kept gnawing at him, and he began to wonder if there was another way to do the deal. An intriguing idea popped into his head, but he was distracted by a commotion up ahead. He saw Villareal stomping towards him.

"Are we fucking there yet?" LeDoux asked irritably.

"Si, I think," Villareal said, jerking his head up the trail. "There ees a man up there, who says he ees waiting to see you, senor."

"About fucking time." LeDoux wiped his forehead and followed the little soldier up the trail. They pushed through the underbrush and stepped into a clearing. There stood Anton LeDoux's contact man ringed by nervous Guatemalan soldiers. LeDoux stepped through them and approached the man, both hands gripping the precious bag. The other man was in the process of raising a silver flask to his lips, and he raised it in a little salute.

"Do you have it?" LeDoux demanded.

"I do indeed, ya can be sure 'a that," Tavey Bohanon said with a boozy smile, "'n did ya happen ta bring tha' money?"

CHAPTER NINETEEN

"Nice meeting place." LeDoux grumbled, "Middle of the fucking jungle. I don't see why you couldn't bring the goddam thing to Guatemala City. And why such short fucking notice?"

"Opportunity knocked, ya see," Tavey Bohanon said, smiling easily, "thar's a power outage in tha place, 'n it's knocked tha whole buggered buildin' out. All tha security's down, n' it gave me a chance to get inta the lab and swipe tha thing. An' as far as meetin' out here, lad, ya know goddamn well I canna be gone from tha sod'n place more'n a couple 'a hours."

LeDoux opened his mouth to say something, but Bohanon raised a stubby finger and nodded towards Lieutenant Villareal. The little soldier was standing a few yards away, nervously pulling at his mustache and watching them with interest.

"Take your men down the trail, and wait for me," LeDoux ordered.

Villareal shrugged and shouted something to his troops, and the two men watched in silence until the soldiers were out of earshot. Then LeDoux turned back to Tavey Bohanon.

"Allright, where the fuck is it?"

"I've got 'er right here," Bohanon said merrily, reaching back to tap on a pack strapped across his broad back. "She's sittin' in me pack, jest as bonnie 'n healthy as she can be." LeDoux started forward, but Bohanon raised a thick hand.

"I'll be seein' tha color a' ya money first, if ya don' mind."

LeDoux opened the gym bag and showed him the contents. Bohanon grinned hugely at the sight of it, and rubbed his thick hands vigorously together. "Alright, then, I'll show ya what ye've bought fer yerself," he said, and reached around to pull off the backpack. He unbuckled the straps, then reached inside.

Bohanon removed the jobara plant and thrust it towards LeDoux.

"Thar she be," he beamed, "aren't she grand now?"

"That's what this shit's all about?" LeDoux said incredulously. "That fucking weed? Everybody in the fucking pharmaceutical world wants to get their hands on that thing?"

"Beauty's so often 'n tha eye 'a tha beholder, now ain't it," Bohanon said, "besides, there ain't more'n a dozen 'a these little beauties that exist, 'n rare things 'r so much more precious. Nobody 'n tha warld except fer Nova Labs' has ever had one 'a these plants, until right now. You've jest bought yerself somethin' that's warth a lot ta any research outfit 'n tha world."

"An' now," the stocky man nodded at the gym bag, "I'll be takin' me money."

LeDoux reluctantly handed over the bag, and the resentment came boiling up again. Hatred seized the man's skinny body, racking him with a shudder of frustration. It was so fucking much money, to just hand over to this ignorant fucking Irishman or Scotsman, or whatever the fuck he was. Either way, the goddam potato farmer didn't deserve all this cash.

LeDoux wanted it.

He'd never before laid hands on this kind of money. The simple act of releasing the bag set off another round of fury. Like all thieves, he'd spent his miserable life waiting for the one big score. He'd never touch this much cash again.

Tavey Bohanon grabbed the gym bag and took another peek, then gave LeDoux a jaunty two-finger salute. He made his way back into the jungle, whistling a tune as he departed. LeDoux watched the money as it grew legs and started walking out of his life. He couldn't let it happen. He couldn't ignore his instincts. He was a thief, and every fiber of his shabby being screamed at him to do what came naturally.

Steal it.

LeDoux looked wildly around. There was nobody watching. No cops. No witnesses. Just this drunken fuck and a goddam gym bag loaded with a quarter-million dollars in cash. It was about to slip through LeDoux's grubby fingers. Nearly wild with panic, he pulled the silver pistol from his coat pocket. Heart thudding in his ears, he raised the weapon and ran shakily towards Bohanon.

Then he shot him.

The pistol made three cracking sounds that rang simultaneously with the heavy thunks of the bullets slamming into Bohanon's back. The man groaned and slumped to the ground, the khaki shirt on his broad back slowly staining crimson with blood. LeDoux ran forward and grabbed the gym bag, spilling bundles of cash onto the ground. He felt a surge of exhilaration as he greedily began scooping them up.

Now he had the money and the plant. He would give the goddam weed to the buyer. It would solidify his reputation and signal a move into the big leagues. Word would get out that Anton LeDoux could make the big deals. Maybe now he'd broker transactions himself and get away from this middleman bullshit. He'd be a player, a man to be reckoned with, and best of all he had the money. LeDoux did a little basic math, and let out a joyous whoop.

Three hundred and twenty-five grand! My biggest fucking score ever. Three hundred and twenty-five fucking grand! All mine!

His fevered mind began concocting schemes. He decided to lay off working for a year. He'd buy that new Beemer convertible. The James Bond car. He'd fly to St. Croix, in fucking first class, and he'd sit smugly sipping wine as coach passengers filed enviously past. When he got to the island, he'd celebrate his ass off. He'd get piss-drunk, then go down to the water and buy himself the most expensive piece of pussy on the beach. He'd order a new suit, one tailor-made instead of the off-the-rack piece of crap he was wearing.

His fantasies were interrupted by the sight of Villareal jogging up the trail towards him. The Guatemalan soldier skidded to a halt at the edge of the clearing. His eyes grew wide when he saw the cash scattered on the ground. He unleashed a staccato blast of Spanish over his shoulder and began fumbling to unsling his rifle.

"Fuck," LeDoux whined in frustration. He'd forgotten about Villareal and his troops, now crashing through the underbrush towards him. He took out the silver pistol and popped off a couple of rounds in Villareal's direction. The little man dove for the ground and rolled away. LeDoux grabbed the gym bag and sprinted into the jungle.

He ran like a wild man through the dense terrain, clutching the bag in a death grip. The jungle erupted in a cacophony of shouting and gunfire. A stream of bullets went zinging through the air. LeDoux kept running, ears filled with the distempered sounds of his breathing and mind filled with glory and riches. He had the goddam money, and nobody was going to catch him. The gunshots stopped, and LeDoux slowed to a walk. He heard them beating through the brush somewhere behind him, but that sound eventually faded as well.

The exhausted man dropped to the ground and leaned against a tall kapok tree. A few minutes later he heard the heavy whumps of choppers. He watched the pair of helicopters rise above the tree line and slant away to the South. He laughed contemptuously at the idiot Villareal. LeDoux waited until the choppers were gone from sight. The silly grin gradually faded away as he frowned in concentration. A thought insinuated itself into his thick head.

A hundred and sixty miles of uncharted jungle lay between him and Guatemala City. His transportation had just disappeared beyond the horizon. How the fuck would he get back?

"Motherfuckers!" He jumped up and emptied his pistol into the sky. The furious man issued a stream of curses and slammed the gym bag to the ground. His voice echoed through the jungle and died away. The sudden silence served to remind him that he was alone in this place. LeDoux stared into the dense foliage and felt a shiver of fear run up his spine. He noticed the sun dropping below the treetops. He nervously reloaded the pistol, then snatched up his satchel of money. He spotted a narrow game trail snaking into the jungle.

LeDoux had no desire to spend another second in this place. He clutched the money bag to his chest and began moving cautiously down the trail.

LeDoux trudged along the path, all the while cursing Villareal, Bohanon, and fucking Guatemala every step of the way. Everything had gone to shit in the space of five minutes. LeDoux was furious at everybody but himself. The fucking drunk Bohanon should have picked a better meeting place. If the prick hadn't been so greedy, LeDoux wouldn't have been forced to shoot him. And Villareal. The fucking spic tried to steal the money he had worked so hard to take for himself. After already ripping him off for fifty grand. Then the asshole flew off and abandoned him in the middle of fucking nowhere.

He began plotting his revenge. He would track down the weasel Villareal. He would follow the little asshole to wherever he lived, and then he'd take care of Lieutenant fucking Villareal. He'd kick down the door and shove his pistol in the fucker's mouth. Bring the little spic to his knees, that's what he'd do, and teach him about double-crossing Anton LeDoux. He imagined the terror he'd see on Villareal's face. He saw himself pulling the trigger and blasting the bastard to hell. He savored the image, and the feeling of power it gave him.

Villareal would be taught a valuable lesson. One that he would pay for with his life. People might have fucked with Anthony Ludinski, but nobody in this shithole world would ever again fuck with Anton LeDoux

The man continued to push savagely through the dense undergrowth, his mind filled with thoughts of revenge. He ducked to avoid the sagging branches of a huge acacia bush and found himself standing on a narrow dirt road, overgrown and rutted with deep parallel ditches.

LeDoux squatted and saw fresh tire tracks, and felt a surge of relief fill his scrawny body. He remembered Bohanon telling him there was a village, and that Nova Labs had built a dirt landing strip. All he had to do was find either one, and he'd figure out a way to get to Guatemala City from there. Then he'd settle matters with one scrawny Guatemalan lieutenant.

The man glanced up and down the narrow road, then squinted at the sky as if the fading sun would clue him in on which way to go. Finally he shrugged and turned to the left. Like so many other things Anton LeDoux had done during this miserable day, it would prove to be a bad decision. He began walking down the road, moving away from the village and deeper into the vast rain forest.

———◦———

Tavey Bohanon lay motionless on the ground as the early evening gloom turned into the pitch black darkness of night. There was no indication that he was alive, save for the tiniest rhythmic movement of his rib cage. Eventually he stirred and groaned, then he tried to raise his head. A stab of pain lanced through the middle of his body, and the man collapsed back to the jungle floor. The movement caused fresh waves of pain to pulsate from his back, and Bohanon felt the world start to spin. He let loose a low moan and lapsed into unconsciousness.

Forty yards away, a jaguar lay concealed in high grass. Its yellow eyes focused intently on the unconscious man. A big male in its prime, glistening black and weighing nearly four hundred pounds. The animal stretched eight feet from nose to tail. Its distended belly revealed the cat had fed earlier in the day. Just after sunrise, it had run down and killed a full-grown boar, eating half the animal before picking up the two hundred pound pig and stashing its remains high in the fork of a tree. The big jungle cat wasn't the least bit hungry, but it was interested in the man lying unconscious on the jungle floor.

Jaguars kill for reasons other than hunger. Big males will brutally attack any male jaguar they encounter. They attack their mates, and mothers sometimes kill and consume their cubs. Males attack any creatures that wander into their carefully marked territories. This cat had lain in concealment for nearly a half-hour watching the motionless man and carefully processing the variety of scents and signals it was receiving.

If the man were alive, the jaguar would pounce and kill him. If dead, the big cat would carry the carcass away and conceal it for future consumption. When the wounded man groaned and struggled to rise, the cat had hunched down and gathered its powerful legs to launch an attack. Now the jaguar settled back and continued to study its prey. Finally it sniffed the air once again, then the animal rose and began cautiously slinking into the clearing, moving towards the helpless man.

An overpowering scent assailed its nostrils, and the big cat dropped to the ground. It raised its head and tested the air. A rustling in the undergrowth. Something was coming, heading for the big cat and its helpless prey. The jaguar flattened its ears and emitted a low rumbling growl, revealing yellow three-inch fangs. The cat processed the scent once again, then slunk away into the darkness.

Seconds later another kind of animal entered the little clearing. It was huge and fur-covered, and shuffled on two legs. The creature stood in the blackness, sniffing the air and gazing in the direction of the departed jaguar. Then it turned its attention to the motionless man, and began to move slowly towards him.

Tavey Bohanon startled into consciousness. He was lightheaded from the loss of blood, and waves of pain continued to rack his body. The man spasmed into a racking cough, spitting up a scarlet mouthful of blood. It was pitch dark, with only the dim glow of a quarter-moon to illuminate the jungle. Bohanon didn't need the light to realize that something was standing over him.

He moved his head slightly, wincing in pain as he did so, and squinted up at the creature. Bohanon had spent most of his life tromping around one jungle or another, and was familiar with all manner of wild animals. At first he couldn't recognize what it was, but an instant later he did.

The realization caused a new burst of adrenaline and fear to electrify his ravaged body.

"Alfie?" He asked in a hoarse voice.

Bohanon received a rumbling growl in response. The creature leaned over him and bared gleaming misshapen teeth, and the delirious man again fell blessedly unconscious.

The animal drank in the man's scent. It was familiar, and a keening rumble left the beast's chest. Some recess of its primitive brain opened and a stream of images tumbled out. A gleaming laboratory. A little cage and a favorite toy. Chattering animals. And creatures like this one, with shiny eyes and white coats, who had jabbed things into its body.

It stood a long time, staring at Tavey Bohanon. Then it raised its head and tested the air, detecting another scent in the warm night. The creature whimpered, like a puppy craving attention, then it turned and shuffled away, moving down the narrow jungle path.

Following the scent of Anton LeDoux.

CHAPTER TWENTY

Tikal Research Center,
Guatemala

Will was dreaming.

Tamara stood in the darkness at his bedside, dressed in a gauzy white shorty nightgown that barely covered her shapely ass. He saw the glistening reflection of her lipstick in the dim light. The sweet scent of perfume drifted through the night to envelop him. He inhaled deeply, drinking in the woman's aroma. She stood silently by his bed, body languidly swaying to a silent rhythm.

She raised her arms and slowly pulled the nightgown over her head. She released it and he watched mesmerized as the silken garment floated to the floor. Despite the darkness, Will could see the shape of her full breasts and the luscious curves of her naked body. Her nipples stood out like ripe raspberries, and she had a knee turned coyly inward. She seemed to hover above him – a voluptuous shimmering vision pursing shiny lips and pouting at him. He felt himself become turgid.

He raised his head and blinked, trying to adjust his eyes to the darkness. The erotic vision remained above him, smiling dreamily as she cupped her tits and sensuously stroked them with her thumbs. She rolled her head, tossing her frizzy hair and exposing the graceful curve of her neck. She flitted her eyes toward the ceiling. Then she lowered her head and smiled, floating closer to his bed.

He felt the mattress shift as she crawled onto the bed. Her radiant warmth embraced him as she slid under the covers and moved closer to him. The shock of reality was electric. He wasn't dreaming. He was wide awake, and this was happening. Tamara was in his bed. She climbed atop him and wrapped her arms around his neck, pushing her tongue into his mouth in a passionate kiss. Will groaned and felt his body's instant response to her gyrating hips. He frantically shucked his boxers and began moving in response to her rhythm.

She whispered something in his ear. He didn't hear her as he ground against her pelvis and moved a hand to cup her breast. Tamara whispered more urgently. This time he heard her.

"We have to talk," she hissed.

"Not now," he moaned. He reached down and stroked between her legs, feeling her buttery wetness. She grabbed his wrist in a vice-like grip and pulled it away, then stuck her mouth back in his ear.

"We have to talk now," she said in a harsh whisper.

"Right now?"

"Shut up," she hissed, "keep your voice down. They're probably watching us right now."

"What?" He tried to rise off the bed, but she pushed him back and continued her gyrations.

"Goddamit." Her whisper took on an urgent tone. "Get some blood back into your brain and listen to me. We may be in danger. I've got to talk to you about what's going on, and this is the only safe way to do it." She paused a moment to emit an orgasmic moan, then moved her mouth back to his ear.

"Yanni left a note in my briefcase. He believed something was wrong in the labs. With the way they're doing research. He was suspicious of Hermann. He found a camera hidden in the ventilation grills." As a shudder coursed through her body, Will felt the wetness of her tears.

"They tried to kill him. He said in the note if anything happened to him, we shouldn't believe it was an accident."

Will tried to shake off his sense of unreality. Was this an erotic dream? A voluptuous woman had appeared like a naked ghost and climbed astride him. Now she was urgently whispering about conspiracy. He felt the excitement down below begin to fade and tried to get his sluggish brain moving.

"Keep humping," she whispered, "in case they're watching."

He was happy to comply and continued to move his body against hers. His heart was pounding like a jackhammer. He felt himself growing excited again as he ground against her velvety flesh. "Why would they fake research? Or try to kill someone on the inspection team?"

"I don't know," Tamara said. He felt her shake her head against his chest. He heard the frustration in her voice. "People fake research all the time. There's something bad going on in this place. Yanni knew it. They found out and somehow caused him to have a stroke. We've got forty-eight hours before this inspection ends. I intend to use the time to find out what happened to him."

"We could call in the authorities," he said. "Or just get out of here."

"If you checked your cell phone, you'd know there's no service down here. You can't call anywhere on the room phones. And how would we leave? We're stuck in this jungle. Besides, look what they did to Yanni. We'd put ourselves in danger if they suspect we're onto them. We have to work this out ourselves, Will. Are you going to help me?"

"Of course," he whispered into her ear. "But we can't do anything tonight." He gave her another passionate kiss, and she responded with heat. When they came up for air, he drew away to look at her.

"What should we do now?"

Tamara Rodgers raised her head and stared wide-eyed at him.

"Make love to me, you idiot."

It had been a long time since he held a woman in his arms. As he lay in the darkness holding Tamara, he had trouble believing this was more than a dream. She made love the same way she did everything else – full-bore and loud. She'd passionately consumed his body, wrapping her long legs around him and taking him deep inside her, then she lost herself in a kaleidoscope of passionate gyrations. She seemed to have forgotten that someone might be watching them, and after a while she climaxed in a series of shuddering cries. A minute later he followed with his own moaning release. She collapsed on top of him, sweaty and spent. Then she slid beside him demanding to be held.

"I don't know anything about you," he murmured. "Suddenly I want to know everything."

She remained quiet for so long he began to wonder if she'd fallen asleep. "I am born," she finally sighed. "I live. I fall into disgrace."

"Dickens so soon after sex?" He grinned wryly at her.

"Yep," she said shortly, then fell silent.

"That's all I get?" He offered her a smile of curiosity.

"This isn't the time or place." She flitted her eyes upwards, and he remembered what she'd said about cameras. He felt his face warm at the thought that others might have witnessed what they'd just done.

"No, it isn't," he murmured. He pulled her against him, but a minute later raised his head and cocked it in puzzlement.

"Did you hear that?"

"Yeah," she said. They heard the sound again, a low moaning growl that seemed to come from a great distance.

"There it goes again."

She rose on an elbow and frowned as she concentrated. "It's coming from outside this place. Out in the jungle. Sounds like something screaming or howling. What is it, Will?"

"I don't know, but it doesn't sound happy."

—————— ◆ ——————

Anton LeDoux spasmed in terror as he stumbled wearily along the narrow road. At first whatever was following him moved stealthily in his wake, remaining silent and invisible in the blackness of the night. It was only when he abruptly stopped and cocked his head that he heard the sounds coming from the jungle behind him. The animal was no longer making any attempt at stealth. He could hear it grunting as it crashed through the undergrowth and closed in on him.

LeDoux could see the glow of the research center's lights in the distance. He ran awkwardly towards them, limping heavily, staggering from the weight of the gym bag. It had been a horrible night. He had wandered exhausted and disoriented for hours along the dark trail. Then this fucking animal started following him, and he'd begun running. A sharp pain was stabbing at his gut and his lungs were on fire, causing the asthmatic LeDoux to hack and cough as he stumbled along. A thousand times he'd thought of throwing the goddam bag down, but he couldn't make himself drop it. This was his money, his big score, and nobody was taking it from him. Not even the fucking thing chasing him, whatever it was. LeDoux had his pistol, and if the goddam thing caught him he'd blow its fucking brains out.

He stepped into a clearing and spotted the research center a mere hundred yards ahead. LeDoux heaved a sigh of relief. He was going to make it to safety before the fucking animal could catch him. He set his feverish mind to work concocting a story. What fucking reason could he give for wandering around in the jungle in the middle of the night with a bag full of cash and a stolen jobara plant?

At the moment he didn't give a shit. He'd get inside that gate and away from whatever the fuck was out here, and then figure out his story. He'd give the dumbasses some bullshit line. Maybe return their precious fucking plant in exchange for a ride to Guatemala City.

Something stepped into the roadway in front of him, a shadow profiled in the glare of the building's lights.

LeDoux squinted at the thing, then he shit his pants. In the moment of his death, everything came back to him. The cabbage-smell of the shitty little apartment, and the vacant look in his parents' eyes. His constant need for them to recognize he existed. It all flashed though Anton LeDoux's mind, and for the first time he felt remorse for the emptiness of his life. He felt his knees buckle, and the bag dropped to the ground. He didn't care about money now. LeDoux had the presence of mind to take out the little pistol and empty it into the thing as it descended on him, but it did no good. He let loose a strangled scream, then it was on him. The jungle fell silent as the creature did its grisly work.

It moved away from the mangled body and stood in the darkness at the jungle's edge, twenty yards from the perimeter fence of the Tikal Research Center. Its hairy chest was heaving, and its breath came in shallow pants as it stared at the high wire fence and the structure standing just beyond it.

The animal's snout was smeared with blood, and its belly was distended from feeding. LeDoux was dead almost before he knew he was being attacked, and the ravenous creature had devoured most of the man's stringy flesh in a frenzy of slashing teeth.

The animal turned its deep-set eyes towards the building, and again felt the wave of familiarity sweep over it. Driven by its biological imperative, some dim recess of the creature's devastated brain commanded it to come to this place. Once again, the creature raised its head to the black sky and screamed out the jumble of tortured emotions that filled its mutated soul.

CHAPTER TWENTY-ONE

Aboard the SteeleHead,
Twelve Miles Southeast of Port Aransas,
In the Gulf of Mexico

Andrew Glass leaned against the railing of the gleaming yacht and stared out at the rolling sea. Despite the dark night, there was light everywhere. Twelve miles away the clustered lights of Corpus Christi bounced off the gauzy atmosphere and illuminated the Western sky. Along the coastline, he could see a thousand twinkling lights flung along the narrow strand of beach that constituted the Matagorda Peninsula. Off the ship's port side was open sea, and only a constellation of glittering stars defined where the deep water ended and night sky began.

The sounds of a party drifted from below decks.

Glass had invited a dozen people aboard, including Barney Fried and Elliot Masters. The diminutive Scottie Bowers had flown in from Chicago, and several of Glass' high-roller buddies were in attendance. The ship had three full-time crewmen, and Glass had arranged for a pair of hostesses to serve up food and drinks. He'd also imported a couple of high dollar escorts from Houston. Glass was married to a gorgeous South Texas socialite, but had left his wife at home this evening. This wasn't a night for spouses.

Masters stepped onto the deck and leaned on the railing. The trim attorney was nattily attired in a bespoke blazer, silk slacks and expensive deck shoes. A matching skipper's cap set off the ensemble. Masters stood in silence, sipping Perrier as he stared into the starry sky.

"Makes you feel puny, doesn't it?"

"We think the world's small and we're large," Masters replied. "Sometimes we need perspective."

"What inspires you, Elliot?"

"I don't know," the man shrugged. "The good life. Wanting to leave a mark. That kind of stuff. What about you?"

Glass raised his glass to the sky. "The stars."

Masters let the comment hang and sipped at the water. He turned towards Glass. "I heard news."

"Dowd-LaPorte?"

Masters smiled tightly. "Talked to a buddy whose firm handles their corporate litigation."

Glass took a slug of the booze and gazed at the sky.

"The split's still there," Masters said, "and it's about to get nasty. It's tearing the place apart. The growth faction is dead-set on taking the company public. The old guard's fighting it tooth and nail. They want to keep the family atmosphere that made them successful. Both sides are threatening litigation."

"What about the holdings?"

"Nothing's changed," Masters said, pausing to wet his lips with the Perrier.

"Malcolm Dowd's still the controlling partner?"

Masters nodded. "The old man died a couple of years ago. Left young Malcolm half-ownership of the company."

"What about the public offering?"

"He doesn't give a shit. He'd love to torpedo the whole thing."

The men fell silent, and Glass gazed at the starry panorama.

Forty years earlier, Dowd-LaPorte had sent a research team to northern Guatemala, seeking plant life with medicinal potential. The expedition returned with a ton of plant and arboreal life. Included in the clutter were three jobara plants. The company's scientists paid them scant attention and they were stored along with everything else in the California lab.

When Glass learned of the company's long-ago expedition, he became curious. He put Scottie Bowers to work. The little investigator didn't attempt to break into the Dowd-LaPorte laboratory, as it was under tight surveillance. He breached the company's computers and located an electronic inventory that included photographs of every plant found in the jungles of Guatemala.

The company's scientists had no idea of the jobara's research value. But Glass had no doubt what would happen after Novix hit the market. Dowd-Laporte would develop its own version of the drug. This could cost Steele Pharmaceuticals billions down the road.

So Glass decided to move on Dowd-LaPorte. It was a stroke of brilliance. He would acquire a profitable company and expand his corporate portfolio. He would also possess every jobara plant in the world. Just one problem – Dowd-LaPorte wasn't for sale. His early overtures had been swiftly rejected. The only option was a hostile takeover, and Glass was up for the challenge. He gave Scottie Bowers another assignment - find leverage. Bowers sniffed out Malcolm Dowd, the twenty-seven-year-old heir to the company fortune. A lazy do-nothing who loved fast cars and hard drugs. Dowd spent his days shoving cocaine up his nose and wrecking expensive automobiles. Malcolm had inherited half ownership of Dowd-LaPorte but had long been expelled from the company boardroom. His salary insufficient for his reckless lifestyle. Glass had coddled the man for months, listening patiently as Dowd bitched about his family and supplying him a steady stream of designer drugs.

Glass capitalized on the man's festering hatred towards his family. He pitched a buyout offer, promising to make Malcolm filthy rich. He would confer on Dowd the nominal title of company president. Along with the title would be the privilege of personally firing everybody in the company. The spaced-out Dowd eagerly accepted the offer but wanted nothing to do with stock transfers or letters of credit. Dowd wanted to be paid in hard cash. Corporate lawyers were busy preparing merger and acquisition documents. Within the week, Glass would drop a bombshell on Dowd-LaPorte.

Glass' reverie was interrupted by Masters. "You're over-capitalizing the purchase," he was saying.

"You doubting me, Elliot?" He turned to focus his cold eyes on the other man.

"It's my job to plan for contingencies," the attorney soothed. "A hundred million's a lot of cash. I just want to make sure you can raise it."

"I'll raise it."

"Mind telling me how?" Masters ventured.

"It'll be there," Glass said. "That's all you need to know."

The two men contemplated the dark sea. A wind had arisen and swells gently rocked the ship. After a while Glass laid a hand on the other man's shoulder. "Don't worry, Elliot. I'm on top of this."

"Alright," Masters said. He nodded and went below decks.

Glass returned his attention to the sea. He gazed into its blackness, enjoying the sensation of the breeze cooling his face. This was a celebration cruise, and he allowed himself to savor the moment. Steele Pharmaceuticals was in good standing with the Securities and Exchange Commission. He had played the pompous Raymond Towles like a banjo. Glass chuckled at the thought of the wrinkled dinosaur and his imperious display of authority. Midlands Investigations had uncovered the man's weak spot, and Glass had artfully exploited it. Everything else was clicking into place. The inspection in Guatemala would be over in two days. Novix would be approved for human subjects testing. The takeover of Dowd-LaPorte was all but done.

Raucous laughter from below. Andrew Glass raised his glass to the night, toasting his brilliance and foresight. He gazed at the glittering stars, confident his own was ascending. Glass drained the drink, then threw the tumbler into the sea. He went below and headed for the red-haired hooker. Someone handed him another drink, and he chugged it down. He allowed himself to be carried away by the intoxicating taste of victory.

CHAPTER TWENTY-TWO

Tikal Research Center
Guatemala

"We're in danger."

Tamara leaned in close and whispered into his ear as they slowly circled Ponce De Leon fountain. A rainbow plume of water roared into the air and crashed to earth in a noisy spray. The dome was cranked open and sunlight streamed into the garden. Birds chirped, and the ivy smell of spring was in the air.

Will gazed across the lush garden with its genetically programmed plant life. He tilted his head and stared at the vast dome that crowned the facility. World-class researchers were busy creating genetic wonders inside these laboratories. "I'm not so sure," he said.

"You agreed with me last night."

"Last night it made some sense. In the light of day it seems...I don't know...unrealistic." He swept an arm around the facility. "Look at this place. It took genius to conceive it. Millions to build it. They've recruited credible researchers. Invented genetic technology that advances science by decades. They're creating miracles here. You think they'd risk it all by trying to kill a world-renowned physicist?"

Will didn't want to derail their budding romance. He really didn't want to upset Tamara, but he could see it was too late. Her chest was heaving. Arms were crossed. She exhaled slowly and deliberately.

"Ever been to Disneyland?" she said. "You enter the Magic Kingdom and lose your sense of reality. You forget it's fantasy. That's what they're trying to do here. Make us suspend disbelief. Razzle-dazzle us with genetic technology so we don't look behind the curtain. Make us forget there's someone behind it. Pulling levers. Something's not right, Will. This place is too perfect. Too amazing. It's Disneyland in the jungle. Something's going on in this place. I can feel it. Yanni felt it."

They made a silent circuit of the fountain. He tried to control churning emotions. His fear for Mollie, and worry about the clock ticking away precious minutes of her life. His attraction to Tamara. The desire to please her. The possibility of a relationship. He took a breath and forced himself to reason. To seriously consider what she was saying. It made some sense. Events had occurred that couldn't easily be explained. Tamara's kidnapping by natives she described as children. An animal in the jungle the villagers said came from the facility. Video monitors in the grills. Shimota's sudden stroke. Bohanon's disappearance.

"You know why I'm here?" he asked.

She nodded. "Yanni told me." They made another circuit before she stopped and put a hand on his arm. "I don't want to pry. Can I ask about the condition of your daughter?"

"She's got a few weeks. Maybe a month."

"You believe there's something here to help her?"

"It's a long shot," he said. "But it's possible."

"I hope you find whatever you're after," she said. "But if they're lying to us and engaging in dishonest research, you won't find answers here. You must know that. We need to know the truth, Will. Don't forget they tried to kill Yanni when he got suspicious. What makes you think they won't do the same to us?"

"Let's say you're right. I don't see what we can do about it. We're isolated down here. A couple of thousand miles from civilization. They're monitoring us. Why don't we finish this inspection, get out of here, and notify the authorities?"

Tamara seemed exasperated. "Don't you see? That's what they want. It'll give them time to cover up everything. An investigation could take years. They'll get away with it. We have to do something."

He raised his hands in surrender. "Okay. We do something. I just don't know what."

"For starters," she said, "we don't know enough about these people. Or this place. We need more information. I'd love to know more about Steele Pharmaceuticals. The people running it. And Joseph Hermann."

"Didn't Shimota say something about Wayne Storsky?"

"In his note. He said you should study Storsky's research, whatever that's supposed to mean." She frowned in concentration. "There's no cell service here. We've got to figure out a way to communicate with the outside world."

"They have satellite phones. Russell told me they send electronic dailies to Houston. They're obviously wired to the internet. Shouldn't be hard to get into their system."

"Work on it," Tamara said. "I want to contact my research assistant. Mary Wells. My bulldog. She can find out everything we need to know. Meanwhile, I suggest you continue with the inspection. Play the game."

"Okay." He leaned in close. "You better give me a kiss. In case they're watching."

Tamara pecked him on the cheek. He stepped back and studied her. "I thought last night meant something."

"It meant something," she said, "I'm not sure what."

"I hope we can talk about it at some point."

She stood on tiptoes and gave him a better kiss. "Now's not the time. Let's get to work."

Four men stood around a video monitor, watching the activity in Renewal Gardens. "What the hell are they doing?" Travers raised a hand to massage his fleshy neck.

"Beats me." Gene Johnson took a drag from a Camel. He exhaled a plume and stared at the screen, absently scratching at his pock-marked face. "They strolled into the garden ten minutes ago, and they've been bunched together ever since. Whispering back and forth."

"Probably planning their next hump session," Woody grinned. "Did you catch the show last night?"

"Yeah," Johnson said. "That's one fine piece of ass. She can sneak into my room and jump my bones anytime."

"Enough," Travers said testily. "Can you improve the audio?"

Johnson manipulated a slider on the control panel. On the far wall of the dome, a unidirectional microphone rotated in the direction of Will and Tamara. As they stood beside Ponce De Leon fountain, engaged in huddled conversation, Johnson fiddled with the volume control before giving up.

"I'm gettin' zilch," he said, taking up his cigarette. "They're movin' around, talking low. Plus, they're standin' by that friggin' waterfall. Sounds like rush hour in L.A. I can't pick up a thing."

Travers drummed pudgy fingers as he stared at the activity. "I don't like this crap," he said to Joseph Hermann. "They're up to something, and I want to know what it is."

Hermann had a skeptical look on his face. "A washed-up geneticist and a ditzy anthropologist playing grab-ass? Neither one of them has a clue."

Travers broad face was stony as he stepped in close to the blocky scientist. Hermann wiped the cynical look from his face and took a step backward. His perception of Travers had changed in a big way. He'd thought of the man as clownish, with his flushed face and ingratiating style. An eager-beaver P.R. man, constantly pumping hands and slapping backs.

Then Hermann witnessed the man take out Yanni Shimota. He remembered Travers' detachment as he'd rammed a long hypodermic needle into Shimota's exposed neck. Travers had efficiently dispatched the old Asian with the indifference of crushing a fly. Hermann had come to realize the corn-pone routine was the guise of a cold-blooded assassin.

"Never underestimate anyone." Travers emphasized each word, then curled his hand into a pistol and pointed an index finger at Hermann. "It can bring you harm. Those two aren't as stupid as you think. They're educated and intelligent, and right now they're suspicious. Keep in mind

Shimota figured it out. Watch them around the clock. Let me know if they do anything unusual."

"I'll keep an eye on them," Hermann promised.

Travers turned to Gene Johnson. "As soon as they're out of there, install more microphones. Make sure every inch of the place is covered, including the area around the fountain. They'll return to that spot, and next time I want to know what they're talking about."

"Okay, boss," Johnson said. "Soon as they're out of there."

Travers spun and strode from the room.

CHAPTER TWENTY-THREE

Joseph Hermann was poking at a salad when his phone buzzed. He ran restless eyes over the text and saw his presence was urgently requested at the Horticulture Laboratory. He pushed away the plate and jogged through the corridors to the West Wing. The plant lab took up half the facility's space. A cluster of climate-controlled rooms where plant generation experiments were conducted. This was where the miracle tomato and other wonders growing in Renewal Gardens were developed through the magic of genetic engineering.

A monument to arboreal clutter, the wildly growing plant life resembled the overgrown jungle outside. The humid temperature of a hothouse was maintained, and multitudinous varieties of plants were scattered in disarray. Typically, groups of researchers gathered around tables, engaged in noisy dialogue. That wasn't happening today. A grim cluster of scientists waited with crossed arms as Joseph Hermann entered the room.

"What is it?" Hermann glanced pointedly at his watch. He had other gardens to tend this afternoon.

Meredith Tansey, a tall plant biologist whose rough hands reflected a lifetime of working in dirt, stepped forward. "Better let me show you."

They walked toward the back of the plant lab. Hermann realized where they were heading and felt a tremor of apprehension. Plant biologists were an isolated bunch, preferring to do their work without his involvement. Hermann was never contacted unless they'd discovered something either very good or very bad.

It was apparent Tansey wasn't about to unveil her latest advance in crossbreeding technology. She led him to a heavy steel door, where she punched a security code into a keypad. She stepped aside and allowed Hermann to enter. He pulled on sterile gloves and a surgical mask. Meredith Tansey did the same, then walked stiffly through the room.

It was even warmer in here. The room was monitored by sensors that regulated the internal environment and maintained precise climate control. Unlike the other plant laboratories, this room was meticulously maintained and germ-free. Overhead banks of solar simulators provided artificial sunlight, and a misting sprinkler system was installed in the ceiling.

A mainframe controlled the interior environment. It was programmed to provide the identical climactic conditions as those outside the facility. When it rained in the jungle, precipitation fell in this room. When the afternoon sun blazed above the rainforest, the room's solar lamps were activated and duplicated the outdoor temperature. Jungle air was captured by a mechanical ventilating system, sanitized, and circulated through the room.

In the middle of the room, twelve tubular glass canisters sat in a row. Each was dripping condensation from the humid air. Hermann walked past, glancing into each tubular container as he passed.

Each was designed to hold a jobara plant.

Despite ten years of searching, only a dozen had been discovered. Each jobara had been unearthed like the rarest archaeological treasure and transplanted into this room by Hermann's botanists. The jobara plant was the oldest living matter on Earth, and each was precious beyond calculation. The plant was the foundation of the Tikal Project. The jobara's unique manner of cellular preservation had led to the discovery of the third messenger strand. A commercial genetics lab possessing just one plant could duplicate the messenger technology in a matter of months.

Tansey had moved ahead and was standing beside the last container. Hermann stepped beside her and glanced inside.

It was empty.

"Mother of God." Herman felt his knees give way as he reached to the wall for support.

Will was lying on his bed, staring at the ceiling. Emotions churned through his body like a mix master. A merry-go-round of thoughts and images whirled through his head. Mollie twirled in and out of awareness, the third messenger strand entwined around her body like a serpent. Everlasting fruits and an immortal chimp. His purpose in being here. The responsibilities he'd been ignoring.

Lustful fantasies of Tamara spun in and out of his mind, taking center stage and impossible to push away. It had all congealed and intensified into a massive ball of confusion, compressed into this single moment in time. He focused on his breathing, gradually slowing the rampant thoughts.

One problem at a time.

A badge dangled from his neck. He raised it to his eyes and examined his picture and title. It identified him as a member of an FDA inspection team. As he rubbed a thumb across the badge, he wondered why he was here. Why he'd been selected. He had torpedoed his professional life. No research in over a year. Fired from his job. No academic standing in the scientific community. Yet chosen at the last minute for a prestigious team inspecting the most important drug in history.

He shook his head in disgust as he reviewed his behavior over the past two days. He'd behaved like an adolescent on a field trip. Wide-eyed with wonder. Believing everything. Questioning nothing. He turned his thoughts to the morning's conversation with Tamara. She was terrified and thought they were in danger. Convinced someone tried to kill Shimota. Viscerally feeling something was wrong in this place. Trying to warn him.

He hadn't felt it. Hadn't wanted to see it. Blinded by his obsession with healing Mollie. Made stupid by lust for Tamara. The thought of her aroused every one of his senses. Her scent. The softness of her kiss. The incredible feeling of their entwined bodies. The passion of her love-making. Emotions new and powerful, unlike anything he'd ever felt. Demanding his attention. Distracting him.

She was a complicated woman. Afraid of dying. Needing his help. Just like Mollie. He didn't want to disappoint either of them but wasn't sure he could help them both. Either way, he stood to lose something precious.

He opened the thick inspection binder. He'd barely glanced at it a week ago. Now he went through every page. He'd been assigned to inspect the research design and methodology for Novix. Toxicity studies. Tissue rejection statistics and compatibility studies. Failure rates. He pulled out a yellow legal pad containing his inspection notes. He leafed through a few pages, then threw the pad on the bed.

He found Mollie's picture. He brought it close and kissed her face. He whispered an apology and repeated his promise. Then he grabbed the binder and marched down to Laboratory Four, where Dave Russell was standing by. The man started to say something, but Will raised a hand to cut him off.

"We're starting over," Will said. "The clinical studies you showed me yesterday? I want to see them again. Get out the studies on the orangutan and the chimp. I don't want enhancements or models. Give me hard copies of everything. We'll start looking at tissue studies under the microscope."

Russell started to object, but Will stopped him.

"And rejection studies dating from the day you opened this place."

Russell paled. "I.....I don't k-know if I can do that," he stammered, "some of those records are in storage. I'll have to get Doctor Hermann's approval."

"Get it," Will said, "and bring in Sheila. I want to draw more tissue samples. Can you do toxicology screens in this place?"

"Yes, but I don't know....."

Will cut him off and nodded at the phone. "Call your boss. Get your ass in gear."

Russell sent Joseph Hermann his second urgent call of the morning. He engaged in a terse conversation, then put down the phone. "Doctor Hermann says to give you what you want."

Will opened his binder and got to work. They spent the morning re-examining studies, beginning with the earliest ones in the database. Sheila was brought in, and he drew her blood sample. Russell stepped aside and allowed Will to do it all. Things gradually relaxed as they fell back into the routine of the lab.

After several hours, they took a break. The two men sat at a lab table, chatting about their lives. Russell said he lived in Dallas. He had a wife and two daughters. One in kindergarten, the other still nursing. Will asked about the man's work arrangement.

"I signed on for three years," Russell said. "Every six months I get two weeks at home, expenses paid. At the halfway point I get a month." He shrugged. "I miss my girls. But the pay's incredible. I'll be set for life after three years."

"How do you stay in touch?"

Russell pointed to the laptop computer sitting in front of him. "Wireless. The big antenna on top of the building hooks up to a satellite. I email my wife every day."

Will nodded in interest.

That evening, Will stood on a chair and used a flathead screwdriver to remove two screws. He gave a tug and the ventilation grill dropped into his hands. He handed it to Tamara, then peered into the duct. The camera was recessed into the shaft. It was a Sony, mounted onto a swiveling base. A length of coax was screwed into the rear of the camera, and the cable snaked into the shaft.

He disconnected the camera, then hopped to the floor and gave her a Stan Laurel nod. "Now we can talk."

"Think they'll get upset?"

"What can they do? Bust us for disconnecting the camera they're using to spy on us?"

She waited while he took a moment to organize his notes. "I took a closer look at things today," he said. "Drew tissue samples. Prepped slides. Double-checked everything through the 'scope. I made them show me every study they've done the past ten years. I checked placebo and control group outcomes, and re-ran data for the critical studies."

He flipped to another page. "They've been experimenting with the synthetic strand for ten years. They've run a lot of primate studies, mostly with chimps, and on paper they've had a string of good results. They've looked at nearly every area of genetic programming, and they're convinced the technology might be used to fight killer diseases like AIDS and cancer. Right now they're focusing on aging. They used the third messenger strand to produce Novix, and here's something that might surprise you – the drug works."

"You're saying they're legit?" She was sitting cross-legged, buffing a fingernail.

"Novix is for real. There's nothing fake about it. But there are problems they didn't mention. Yanni was right, Tam. They've been lying to us."

"I knew it," she whooped, pumping a fist in vindication. "What kind of lies?"

"Tissue rejection, for starters. That's always the problem with a synthetic genetic strand. The third messenger's an artificial piece of tissue, even if it's an exact clone of living material. Any organism is programmed to do one thing the instant you introduce something artificial."

"Reject it?"

"Exactly. But they don't report any problems with tissue rejection. Russell claims they've used the strand on thousands of lab animals without a single case of tissue rejection. Russell has no explanation. It just works." Will smiled dubiously. "Science doesn't accept magic to explain how something works. This afternoon I started looking for answers. It didn't take an hour to figure it out."

"How'd you do it?"

"I ran tox screens, but I didn't use the computer. I ran the studies myself using Sheila's tissue samples."

"And you found?"

"Cyclosporine."

Tamara shrugged helplessly. "What's that?"

"An immunosuppressant. It's used when they do transplants, to prevent the rejection of donor organs. But high dosages tend to weaken the body's defense systems. Toxic levels of Cyclosporine, like I found in Sheila, destroy the immune system. It's fatal to the organism."

"You're saying," she said slowly, "that Novix is a legitimate drug. It can make you grow younger. But to use it, you'd have to take another drug that would kill you. And they're hiding that problem from the FDA inspection team?"

"That's what I think."

"Why would they lie? They wouldn't dare test Novix on humans, even if you guys approved it. These people wouldn't be killing monkeys, they'd be killing people. It wouldn't be just unethical, it'd be criminal. I don't see the point."

"Tissue rejection's not an unsolvable problem," Will said. "I'm guessing they need another couple of years to overcome the tissue rejection issue. For whatever reason, they don't want to wait." He paused, thinking about it. "What was it you said the other day? About private-sector research?"

"Advancing science isn't the objective," she said. "This kind of research is motivated by money."

"Maybe they want to rush this drug through clinical trials and to market for financial reasons. They're willing to shortcut research to do it. But I can't figure out who's behind it. It can't be Hermann."

"Did you find out anything about communicating with the outside world?"

"It's obvious they want us cut off. Our phones don't work down here. No cell coverage. But everyone on staff communicates just fine with the states. Including Russell. They have a satellite phone system. And they use email."

Connors nodded at her laptop. "I'm assuming that's wireless?"

She nodded.

"They have a secure wi-fi network. All we need is a password."

"That's beyond my skill set," she said. "Can you get it?"

"I already did."

It hadn't been difficult. Russell talked about little else but his daughters. Kailee and Emma. How amazing and beautiful they were. He wanted to show Will pictures. Connors had watched as the researcher went online and retrieved them. Russell had punched in his screen name and password. *DrRussell. kaileeandemma.*

"Cool." She gave him a nod of approval. "What now?"

"We'll get on the network later tonight. Try to get in touch with your assistant."

"Okay," she said.

Will moved over and sat by her. "We still haven't talked."

"What about?"

"You and me."

She tilted her head and allowed the hair to cascade over her face. She tried to twist a crick from her neck. "What do you want to talk about?"

"Are you involved in a relationship?"

"Not at the moment." Tamara grabbed the nail file and resumed buffing.

"Are you interested in one?"

She kept her head down, concentrating on the nails. "I don't know."

"Didn't the other night mean anything?"

She seemed weary as she pushed a hand through her tangled hair. "Can't it just be something nice that happened? Your lucky night, or whatever? I should have known better," she muttered. "Things can never stay simple."

"I'm sorry," he said. "They can stay simple."

"Now you're hurt." She threw up her hands. "It wasn't just sex, okay? It was wonderful, a night I'll remember. You're a nice man, and I like you. But….." She shook her head and resumed buffing.

"But what?"

Tamara studied his face. "Last night changed things between us."

"And that's a problem?" Will watched as her walls came down. The sassy assertiveness was gone. Now she seemed worn and sad.

"I'm poison," she said.

"Poison?"

"I've racked up two divorces. You know how much divorce hurts? I've had two, and I'm not interested in another. There's more about me you wouldn't like, but that should be enough." She clamped her jaws together. "Still interested?"

He reached for her hand. She resisted, then relented. "There are two people in a relationship. Sure it's all you?"

"I'm selfish and stubborn. I want things my way. I want everybody to change for me. I always hurt the one who loves me. I get crazy about someone, and I'm quick to make commitments I can't keep. Things change, and I have to get out. Somebody gets hurt. Then comes the divorce and even more hurt."

"Divorce isn't a criminal offense."

She leaned her head against his shoulder. Soft tears began to flow. "I hate myself for hurting people who didn't deserve it. I can't change. I've tried. I didn't intend to leave a trail of destruction and pain, but it's what I did. I'm not going to do it anymore."

He pulled her into his arms. She let him put his arms around her, resting her chin on his chest. "I spent a lot of time in therapy," she said, "and all I uncovered was the pattern. I fall in love with nice guys. When it's compromise time, I can't do it. The first couple of times, I figured it was bad luck. Then I started blaming men. It took me a long time to understand I was the one causing problems."

"So you've sworn off love?"

"I don't want to hurt you."

"Does it matter what I want?"

"Not at this point," she said softly. Mollie's photo lay on the nightstand. She nodded towards it. "Besides, your plate seems pretty full right now."

His eyes followed hers, and he stared at his little girl's face. He sighed and released Tamara from his arms. "Dammit, you're making sense," he said. "The time's not right. Sorry I got all emotional. I'll get myself under control. I'm ready to get back to business. First thing is to get some information. You ready to send your message tonight?"

She nodded.

"It might open up a big can of worms. Sure you want to do this?"

"Absolutely," she said.

CHAPTER TWENTY-FOUR

Department of Human Anthropology,
University of Illinois, Champagne

"All right!" Mary Wells exclaimed.

The woman munched an oversized Snickers Bar as she studied the computer screen. An e-mail had arrived from Tamara Rodgers. There would be news from Guatemala, and Mary was eager to read it. She printed a hard copy and stretched to pick it up, but her movement caused the nearby whining noise to increase in volume. She sighed and turned to the gaggle of graduate students lined three deep at the counter. Midterm grades had been posted, and a group of entitled Gen X babies had made a lunchtime assault on the division office.

Mary was a wide-bodied woman who efficiently carried two hundred compact pounds on her stubby frame. She tended to dress in sandals and flowing dresses. With her scarlet hair and flushed face, she resembled an over-inflated kewpie doll.

But Mary Wells was no softie. A hard-nosed overachiever and a meticulous researcher, she possessed a high IQ and a bulldog's tenacity. Mary efficiently juggled graduate school, three kids, and a thirty-hour a week job in the Anthropology Division office. She also happened to be Tamara Rodgers' personal assistant.

Mary studied the bleating herd and was reminded of how much she hated graduate students, although she was one herself. They were all crybabies, uniformly convinced their problems were of the same magnitude as a nuclear attack. This bunch obviously felt maligned by the offending grade list and had rushed *en masse* to the division office. Desperate to avoid the unthinkable fate of being considered average, they were clamoring to see their professors.

"Alright," she slapped a hand on the counter. "Quiet down, people. Nobody's here but me, and I can't help you. I'm a lowly graduate student, just like you. You can all come back this afternoon and submit your appeals." They glared and muttered as if their problems might be Mary's fault, then someone made a move for the door. The rest followed like educated bovines.

Mary tore off another slug of Snickers while contemplating the blinking phones. She'd put everyone on hold when the students had made their assault and was surprised to see the callers still waiting. Mary began working through the calls, occasionally gazing wistfully at Tamara's message. She couldn't wait to learn what was up with her favorite professor.

Mary idolized Doctor Rodgers, who was everything a university professor shouldn't be. She didn't give a damn about departmental politics and fiercely defended her students. There was a long wait-list for her classes. Safely tenured and uninterested in advancement, she never failed to exasperate colleagues and thrill students. She spoke her mind at all times and took crap from no one. Dr. Rodgers actually cared about teaching, and made student education a priority. Invariably noisy and spontaneous, her office door was always open with rock music issuing forth. Even her clothing was a wild splash of color in the drab landscape of academia.

Tamara Rodgers was the reason Mary was in the program.

Mary Wells had been an over-weight and over-forty mother of three when she'd applied for the graduate program. Her grades were questionable and she was a long shot to get admitted. Tamara was on the screening committee and saw something in the plucky woman. She voted for Mary's admission, then took the woman under her formidable wing. She'd even arranged a fellowship to pay Mary's tuition and expenses.

The phones hit their mid-afternoon lull and Mary took a break. She closed the office door and picked up the message. She gave it a quick scan, then Mary went through the message more carefully. She wondered if Tamara was in some kind of mess.

Mary knew her boss was in Guatemala to study a Mayan tribe and to participate in an inspection. Tamara had been excited and for weeks had talked of little else. But the email message hinted something had gone wrong. She needed information and said it was urgent. Mary got out a marker pen and began highlighting.

It was Mary's policy that anything Dr. Rogers needed would receive the highest priority. She swiveled to the computer and began Googling. She located some information but soon realized she needed assistance. She mentally measured the candy bar sticking from her purse. She fought off the urge as she considered who to call. A name came to mind, and Mary snapped her fingers. She reached for the Rolodex, flipping through it until she found Steve's number. A journalist who worked for a newspaper in Chicago, Steve McNeal was Tamara's ex-husband. Mary knew he would help.

She punched in the number, thinking about her own ex as she waited for an answer. The man was a slug who lived in Florida with his skinny wife. He skipped child support payments as often as he made them and had visited the kids once in the past three years. Mary made no effort to conceal her contempt for the man. She couldn't imagine calling him for anything.

On the other hand, Tamara's former husband adored her.

The two of them still dated, and occasional Monday morning flowers would arrive for Tamara. Mary didn't know the details of the divorce, although once after too much wine Tamara confided she wasn't good at marriage. The relationship had survived the divorce, and Mary knew Steve would jump at the chance to help Tamara. She got him on the line and made small talk, filling him in on her life and Tamara's latest escapades. Then she told him the purpose of her call. Steve instructed her to wait forty-five minutes, then check her e-mail.

Mary waited thirty minutes before giving in to the candy bar.

While she munched, she took another look at the message from Guatemala. There was something about the tone she didn't like. Tamara's requests were usually for uncomplicated things like express-mailing favorite earrings or rescheduling meetings. She often filled her notes with song lyrics and stern warnings against gorging on sweets. This message was different. It sounded serious. A niggle of worry wedged itself into Mary's head.

She checked her watch and logged onto the computer. Her e-mail inbox had blown up with messages from McNeal. They were filled with references and each one had multiple attachments. Mary downloaded it all into a file, then she composed a message and forwarded it all to her favorite professor.

CHAPTER TWENTY-FIVE

Tikal Research Center,
Guatemala

Eugene Robinson stood motionless, squinting into the jungle.

His eyes darted back and forth as he strained to see into the shadows. His head was cocked, listening for the tiniest sound. The Paragon security guard was crouched inside the perimeter fence, pressing a flat gray assault rifle to his shoulder. The wiry man twisted his mouth and spat a stream of tobacco juice into the dirt. His eyes never left the jungle.

There was something out there.

A big animal was prowling the dense brush just inside the tree line. Robinson had never seen the thing, but nearly every day he heard the sounds of its movements as the creature stalked the jungle beyond the perimeter fence. He felt the hair rise on his neck as an instinctive part of his body released a surge of adrenaline. A blast of energy electrified his system and set off a primitive alarm. Robinson fought off the urge to turn and run.

The jungle had fallen silent, allowing him to hear the tiny rustling sounds. He remained motionless, listening as a different sound arose from the jungle - an undulating, ragged groan that he couldn't identify. Robinson shook his head in puzzlement. He sucked in a deep breath and clicked off his weapon's safety.

Twice in the past month he had stood in this exact spot. Drawn here by mesmerizing sounds. Determined to track down the animal making them and empty his assault rifle into it. Both times superstitious fear froze him in place.

Now again at the jungle's edge, Robinson stared into the jungle a long minute before releasing a breath. He lowered the rifle, then turned and walked back into the compound.

Robinson was an angular kid of twenty-one who'd grown up among the rolling prairies of Southwest Texas. He'd been a roughneck kid who never backed down from a scrap. He worked the Brownsville oil fields at seventeen, and now a couple of years later was a proud Paragon security officer. Robinson liked the work and took his job seriously. He craved excitement, and the job offered him the chance to carry a weapon. He subscribed to Soldier of Fortune and could cite specs on all the latest ordnance. Robinson was convinced this work would be a stepping-stone towards bigger things. Private security. Maybe personal protection for celebrities. He was proficient with a variety of weapons and possessed a fair amount of courage. Robinson never met anything in his young life that caused him to feel an instant of fear.

Until he came here.

The jungle scared him. Every night he used a stubby pencil to mark off another day on his wall calendar. He was nearly through a six-month rotation and swore he'd never return to this place. He hated it. The heat. The work. The isolation. The place was nothing like he'd thought it would be. He had imagined a big adventure, world travel, and a chance for action. He'd jumped at the chance to work in Guatemala. The pay was double what Paragon paid anywhere else, and Central America sounded exotic. The opportunity for a real adventure.

But there was no excitement here, just alternating extremes of boredom and danger. Lately there had been too much of the latter. Robinson wanted nothing more than to get his ass back to the hill country, and never again pull duty guarding against the jungle. This was a dangerous environment. The natives had been friendly at first but turned nasty and killed two of his buddies with poison arrows. The tribe vanished into the jungle, but Robinson knew they were still out there. And the animals were like nothing he'd ever seen.

Especially the jaguars. More than once Robinson had seen the powerful cats prowling the perimeter fence or crawling through the bushes, waiting to pounce on anything venturing near. A couple of guards had already been attacked by the beasts. He had seen twenty-foot snakes, rats the size of beaver, and poisonous insects that buzzed like aircraft. The wild pigs here were nothing like the ones on his daddy's farm. These things were the size of ponies and had wicked tusks that could slash a man in half.

That wasn't all.

Something else lived here. He'd never spotted the thing although he had found evidence of its handiwork, usually the remains of jungle animals that had been ripped apart.

Deer carcasses. Reptiles. Even the greased-lightning pigs. Once he'd discovered what was left of a jaguar, hacked to shreds. Robinson couldn't imagine what kind of animal could tear apart a big cat like that.

The sun was high in the sky when Robinson arrived for his swing shift. Sipping coffee and flipping through a dog-eared magazine, he heard the sound echo from the jungle. Not the usual grunting and growling. He turned up the volume, straining to identify it. He couldn't figure out if the sound was human or animal, but it was evident the thing was in distress. Robinson chewed absently on the tobacco plug as he listened. He had ventured three times to the jungle's edge to investigate, but lacked the guts to step into it. He'd since been berating himself for his cowardice. After a period of self-examination, he spit the plug into the coffee can and picked up the assault rifle.

The day was losing light and the air superheated as he again left the security room. He marched towards a heavy metal gate on the backside of the compound. The towering trees cast the jungle in a canopy of deep shadow, making it impossible to see more than a few feet past the fence. There was no movement, and no sound except the dense buzzing of insects.

He swung open the gate and stepped through it, pulling the gate closed behind him. He cautiously moved to the jungle's edge. The moaning suddenly grew louder and nearly continuous. Robinson took a deep breath. This time he wouldn't turn back. He double-checked his rifle, then he stepped into the jungle. He instantly lost visibility as heavy brush reached out to grab him. The noise increased in volume, and he knew he was getting closer. He again felt the hair prickle on his neck as he stumbled forward. He heard a shallow panting and rustling of leaves. The man again nervously checked the rifle's safety, then he pushed through the thick branches.

"Holy shit," he shouted. Robinson lowered his rifle and ran forward.

A man lay on the ground, nearly unrecognizable beneath a congealed mass of jungle grime and blood.

It was Tavey Bohanon.

———————◆———————

Joseph Hermann's hellish day continued.

A stab of pain behind his broad forehead announced the arrival of a migraine, and he reached back to massage his thick neck. He rummaged through his desk for aspirin, then dry-swallowed three of them. He waited a couple of minutes for the medicine to take effect, then returned to his problems.

A missing jobara plant was a catastrophic development. He hadn't yet summoned the nerve to call Houston. Also missing was his security chief. He was certain the two disappearances were connected. Shimota lay comatose in the infirmary, awaiting transport to Guatemala City. Nearly every primate in the facility had been slaughtered. Two members of the site team, Connors and Rodgers, had started to act up. The calls from Houston were coming more frequently.

Hermann rubbed his temples with stumpy fingers. What a mess this had become. It had started out so simply. He came here to do research. The Tikal Project was all-consuming for Hermann. He had no family, no friends, and no interests beyond work. After his humiliation at Harvard, he also had no reputation. His sole mission was to restore his name and prove to the pompous assholes who'd terminated him they were wrong.

He considered himself a genius. He gave himself sole credit for the genetic advances created in this remote laboratory. The third messenger strand was just the beginning. There would be much more. His research would change the world. A Nobel wasn't out of the question. That would restore his standing in the scientific community. Everything had been on track. But now there were these complications and he could no longer concentrate on his research. He massaged his throbbing temples as the phone rang. He picked it up and listened, and a tight smile crossed his face. He slammed down the handset and went running for the infirmary.

As he pushed through the door he saw Bohanon lying motionless on a narrow cot, eyes closed and breathing rapidly. A gastric tube snaked down from his nostril, and an IV dripped a glucose solution through a hypodermic needle taped to his arm. Hermann noticed Bob Travers standing beside the bed.

"What happened?" Hermann asked the question of Wiley Donaldson, a stoop-shouldered researcher who doubled as infirmary chief.

"Somebody shot him." Donaldson raised an X-ray to the light. "Three times. He took a slug in his shoulder blade that did serious damage. You can see the thing right there. There's another one five centimeters off the spine. Barely missed a kidney. He also caught one in the right thigh. All three slugs are still in his body."

"Will he live?"

Donaldson tossed the film on a surgical tray. "He's been in the jungle two days. From the looks of his knees and hands, it's obvious he made it back here by crawling. Either of the upper body wounds is potentially fatal, and he's nearly bled to death." Donaldson chewed on a lip as he studied the Irishman. "The wounds are infected, he's bradycardic and nearly comatose. He's stabilized, but we need to get him to Guatemala City. There's not much more I can do for him."

Hermann glanced at his watch. "The plane's due in twenty-four hours. Keep him comfortable with pain medications. If he's still alive tomorrow, we'll take him to Guatemala City."

"Did he say anything?" Travers had asked the question.

"Nothing that made any sense."

Herman turned his attention to Robinson, who was standing nervously by the door. "He have anything on him?"

The guard shook his head.

"He say anything?"

"No, sir," he said.

Hermann jerked his head towards the door. The guard and doctor left the infirmary. Hermann closed the door behind him then nodded to Travers, who moved to the bed and leaned in close. Travers pressed his knuckles on Bohanon's chest. The man groaned and shifted in the bed. Travers pushed harder, and a look of pain creased Bohanon's face. His eyes fluttered open, and he erupted in a spasm of coughing. He turned his head towards his tormentor.

"'Shoulda known 'twas you." Bohanon said weakly, pulling his mouth into an agonized grin.

"Did you take the plant?"

"Ya know Ah did, sar," he rasped.

"Where is it?" Travers thumped again, eliciting another gasp of pain. Bohanon stared at the ceiling until the agony receded.

"Ah handed it over ta LeDoux. Just before tha weasel put three slugs in me. But Ah wouldn' be warrying much about him." He turned his head and looked at Hermann. "Ah saw Alfie."

"Alfie?" Hermann blinked behind steel-rimmed glasses. He shook his head in dismissal. "You were hallucinating. That animal's long dead."

Bohanon flashed a bloody smile. "Bugger off, doc. We both know better'n that, now don't we?"

CHAPTER TWENTY-SIX

Tamara sat cross-legged on the bed, biting a lip in concentration as she focused on the laptop screen. She found the facility's network, then entered Russell's screen name and password. She drummed her fingers while invisible connections were made in the electronic universe. Once online, she browsed to her email account. She scrolled through a series of messages and saw one from Mary Wells. A string of files attached to it. She felt a surge of affection for her grad assistant. Tamara downloaded the records and signed off the network.

She began opening attachments and saw that Mary had been thorough. She'd attached research studies, and stories from business magazines. Profiles of the people associated with the Tikal Project. Stock reports including an analysis of Steele Pharmaceuticals. Tamara scribbled notes on a pad then handed over the laptop to Will. She examined her notes while he browsed.

He placed the laptop between them on the bed. "I had hopes that Storsky's research might tell us something."

"Who is Storsky, anyway?"

"Big name in genetics," he said. "Worked at Yale with Shimota. About a zillion years old. Storsky's specialty is inter-species breeding and genetic transplants. Impregnating a lion with a tiger's sperm and getting a 'liger.' Implanting a zebra's kidney into a horse. He's a pioneer in the field of modifying animals for use as organ donors for humans."

"They doing that kind of research down here?"

"Not that I've seen. Anyway, Storsky's studied the genetic compatibility of related species. Putting a frog's DNA into a lizard, or a baboon's bone marrow into a chimp. Mixing together genotypes. Outcomes haven't been promising. They've had a hard time preventing rejection of genetic materials. Some of their experiments got out of hand. Uncontrolled cell growth, mutation in the host organism, toxicity."

"I don't see how that connects to this place."

"Me either. You find anything interesting?"

She resumed chewing her lip as she stared at her notes. "First of all, who's William Bernard?"

"An original member of the site team. I replaced him."

"Any idea why?"

"No idea," Will said. "I was told he dropped out. No reason was given."

"Well, he's dead. Killed in a car accident in Atlanta. Couple of weeks ago."

Tamara grabbed the laptop and scrolled down the screen. She flipped it around to show him the story. He skimmed it and raised his brows in surprise.

"This is getting stranger and stranger," Tamara said. She returned her attention to the computer screen.

"Here's a profile on Steele Pharmaceuticals. The company's been around a long time. Got started by selling drugs to the government during the Second World War. They were big in blood pressure medicines, and had a huge share of the over-the-counter acid reflux market. Looks like they started to decline about ten years ago. Stock's been dropping like crazy. Two years ago it was selling at a hundred a share. Now it's dipped under thirty-five. Steele hasn't put a new drug on the market in three years."

"Confirms our idea that the company's in trouble," Will said.

"It doesn't explain why they'd commit fraud. Why fake research to get a drug approved if the medicine doesn't work? Think of the risk. Something like this would destroy the company. The idea's inherently stupid. There's got to be more to the story."

They continued to pass the laptop back and forth. "Here's something interesting," Will said. "It's a list of Steele's biggest stockholders. Number one on the list is the CEO of the company – somebody named Andrew Glass." He scanned the list, then turned the laptop her way.

"Check out who else made the list of big-time shareholders."

"Joseph Hermann," she said thoughtfully.

"The top man at Steele Pharmaceuticals and Hermann are among the company's biggest stockholders." He continued to study the list, running his finger across columns of information.

"There's a lot of financial information here," he murmured. "Your buddy Mary must know somebody in the stock market."

"She probably contacted Steve."

"Steve?"

"Ex-husband number one. He's a journalist. Knows how to dig up information."

Will went back to the list. "Here's something weird. Glass has been buying back company stock like crazy. Seems like the further the stock drops, the more he buys."

Tamara gazed upwards in concentration. "So what happens to the stock price if the FDA approves Novix for human subjects testing?"

"It would shoot through the roof." He pulled up the shareholder list and scanned it. "Whew," he exhaled sharply, "Glass recently picked up options on a million shares of Steele's stock. He'd stand to make an obscene fortune."

"How about this for a scenario," she said. "Steele Pharmaceuticals is about to go bankrupt. They need to get Novix on the market. Billions are at stake. The inspection's standing in their way. So they play dirty. Tell lies. Spy on us. Fake research. Maybe kill people."

"That would explain a lot. Except for Hermann. I'd be surprised if money motivated him. I've been around obsessed researchers. For people like him it's all about the science. And reputation."

"At least we have the answer to one question."

"Where the money leads us?"

"Exactly."

Will pinched the bridge of his nose and yawned. "I'm getting sleepy," he said. "Can I stay with you tonight?"

"Yeah," she smiled. "Just don't try to propose or anything." She crept into his arms.

"Are we in danger? Or am I being silly?"

He gave it thought before answering. "Yesterday I thought you were over-reacting," he said. "Today I'm not so sure. This situation's getting complicated. There's more to it than I've been seeing. There's a big corporation behind all this. Big dollars. Reputations."

"I just know they did something to Yanni. And this guy Bernard's dead." She shuddered and moved deeper into his arms. "I'm scared, Will. We're a long way from home. Surrounded by nasty jungle. We have no way to protect ourselves."

"We can't fight them," he said. "No way to call for help. That leaves one alternative."

"Getting the hell out of here?"

He nodded.

"We finally agree on something," she said.

CHAPTER TWENTY-SEVEN

Tikal Research Center,
Guatemala

The chestnut-colored stream of juice landed square in the Folgers can. Eugene Robinson grinned at his marksmanship and wiped a line of spittle from his chin. He rearranged the plug in his jaw and returned his attention to the bank of security monitors. A dozen screens provided video feeds from various areas of the compound. Most were trained on the electrified fence and the jungle beyond it. For a change, all was quiet. A dappled sun illuminated the rainforest. No sound interrupted the morning calm. No movement set off the motion sensors.

Robinson was operating on autopilot, two hours into a dull shift and absently scanning the monitors. He was about to replace the plug in his cheek when something caught his attention. Something out of place. He squinted into a monitor then leaned forward and cranked a dial controlling a perimeter camera, zooming the camera for a closer look.

He spotted the animal lying against the perimeter fence.

A large Brocket deer, fried to a crisp and rigid in death. This was a routine occurrence down here. The local creatures never learned to avoid the five thousand volts running through the electrified fence. Every day something was zapped. Rounding up victims was one of Robinson's regular chores. Removing the carcasses required him to shut off the juice and drag the unfortunate creature to the jungle's edge for disposal. The scent of death spread quickly through the humid air. It wouldn't take long for something to slink in and take advantage of the free meal. Robinson decided to put off disposal detail until end of shift.

A grimy calendar was pinned to the wall. He pulled it down and marked off another day in his tour of duty. Robinson was due to rotate in forty-seven days. He couldn't wait to get back home. He ran his restless eyes around the room. The shift had barely begun and he was already bored. Robinson took another look at the fried deer. It had run head-on into the fence as if something were chasing it. Part of the animal's flank had been torn away. Looked like something had taken a big bite.

He returned his attention to the wall calendar. This month's picture was a collage of Texas wildflowers. Purple and orange Indian paintbrush. Bluebonnets of indigo and lavender so bright they looked artificial. Mexican hat with its tall sombrero crown. A sunny meadow bursting with Brown-eyed Susan. Robinson thought about Texas and felt a pang of homesickness.

He pulled out a notepad and began writing a letter home. His parents were country folk who didn't own a computer. Email was an alien concept. So Robinson communicated in the old-fashioned way. He wrote them letters. He knew they eagerly awaited the mail's arrival. He imagined his father walking down the dirt lane to the mailbox. Sitting at the kitchen table, reading glasses perched on his nose as he read the letter aloud to the family. The old man was a dirt farmer who wore bib overalls every day of his life and had never ventured outside Val Verde County. Eugene was his pride and joy. The son who had made good. Out in the world having adventures. Sending home a few dollars or an exotic photo. He knew they showed his letters to half the farmers in the county.

Robinson finished the letter and folded it into his pocket. He drummed his fingers and looked for something to do. He rummaged through a drawer for the dog-eared Soldier of Fortune. He turned to the article on hunting Texas javelina. Since he was a kid Robinson had stalked and hunted the pigs. The magazine story was pure bullshit, portraying the javelina as dangerous and unpredictable creatures. The writer recommended hunting them with high-powered rifles and scopes. Robinson chuckled at the absurdity. Texas javelina were nothing like the vicious overgrown porkers that ran through the jungles of Guatemala. The ones on his daddy's farm were skinny pigs with ugly fur coats and big teeth. Robinson and his buddies shot the creatures with twenty-two rifles.

The guard stretched his lean body and glanced at his watch, wondering if it was too early to call the cafeteria for lunch. He resumed leafing through the magazine, perusing glossy ads soliciting men in search of adventure. Soldiering was a growth industry these days. Private armies were springing up around the world. Looking for soldiers to fill their ranks. There was action to be found in exotic places.

Africa. Middle East. Central America. Military experience preferred, but not necessary.

He'd figured to return home when this tour was finished. Back to the pathetic farm in Val Verde County. His parents wanted him to help run the place. His father would one day turn the land over to him. Robinson considered the idea of spending his life dragging a plow and shooting javelina with a twenty-two. He began looking more closely at the soldiering ads.

The emergency siren erupted.

He threw down the magazine and scanned the security board. The undulating horn signaled a perimeter breach. Robinson spotted a gaping hole in the electrified fence. He caught movement on another camera. Something running through Renewal Gardens.

He panned the camera and saw a big animal shuffle up to a steel reinforced door on a far wall of the building. It began battering at the door. He felt the building shake with each percussive thump inflicted by the massive creature. He peered in puzzlement at the animal trying to knock down the door. He didn't recognize it. He turned a dial and zoomed in for a closer look. Robinson dropped his mouth in amazement as the thing came into sharp focus.

Again Hermann's phone buzzed. He raised it to his ear, and again he went jogging through the corridors of the Tikal Research Center. He pushed through the double doors of the security room. Robinson was staring into a monitor.

"What happened?"

"That fuckin' thing just tore a hole in the fence and now it's trying to break down the door," Robinson reported in a shaky voice, tapping the monitor with a finger. His face was flushed and he was breathing in ragged gulps. The guard pointed to another monitor, the one showing the fried deer. "The juice was turned on. Five thousand volts didn't faze the thing."

Bob Travers burst through the doors and stood behind Hermann. He stared into the monitor, furrowing his brows in puzzlement. "What the fuck is that?"

Joseph Hermann gazed into the screen and shook his head in resignation. "The product of bad science."

They clustered in silence around the monitor, watching as the animal battered the heavy door. Robinson zoomed the camera, magnifying the thing's image. It was like something from a low budget science fiction movie. The animal had the misshapen frame of a chimpanzee, but huge and mutated. It stood nearly even with the seven-foot door and looked to weigh a half-ton. The shoulders and chest resembled those of a bull. Slabs of corded muscle were layered beneath its furry skin. A reptilian ridge ran along its jagged spine. The mammalian hands were malformed, with razor-sharp claws. The creature's face was an amalgam of a dozen animals. A once-flat mug had extended into a broad canine snout. It had grown rows of what appeared to be shark's teeth. The oddest feature was the ears, which were delicate and human-like. Its red eyes gleamed with intelligence.

Travers swiveled his head and stared at Hermann. "You didn't answer the question. What the fuck is that thing?"

"A lab animal," Hermann said. "An experiment that got out of hand. It escaped the facility. We've been searching for it."

Travers continued to gaze into the monitor. The steel door was beginning to sag under the relentless pounding.

"That's no fucking lab animal."

"It was once a chimpanzee," Hermann said. "We modified it."

"The fuck you mean you modified it? You made that fucking thing?"

"This project's been running ten years," Hermann said wearily. "We were exploring new territory down here. Many of our early experiments weren't strictly controlled. Some studies were trial and error. I was interested in animal defenses. The tactics species use to protect themselves against disease and predation. Nearly every animal on the planet has weapons to protect itself. Claws. Teeth. Strength. Biological defenses. Poisons and toxins. Some are sophisticated and powerful, to the extent that certain species are nearly invulnerable to predation. I explored combining these capabilities."

"You fucking combined animal DNA?" Travers said, incredulity on his face. "And made that thing out there?"

"He was our first chimp. Designated as Alpha One," Hermann said. "We called him Alfie. He was once a normal lab animal. We isolated genetic codes for biological and physical defenses in various species, and I wanted to incorporate them into a single animal. The intent was to create a creature invulnerable to predation. Alfie was our earliest test animal. We injected everything into him. From every imaginable species. Sometimes just to see how it would affect him. We kept modifying the structure of his DNA, and he started to change. Almost overnight he turned into that thing. We couldn't stop it. He kept mutating and getting bigger. Six months ago he broke out of the lab and ran into the jungle."

Travers continued to stare into the monitor. "So why the fuck's it trying to get back in?"

"I can only speculate," Hermann said. He ran a hand through his hair and shook his head. "The electrical circuits in his brain are haywire. He's become violent. Created mayhem in the jungle. He's attacked the villagers. Destroyed anything that got in his way. He's broken into the facility a couple of times already. Killed off nearly all our primates. I'd guess he's ready to come home."

"Well, it can't fucking come home," Travers said, "we have company on the way." He turned to Robinson, who had an assault rifle slung across his shoulder. "Get out there and kill the goddam thing."

The guard began to move towards the door, but Hermann raised a hand to stop him. "You can't just shoot him," he said. "Remember we programmed Alfie to be invulnerable to predation. To an extent we were successful. He's got a lot of armament. He's developed defenses to handle bullets and projectiles. Five thousand volts of electricity didn't slow him down. I'm not certain he can be killed, at least not in any conventional way."

Travers tapped at his watch. "Glass will be here in a couple of hours. He sees that thing, and we'll be the ones fried against the goddamned fence. We need to destroy it, right now."

"I know," Hermann said wearily. "I knew this day was coming."

"What the fuck do we do?"

Hermann stared speculatively into the monitor.

"Let him in," he said.

———— ◆ ————

"**W**hat's that?" Tamara said.

They were in her room, brows knit in perplexity as they listened to the compressive thumping that echoed through the building. Sirens were blaring. Tamara opened the door and watched a cadre of armed Paragon security men jog past the room and disappear down an intersecting corridor.

"Let's find out," Will said. He moved to the open door and glanced down the hallway. "Stay here."

"No way," she said. Tamara stepped into the corridor and stood beside him. He saw her determined look and reached for her hand.

They moved carefully down the corridor, following in the wake of the guards. They halted at an intersection of empty hallways. The rhythmic pounding continued to rattle through the building.

He spotted a heavy steel door beneath an illuminated Exit sign. They pushed through and jogged up two floors before arriving at another reinforced door. He pulled it open and they stepped onto the roof. They moved to the edge and peered onto the facility grounds.

"My God," Tamara whispered. "What is that thing?"

Will stared at the creature, then he nodded in comprehension. "I'll explain it later," he said. "Right now we need to get away from this place."

Tamara followed close behind as he strode swiftly around the building's ridge. He stopped and ran his eyes around the expanse of Renewal Gardens before pointing to a large rectangular structure. Tandem doors stood open. Heavy equipment was scattered in the motor pool yard, along with a half-dozen camouflage painted Jeeps. More vehicles were parked inside the building.

"Run back to the room," he said. "There's a map of Guatemala pinned to the wall. It might be useful. Bring my leather satchel. Mollie's picture's on the desk. Grab it and anything you want to take with you. Get to the front doors fast as you can. I'll be there in a minute."

Tamara nodded and dashed off.

He returned his attention to the activity on the ground. The huge creature continued relentlessly pounding on the door. A cadre of nervous guards surrounded it, assault rifles raised. They appeared to be awaiting an attack signal. Will ran across the flat roof to the other side of the building. He ran his eyes over the terrain and saw the most direct route to the motor pool was through Serenity Gardens.

He hustled down the stairs and burst through a side door. Past the fountain and directly through the middle of Renewal Gardens into the motor pool. He approached the nearest vehicle and jumped inside. He fired up the engine and studied the fuel gauge. Quarter tank.

He moved to the next Jeep and went through the same drill. This time the gauge registered full. He threw the vehicle into gear and bounced along a hard-packed dirt road running tandem to the perimeter fence. He passed guards running in the other direction. None paid him any mind. He skidded to a stop in front of the Tikal Research Center. Tamara came running from inside. She threw a duffle in the back seat and jumped into the Jeep. He spotted the large gate the site team had passed through three days earlier. It was standing open.

He gunned the engine and they roared off into the jungle.

Will raced down the jagged and rutted trail. Tamara bounced beside him. She turned her head and stared through the back window. The concussive thumping echoed through the jungle.

"What was that thing?"

"I think I know," he said.

Hermann was staring through an observation window at a small padded room. It was theoretically escape-proof, built with steel-reinforced studs and a sturdy metal door. This was Alfie's home. He'd lived his entire life in this space. It held the things that brought him comfort. The thick floor pad that served as his bed. A little cloth doll he liked to carry around. Hermann had placed a bunch of bananas in the room, along with a two-liter bottle of Coca-Cola. Alfie's favorite drink.

Hermann recognized what was motivating the pathetic creature. He had created Alfie. Watched it mutate from lovable chimp to hideous beast. He was certain the animal was following a basic instinctive drive. Alfie wanted to come home. Once inside the building, he would head straight to this room. He would pick up the rag doll and lie on his bed. Hermann considered the possibility he might be wrong. His intended actions might result in Alfie tearing him to pieces.

Regardless of what Hermann did at this moment, Alfie would get into the building one way or another. Right now the animal was enraged. He might tear down the building and destroy any living thing in its path. Better to give Alfie what he wanted. Open the door and get out of his way. Welcome him home. Hermann picked up the phone and dialed the extension for security.

"Status?" he asked curtly.

There was a pause as Robinson studied the monitors. "It's still at the door, which is pretty close to caving in. The rest of the facility's secure. The building's on lockdown and personnel are in secure environments."

"Okay," Hermann said. "Make sure the hallways are clear. Then unlock the security door and let it in."

"I should tell you Dr. Rodgers went running through the building a couple of minutes ago," Robinson said. "She went out the front gate. Connors picked her up in a Jeep and they drove through the gate."

Hermann exhaled in frustration, then he rubbed his sweaty brow. "Don't worry about it. We'll deal with them after this is done." He pushed a button and opened the door to Alfie's room.

"Go ahead," he said. "Open the security door."

"Yes sir," Robinson said. The wiry man stepped to the security panel and gazed at the enormous animal pounding at the door. He took a deep breath and punched a code into the computer. The door slowly swung open, and Alfie stepped inside the Tikal Research Center.

The crisis ended without further drama or violent confrontation. Alfie behaved as Hermann had predicted. It shuffled through the open door, made its way through a maze of corridors, and went straight to its little den. Hermann quietly closed the door and sealed the animal inside the room.

The scientist stared through the observation window.

Alfie was on the mat, its body curled into a fetal position. Holding the pathetic raggedy doll to its heaving chest. Hermann flipped open an intercom and listened. Alfie was emitting a rumbling sound of contentment that reminded Hermann of a growling V-8 engine. His face flushed with shame as he considered what he'd done to an innocent lab animal.

He regretted the necessity of putting Alfie down. He had grown attached to the chimp. The animal also had research value and untapped economic potential. Hermann had created an animal more potent than anything on the planet. Nearly impossible to kill. Hermann had intended to genetically create the perfect soldier. The possibilities were endless. Armies worldwide would be interested. Hermann stared at Alfie and wondered if there might be some way to continue this line of research. A thought came into his head. He tucked it away for future consideration and returned his attention to the immediate problem.

He must destroy Alfie.

He raised his head at the familiar whump of an approaching helicopter. "Fuck," he muttered.

Hermann moved to a small electric chiller. He reached in and pulled out a small vial. He slid in a hypodermic needle and extracted a sample. He transferred it onto a slide, which he placed beneath an electron microscope. He gazed through the lens, then nodded in satisfaction. He had anticipated this moment for months. Alfie had mutated into a unique creature, unlike anything on the planet. Its body absorbed projectiles and immediately replaced damaged tissue or organs. Any naturally occurring toxin couldn't poison Alfie. But Hermann understood the animal would have no resistance for artificial toxins.

He'd ordered the horticulture lab to grow a small crop of *digitalis lanata* plants. Commonly called a foxglove, extracts of the shrub's leaves produced digoxin, one of the world's deadliest toxins. Hermann created a synthetic analog for the substance, producing a powerful chemical poison. He had loaded the analog onto the messenger strand, which he'd mated to a scrubbed Ebola virus. The result was a powerful synthetic poison capable of killing any creature. Alfie's body would have no defense against it. The sanitized Ebola virus carrying the poison would infect Alfie's body in a matter of minutes, and the animal's heart would seize.

Hermann moved to the wall separating him from Alfie. He manipulated a lever. A mechanical sleeve swiveled open.

It was an ingenious contraption Hermann had designed to administer injections to lab animals that might be aggressive or infectious. Animals were trained to insert their arms into the sleeve, which contained a button-activated relay switch. When the animal pushed the button, its favorite treat would drop into a stainless steel pan. As long as it kept pushing the button, treats would randomly fall into the pan.

Meanwhile, the animal's arm was affixed palm up in the sturdy metal sleeve, veins and arteries exposed. Researchers could reach through a small rectangular hatch and safely administer injections. This was a routine procedure, and all research animals were accustomed to the process.

Hermann levered the mechanical sleeve open, then he flipped a switch and leaned into the microphone.

"Alfie," he said gently.

The animal turned its red eyes towards him. Alfie slowly rose and shuffled across the room, carrying the rag doll. Alfie obediently stuck his left arm into the sleeve and pushed the stimulus button, dropping the doll as it awaited its reward. Jellybeans. Hermann allowed a few of the treats to drop into the pan, then he opened the hatch. Picking up the hypodermic, he paused to look at Alfie. The pathetic animal turned and looked directly into his eyes. Hermann saw the agony reflected in Alfie's face. He recognized something else in the creatures' visage - an intelligent understanding of what was occurring.

My God. It knows. It wants to die.

Hermann uttered a silent apology to the animal. He reached through the hatch and slid the hypodermic into a vein. Alfie remained passive as Hermann injected the poison into its body. Hermann withdrew the needle and closed the hatch, then he pushed another button that released the animal's arm.

Alfie picked up the little doll and shuffled back to his mat, where he lay down to die.

CHAPTER TWENTY-EIGHT

Tikal Research Center
Guatemala

Will braked the Jeep to a halt.

Insects danced an insane jig in the glitter of the headlights. He gazed into the blackness and listened as a cacophony of jungle sounds filled the night air. Dusk had fallen. The air was muggy and damp. The environment felt alien and hostile. He had the sense of being on a distant planet. The sensation caused a superstitious chill to run up his spine.

There was ancient history in this place. Four thousand years ago, Mayan civilizations flourished throughout Central America. There had been cities and roads. Complex watering systems of canals and aqueducts. Millions lived and died in this region. They worshiped pagan gods and engaged in human sacrifice. Now all were gone, bones ingested by the relentless jungle and spirits released to the sky. Decaying, vine-covered ruins of pyramids and crumbled plazas were the only remnants of these mighty kingdoms. He felt the strangeness of the night and wondered if spirits lingered here. The thought caused a shudder to course through his body. He wanted to be far from this isolated place.

The map was open on Tamara's lap. Her brows were stitched in concentration and she squinted in the dim glow of the dome light. She exhaled in frustration and handed the map to him. "This thing is useless," she said. "The location of the research center isn't even marked off. We have no point of reference. Plus, there's like six roads in the whole country."

He held the map to the light and examined it. "I see what you mean." He tossed it aside, then drummed his fingers on the steering wheel.

"This is the only road out of the place. There's bound to be something up ahead. A village or bigger road. They have a motor pool back there. Bunch of vehicles. They drove them out here from somewhere. This dirt trail can't possibly run all the way to Guatemala City. Let's see where it takes us."

She laid a hand on his shoulder. "You were going to tell me about that thing we saw."

He nodded and thought for a moment. "Remember Storsky?"

"The liger guy? The one cross-breeding animals?"

"Right," he said. "Shimota wanted us to look up his research. Storsky's specialty was combining genetic material from multiple species. Making new creatures by mixing together DNA from existing ones. I think that's what they're doing back there. I think that thing's a chimera."

"Like from Greek mythology? Fire-breathing monster with a serpent's tail?"

"Hermann's version of it," he said. "Looks like he created a Frankenstein in his lab. That thing looks like he threw DNA from a dozen animals into a blender. That was the result."

"Whatever it is, it's horrible," she said. "It'll stay in my nightmares. But why would he….."

A thundering from above. Tall trees swayed wildly as an aircraft passed overhead. Harsh floodlights illuminated the roadway. The air was filled with swirling dust as the helicopter sat down at the intersection of the two roads.

A man ducked from the chopper and stepped into the bright lights. He was trim and fit, not dressed for the jungle. Wearing a tailored three-piece suit, his dark hair slicked back. A gold watch dangled from a wrist. The man shouted something to a pair of security men who dropped from the helicopter. The guards jogged to the Jeep and flanked it with weapons pointed to the ground. The man approached and leaned into the window.

"Doctors Connor and Rodgers," he said with a smile. "Glad to finally meet you. I'm Andrew Glass."

Glass invited them to exit the Jeep and pointed them towards the aircraft. The armed guards made resistance out of the question. The chopper ride took less than ten minutes. No conversation was attempted in the noisy aircraft. Will glanced at Tamara and saw her face tight with worry. He reached over and took her hand.

They felt themselves descending, then the chopper bumped to the ground. The guards escorted them into the facility. One security man took Will to his room and stood at parade rest outside the door. The other guard led Tamara to somewhere else in the building.

Will fidgeted an hour. A hundred worried thoughts ran through his mind. After a while he heard the thumping of the helicopter's rotors. He listened to the fading sound of engines as the aircraft rose and sped off. Not long afterward, the guard opened the door and motioned for him to follow. Will was led through the building and into what he recognized as Joseph Hermann's office. Andrew Glass sat behind a desk, twisting a big ring on his finger. He smiled and extended a hand to Will.

"Apologies for the dramatic entrance," he said. "I hope you'll forgive me. I also hope you will give me the chance to rectify things."

Will ignored the man's hand. "First, tell me why you're holding us against our will."

Andrew Glass raised his hands in a placating manner. "You're free to leave anytime. When we're finished settling our business, I'll fly you directly to Guatemala City. I have a plane standing by at the airport. I'll order the pilot to take you anywhere you choose. You can be home and hugging your little girl tomorrow night." Glass came around the desk and sat in a chair close to Will.

"We have a problem. I can't fix it without your help."

"You've got a problem all right." Will shook his head in frustration. "What the Hell do you think you're doing?"

"Running the country's third-largest pharmaceutical company," Glass said. His voice was calm and rational. "Developing medicines to extend human life. Improving the world."

"Then answer a question. Your scientists are top-notch. Serious about their work. They're creating genetic miracles. What's taking place in this building actually could change the world." Will raised his eyes to meet the other man's. "Tell me why the hell you're faking research."

"We're not faking anything," Glass said. "We're hurrying things along." The man exhaled heavily, as if making an important decision. "I want to help you understand our situation. I believe we can work this out."

Will stared at him, brows skeptically raised.

"Novix will be the most important medicine developed in human history," Glass said. "You've seen the drug's potential. You saw Sheila. Our miracle chimp. Novix is causing her to grow younger. There's no way to fake her age regression. Novix will change the concept of human life and aging. It will alter every aspect of life on this planet. It will improve the human condition. But there's a business side to Novix. The future of my company's riding on the success of it. We have to get the drug to market. Once it's rolled out, the world will buy it and my company will return to profitability. We can fund the rest of our research and continue producing the products you've seen in our labs."

Glass paused and stared intently at Will. "I'll admit we're cutting corners. We're hurrying things along. But there's nothing fake about Novix."

"Except the human body rejects it."

"Granted," Glass said. "You think it's a problem that can be solved?"

"All research problems can be solved," Will said, "if you have enough time and money."

"You've perfectly described our situation. We can solve the tissue rejection issue with sufficient time and money. At the moment we don't have enough of either of those things. There's a simple solution. We pass this site inspection. That's all it will take. Once it's done, we continue to perfect Novix. We continue funding the Tikal project. We perfect the other miracles you've seen. Otherwise it all dies. Try to see it from my point of view. I want to help the world, but I need to save my company. There's billions of dollars riding on Novix."

"So it's about money," Will said.

"Of course it's about money." He benignly smiled and shook his head, as if Will were a child. "You academics think the pursuit of profit is a sin. Surely you're not so naïve as to deny that drug research is about money. How do you think medical miracles are created? Where do you think all the drugs that improve human life are developed? It's not done in some underfunded university lab. All medical research is funded by pharmaceutical companies. It takes years and billions of dollars to develop life-enhancing drugs."

"I want to improve the quality of human life," he continued. "But I run a publicly traded company, and I have to answer to stockholders and a board of directors. I'm responsible for the bottom line. We must make a profit when creating these miracles, and there's nothing immoral about running a successful company."

"It doesn't justify your methods. Your people are doing things no researcher in the world would consider ethical. I saw that thing trying to break into the building. I'd like to hear you explain that monstrosity. As for Novix, you've shown me nothing that convinces me it can be made safe for human use. You want me to rely on a promise." Will shook his head. "I can't sign documents based on falsified studies. I doubt if anyone else will. What about Wilkinson? You think he'll sign off? And Tamara? Where is she, by the way?"

Glass held up a document. "This is a summary of Dr. Wilkinson's findings. He supports approval for human clinical trials. As for Dr. Rodgers, she's on her way to

Guatemala City. She'll be home in a few hours. We talked productively before she left. She's expressed support for our research. She's excited at the prospect of writing academic papers on the local tribe."

Will shot him a skeptical look. "I find that hard to believe. Two hours ago she was terrified and couldn't wait to get out of here. You brought her back here against her will. She's been suspicious of this place from the beginning. She asked questions you haven't yet answered."

"And what were those questions?"

"For starters, what happened to Shimota? Who shot Tavey Bohanon?"

"I explained those unfortunate events to her satisfaction," Glass said. "I'll be happy to do the same for you." He paused and raised his eyes in contemplation before continuing.

"First, let's discuss something far more important. You understand the third messenger strand's possibilities extend far beyond lifespan. We'll soon be able to cure diseases with this technology. That includes cancer. With sufficient resources, an effective treatment could be developed almost immediately. Terminally ill patients might be saved. Imagine the possibilities."

Glass paused and looked Will directly in the eyes.

"Help me save my company," he said, "I'll help you save your daughter."

PART THREE

Novix

CHAPTER TWENTY-NINE

Chicago Daily Sun
Chicago, Illinois

"I'm on to something," Steve McNeal announced.

He leaned back in an ancient wooden swivel chair, feet atop a messy desk, studying a rectangular corkboard mounted to the wall. The board contained a mess of multi-hued sticky notes, news clippings, and photos. Strings of blue yarn and stickpins connected the disparate pieces of information on the board. The tangle of yarn resembled a demented roadmap, crisscrossing and reversing itself in no discernible pattern. The overall effect was one of stupefying chaos.

His editor stood behind him, scrutinizing the board with a quizzical expression. "I've always suspected this is how your mind works," Reed Tobias said. He walked over to the board and thumped it. "I can't decipher this mess and we don't have a cryptologist on staff. Walk me through it."

The men were in McNeal's cubicle, a rectangle of Plexiglas that separated them from the noisy hubbub of the newsroom. Beyond it, dozens of beat writers and editors fixated on computer screens, busily creating and editing tomorrow's news. The cacophony of noise was music to the ears of any newspaperman. The paper was a hundred years old and housed in nine-story waterfront brick tower dwarfed by Chicago's towering skyline. The Sun was one of a few print dailies still managing to stay afloat in the new world of electronic news.

Steve McNeal was a relentless investigator and the paper's brightest journalistic star. He had earned his prized cubicle after a series of bombshell investigative reports exposing the fraud and criminal behavior that had infected Chicago's political apparatus for the better part of a century. Four of the state's past nine governors had served time in prison, including one currently housed in a cushy Colorado federal pen. It was no coincidence that three of the four corrupt politicians had been served grand jury indictments within weeks after publication of a front-page Daily Sun story carrying McNeal's byline.

Reed Tobias was McNeal's nominal supervisor, although the reporter was granted the freedom to pursue any compelling story. Still, Tobias insisted on knowing what scents the bulldog reporter was sniffing. McNeal had graduated summa cum laude from the prestigious Cronkite School of Journalism in Arizona, and the Daily Sun had vigorously recruited him. That was a decade ago, and McNeal looked much the same as he had then. He still appeared in his twenties, with his wide, inquisitive face and deep blue eyes set beneath dark brows. A month shy of thirty-five, McNeal allowed his shock of bushy brown hair to run past his collar. He invariably looked as if his last shave was three days ago.

McNeal walked around the desk and stood by the board. "Let me lay some groundwork." He pointed to a nine by twelve color photo pinned at the top of the messy board. It was a publicity shot of a gleaming office tower, shiny with reflective glass and steel.

"Steele Pharmaceuticals," he said, "is a Fortune 500 company based out of Houston. This company is the poster child for big Pharma, an industry leader for seventy-five years and commanding a worldwide market although lately they've been slipping. They're in the midst of final trials for a drug they're calling Novix. I'm sure you've heard about it. You can't turn on the television without seeing something about Novix."

"The miracle drug that's going to change the concept of life as we know it," Tobias said. "You'd have to be on a desert island not to know about Novix. Keep going."

McNeal pointed to another photo. "Andrew Glass runs the company. He's the latest genius on the planet right now. His profile's approaching that of Steven Jobs. His personal worth's in the billions, mostly because of the turnaround in the company over the past quarter. Four months ago the company was on the verge of bankruptcy and target of a full-court SEC investigation. It was about to blow sky high. The buzz is the SEC found serious violations and was about to drop the hammer. Then they dropped it and walked away. Somehow Glass pulled the company out. This guy's a fucking magician."

"Anyway, the company got back on its feet almost overnight. They started running ads for Novix and the world went crazy in anticipation of it coming to market. Since then Steele's stock has quadrupled. It made Glass a billionaire. And a superstar. Every paper in the country's run profiles on him, including ours. Time Magazine's about to name him Man Of The Year. Scuttlebutt is that a Sixty Minutes crew is with him right now, working up a profile."

"All because of this drug Novix?"

"Pretty much," McNeal said. "They're claiming it will make you young again. They have other drugs in the pipeline supposed to cure just about every known human condition, including cancer."

Tobias waited with a brow cocked as McNeal studied the board. "I presume there's more to the story?"

"Just getting started, boss."

Tobias arched his back and moved over to take the swivel chair. He was fifty and looked a decade older. His face was lined and perpetually flushed and his remaining hair was gray, the product of two decades in the pressure cooker business of print news. He'd endured too many years of bad coffee, daily deadlines and greasy food, all of which left him with high blood pressure and a dangerously protruding gut. He sat heavily and motioned for his reporter to continue.

McNeal was staring at the board. "Where do I start?" he murmured to himself. "Let me begin at the top and work down."

He pointed a finger to a satellite surveillance photo of a modern structure surrounded by jungle vegetation, then McNeal pointed to a series of photos arrayed beneath it.

"This is the Tikal Research Center. For God knows what reason, Steele built a research facility in Guatemala, in the middle of the frigging jungle three thousand miles from known civilization. It's run by Nova Labs, a subsidiary of

Steele. These headshots are of the inspection team the FDA sent down there to evaluate the research and decide if it was ready for human trials." He smiled again at Tobias.

"Got your seat belt buckled tight?"

Receiving a shrug in response, he moved on. "Dr. William Bernard." McNeal used a knuckle to tap a photograph. "Big name researcher from Georgia Tech. Originally assigned to the team. Killed a week before the inspection. A car accident the Atlanta police department classified as suspicious. It's being investigated as a possible homicide."

McNeal moved to the desk and picked up a manila folder, from which he extracted a large question mark cut from red construction paper. A device of his own creation, a visual tag aimed at identifying areas of suspicion. He pinned it next to the photo of William Bernard.

"This guy," he tapped on another snapshot, "is Dr. Will Connors. Appointed to the team following the death of Bernard. This is where the scenario gets interesting. Connors is an enigma, to say the least. Not that long ago he was a heavyweight in science, one of the most brilliant and credible researchers in the world."

McNeal nodded in sympathy to the photo of a wasted Mollie Connors. "Sad story here. Connors' mother died of cancer a couple of years ago, and not long afterward his kid was diagnosed with leukemia. Tragic situation. Connors went over the edge. Threw away his career chasing a way to save her. He became a pathetic figure, something of an outcast in the science world. Connors was unemployed and at rock bottom when picked to replace Bernard on this team. A curious choice, at least to me." Another red question mark went on the board.

"This is where it starts to go haywire." McNeal pointed at another photo. "Yanni Shimota, whom you may recognize. Highly regarded physicist from Yale with tons of publications. Also a television personality." He paused and provided his boss a deadpan look. "He's dead."

Tobias raised his brows in surprise.

"Shimota was in his seventies but reportedly in excellent health when he suffered a massive stroke. Right in the middle of the inspection. Never recovered. Died in Guatemala and his body's still down there. I find that to be odd." Another red question mark went up.

"This one," McNeal pointed to a snapshot of a broad-faced man in a pith helmet who appeared slightly tipsy, "is Tavey Bohanon, their chief of security. While the inspection team was on-site, he was shot three times in the back. It's speculated he was in the process of stealing secrets to sell to this man." McNeal was pointing at the pathetic face of Anton LeDoux. "A petty criminal notorious in the world of pharmaceutical thievery."

"We know this character LeDoux was in the area when this was going down," McNeal said. "There's no indication he returned from Guatemala. He hasn't been seen in four months."

"What happened to the big man?"

"Bohanon survived getting shot," McNeal said. "Then he disappeared." He attached another question mark.

McNeal could see he had his supervisor's full attention. Tobias moved to a swivel chair and leaned back, then ran a hand across his brow. McNeal smiled as he saw the excitement in the man's face.

"You're talking murder, assault, shootings, missing bodies, fraud, and theft," Tobias said. "Starting to sound like Chicago politics, and we're barely halfway down your board."

McNeal pointed to another photo. "Dr. Joseph Hermann's the research chief down there." There was a lengthy newspaper story affixed beneath the man's photo. "Hermann is also a big name in genetic science, but there's a whiff of scandal. A decade ago, he left a tenured chair at Harvard under suspicious circumstances. Accused of faking research. They never proved it, but he got fired anyway. These geniuses at Steele decided he was the perfect person to run the most important research project in human history."

Tobias rose and walked to the board, where he looked closely at a picture pinned beside the other team members. The woman was dressed in a severe business suit that contrasted to her frizzy red hair and gaudy makeup. She was smiling flirtatiously into the camera. Tobias looked at the photo, then stared at McNeal in puzzlement.

"Isn't that your ex-wife?"

"That's Tamara," McNeal nodded. "She's the reason I started looking at this thing. You may remember she's a cultural anthropologist, down at the university in Champagne."

"There's our local hook," Tobias murmured.

"Right," McNeal enthused. "And that's not the only one. There's a private investigator who works for Steele Pharmaceuticals, a guy named Bowers. I keep running across his name in internet searches. He's connected to this deal. His office is about a mile from here."

"Anyway," McNeal went on, "Tamara was invited to accompany this inspection team, to provide an anthropological point of view. While she was down there, her assistant called me. She said Tamara was in a mess and urgently needed information on everyone on this board. I put together some stuff and sent it to her."

"It got you to thinking," Tobias said.

"Not at the time. I figured it was just Tamara on one of her tangents. Then the Novix media blitz started up, and I realized she was connected to it. I got curious, wondering what'd gotten her all agitated. I pulled out the material I'd sent her. Started going over it. The more I looked, the more these question marks kept popping up." He nodded at the board. "This stuff's has had my full attention the past two weeks. I decided it was time to run it past you."

He raised a finger before Tobias could respond. "One more curious thing. I can't locate Tamara. The university says she took a leave of absence. They don't know where she went. She's not returning my calls."

Tobias raised his brows, then swiveled and stared a long while at the chaotic corkboard. It was covered with question marks. "Summarize," he said.

"We're looking at a major conspiracy. Big Pharma shenanigans at their worst. We've got fraud. Stock manipulation, and maybe an SEC cover-up. I'm seeing bribery or extortion. Maybe murder. We've got dead people. Missing people. A supposed miracle drug about to hit the market, approved by the flakiest inspection team in history. Not to mention that my ex-wife is hiding out, and she's never backed down from anything in her life." He moved over and sat down, staring intently at Tobias.

"This is huge, Reed. I want to go hard at it."

"I agree," Tobias said. "This is Pulitzer stuff. Go ahead and run with it. What's the next move?"

"I need to run down these people and interview them. I want answers for every question mark on that board. Then I'll write the biggest investigative story in this paper's history."

Tobias chewed at his lip and considered the man standing before him. Tobias had met nobody like him in the news business. McNeal never backed down from a story. Nothing intimidated him, and danger didn't appear to register on his consciousness. McNeal had earned his reputation uncovering corrupt politicians, and over the years he had charged headlong into a string of dramatic stories about the worst of Chicago's citizenry. He'd exposed drug rings, murderers, gangsters and corrupt politicians. Threats of violence were common. McNeal was not a strong or imposing man. He was not skilled in self-defense. Anyone desiring to do him serious bodily harm would likely be successful. McNeal didn't seem to care.

Tobias recalled an incident that still astounded him. Two years earlier, McNeal discovered an explosive device sitting in the driver's seat of his car. The bomb squad was called to the scene and secured the device, which was later found to be unarmed. It was clearly a warning. Somebody wanted McNeal off the story he was chasing. He thought the situation humorous. He published his story and included the bomb incident as a sidebar. It didn't seem to dawn on him that he might get blown up. McNeal did obtain a carry permit and a sidearm, although Tobias had never seen him carry it.

"All right," Tobias agreed. "Start running down these characters. Start at the tail of the snake and work up to the head." Tobias stood and slapped the younger man on the back.

"Go get your story. And be careful."

"Always," Steve McNeal said.

CHAPTER THIRTY

Rancho Laguna Park
Santa Cruz, California

Will perched atop a wooden picnic table, watching a pair of cliff swallows dance above his head. The birds circled high into the sapphire sky then dove towards the earth, buzzing him like fighter jets as they whirled through their aerial routine before flitting away in the direction of the hazy Santa Cruz foothills. Will shifted his attention to the emerald waters of the Monterey Bay, gazing at the blue ocean lying beyond the crescent-shaped inlet.

A flotilla of sailboats moved lazily in the bay. He studied a sleek bow rider as it powered through calm waters and arced towards the open ocean. The boat left behind a graceful frothy wake. He made out a man standing tall at the wheel. A woman and child in the bow. Both wore oversized sunglasses. Their hair blew wildly in the oceanic wind. They were laughing and shouting at the driver, pointing in the direction they wanted to travel.

What would you do, he whispered to the man in the boat, *if your child lay dying before your eyes. Would you sell that fine boat? Mortgage your home? Decimate your life savings? Abandon your career and reputation? Sacrifice your integrity? Your honor? Your soul?*

The speedboat disappeared into the blue horizon. He pondered life's complexities as he watched the ocean's infinite water absorb the boat's wake and erase any evidence of its passing. He terminated his reverie with a heavy sigh and glanced at his watch. Will rose and walked towards the lab, pausing to look towards the new playground. It had been built on the facility's grounds just last week.

Mollie jumped from the swing and ran giggling to him. She threw herself into his arms and gave him a sloppy kiss, then raced off towards the monkey bars. Tan and healthy, she swung from one ring to the next, shouting for him to watch. She raced to the merry-go-round and whooped in joy as the device spun her around. He watched her happy play and an effervescent rush filled his chest. Joy and gratitude were emotions he hadn't experienced in a long time. He savored the moment. Will watched his child and appreciated the miracle she represented. He allowed his mind to return to the day he brought her to this place. Three months ago. Mollie was at death's door.

Medicine couldn't save her. God wouldn't save her.

Her savior arrived in the unlikely form of Andrew Glass.

Help me save my company and I'll help you save your daughter.

On a dark night in Guatemala, Glass made an offer that changed the trajectory of Connors' life. Will harbored no illusions. He made no effort to fool himself. Glass was no humanitarian. He cared nothing about Mollie. Glass was a calculating businessman who made Will an offer he could not refuse.

Glass laid the inspection report and a fountain pen in front of Will. He asked him to approve Novix for human subjects testing and to keep his mouth shut. That was all Glass wanted. In exchange, he offered Will a chance to save his daughter's life. Glass would grant him unrestricted access to the third messenger technology. Set him up in a world-class laboratory. Provide an unlimited budget. The negotiation was brief and brutally simple.

Sign the paper. Save your daughter.

Will understood that he was bargaining with the Devil, who would demand an exorbitant price. If he signed the agreement, Will would become a conspirator in a criminal enterprise. Turn a blind eye to unethical research. Conceal the deadly potential of Novix. Disregard the assaults on Shimota and Bohanon. He would risk dishonor, disgrace and imprisonment.

Without hesitation, Will gripped the pen in a steady hand. He signed the inspection report without bothering to read it. He affixed his signature to an ironclad nondisclosure agreement. He accepted Glass' extended hand and endured the slap on his back. Both men walked away with a victory. Glass would rescue his company from bankruptcy and himself from disgrace. Will received the opportunity for a miracle.

Early the following morning they departed the jungle and choppered to Guatemala City, where they boarded Steele Pharmaceuticals' private Lear. Glass ordered the pilot to plot a course for Phoenix, where Mollie lay wasting in a pediatric hospice. He accompanied Will on the long flight. They raced in a waiting limousine to the hospital.

Mollie was nearly comatose and barely breathing. Treatment was palliative. Medication prescribed only for pain. No longer able to eat, Mollie had lost weight and was precariously close to heart failure. Snaking tubes fed nutrients into her body. The doctors estimated she had a few scant weeks to live. Mollie was discharged to Will's care without objection.

They flew Mollie to San Francisco in the corporate jet. Glass arranged for a private duty nurse to accompany them on the flight and an ambulance transported Mollie to Santa Cruz.

Dowd-LaPorte operated a small lab in a research park in the beachside community. Glass immediately appointed Will as the facility's chief of research. A lab was converted into a hospital room and round-the-clock medical care was arranged. All expenses billed to Dowd-LaPorte.

Will turned his attention to saving Mollie's life.

He understood that he was taking on a formidable foe. He likened cancer to a zombie horde, a powerful and alien life form of infinite complexity. The disease struck insidiously, arriving silently as it invaded an unsuspecting host organism. Once established, it rapidly multiplied. Cancer's armies relentlessly infected healthy cell bodies with toxic agents, mutating them until they joined the deadly mass. The disease spread voraciously throughout the host body, devouring healthy cells and manufacturing zombie clones. Only when the body it inhabited ceased living would cancer die.

No researcher in the world had discovered a reliable treatment. In Guatemala, Will had been inspired by the messenger technology's miraculous power and its potential for treating cancer. The messenger strand represented Mollie's only chance. He arrived in Santa Cruz with a plan in mind. Only one strategy made sense. Utilize Mollie's own immune system to attack the cancer. She had days to live. There was no time for anything else.

He began by isolating a sample of her cancerous cells. He positioned a strand of the messenger RNA in an adjacent sterile environment. Using a Cas9 enzyme, he chemically sliced away a snippet of the mutated cell. With a microscopic binding agent, he attached it to the messenger strand. This would program the strand to recognize cancer cells in Mollie's body. He retrieved and attached a receptor gene, which provided the guidance system that would deliver the payload to its target.

He succeeded in creating the genetic coding that directed the messenger strand to seek out and recognize cancer. The next task was to synthesize an agent to kill it. This required modification of Mollie's T-cells. T-cells are specialized white blood cells that orchestrate the body's immune system. They exist for the singular purpose of protecting the body by seeking out and destroying invading organisms. But cancer cells are invisible to them. T-cells fail to recognize cancerous cells as invaders and don't attack them. That was the problem Will was determined to overcome.

He began by injecting Mollie with a small dosage of heparin, an anti-coagulant that prevented her blood from clotting. He implanted a catheter into her tiny vein, then began collecting Mollie's blood. He watched as his child's precious life fluid began to flow through the tube and into a cell separator. Her T-cells would be extracted before the blood flowed back into her body.

He pulled a sample from the separator and isolated a single T-cell. Into the cell body he introduced a latent virus that produced a protein called a chimeric antigen receptor. This would allow Mollie's T-cells to recognize and bind to specific proteins found on cancer cells. This would unmask the cancer and make it visible to Mollie's defender cells.

Will bound the modified T-cell to a slot on the third messenger strand, then he placed the strand in a replicator unit. Within an hour, it created millions of copies. Next he needed to return Mollie's modified cells to her body. This involved a simple process of injecting the cancer-killing T-cells directly into her bloodstream. He collected the material from the replicator and prepared it for injection.

When it was ready, he walked to Mollie's bed. She hadn't woken since he brought her to this place. As he gazed at her, the past year streamed through his mind in a collage of images. He placed a hand on her chest and could feel the shallow respirations. Taking a deep breath, he injected the material into her vein.

Then came the desperate hours.

Lying on the floor beside her, his busy mind refusing to shut down. He reviewed every step in the process, searching for miscalculations or errors in logic. Occasionally he rose on an elbow and placed a hand on her chest, reassuring himself she was still breathing. He stared at the ceiling and felt equal measures of hope and fear until finally falling into an exhausted sleep.

He awoke hours later. The room was illuminated by moonlight, and he felt a strangeness in the air. He cocked his head and listened. A whimpering, mewling cry of pain. More animal than human. Coming from Mollie's bed. He felt a prickle of trepidation and rose to his knees. He saw Mollie's profile in the dim light. Her face appeared strange and distorted. She sensed his presence and turned to gaze into his eyes. She had the mug face of a chimpanzee. Her head and neck covered with coarse fur. She smiled and exposed yellowed canine teeth and huge incisors. He hoarsely screamed her name and kept screaming until he startled awake.

Beams of morning sun streamed into the room. His breath was rapid and ragged and he could feel his heart pounding in his ears. He rose on an elbow and looked at Mollie. She was sleeping peacefully. He fell back to the floor and whispered a prayer of gratitude. Images of the disturbing dream remained embedded in his mind throughout the day.

Three days later, she awoke and asked for water. He pulled her fragile body into his arms and cried heated tears of relief. That marked the beginning of her recovery. He continued injecting her with the cancer killer. He studied tissue samples through the electron microscope. The modified T-cells were doing their job. Each day he detected fewer cancer cells.

Mollie gradually grew stronger. Her appetite returned and she regained lost weight. Her boundless energy returned. She wanted to run and play. Her thick dark hair, devastated by chemotherapy, had regrown.

Now he watched her run from one station to another on the playground. Her face flushed with exertion. He glanced at his watch and called to her. Mollie accompanied him to the lab and reluctantly extended an arm while he withdrew a blood sample. Will prepped the sample for analysis and set it aside. She yawned and hugged him, then she settled in for a nap.

He moved to a lab table and resumed working. He was intensely studying the compound that saved Mollie. He had created it in forty-eight hours and now he wanted to document how he'd done it. He was going about it ass-backward. He should have taken a year to conduct these studies before injecting it into a human. Now he was playing catch-up. In recent weeks he had begun introducing various cancers to lab rats and treating them with the compound. It was tedious work that kept him busy the rest of the afternoon. He stopped when Mollie stirred and awoke. He agreed when she advised him it was time to go home.

They climbed into the company vehicle, an expensive European SUV sporting a Dowd-LaPorte logo on the door panels. Exiting the parking lot, he drove through the city and into the Santa Cruz foothills. Will looked into his rearview mirror and smiled as he watched the blue sedan fall in behind him. Anywhere he went, he could be sure the vehicle would be right behind him. Video cameras were installed everywhere in the lab, monitoring and recording his every action. He had no doubt cameras were hidden in the house he was currently occupying.

Andrew Glass had a multi-billion dollar game in play, and Will understood he was in the middle of it. The man's generosity was part of a larger scheme. Not just the one involving Novix. Steele Pharmaceuticals would benefit enormously if Will actually developed an effective cancer-fighting drug. Such a discovery would bring billions more to the company. Anything Will developed in the lab was the proprietary property of Steele Pharmaceuticals. They wanted to keep their secrets safe.

Will traveled high into the foothills before turning into an exclusive housing development built into the hillside. He drove up a curving driveway and pushed a button on the vehicle's rear-view mirror. Wide gates swung open. The home was huge and opulent, built at the pinnacle of the mountain and overlooking the sparkling bay. Eight thousand square feet of luxurious living space, the place was a multi-million dollar property. The home was a Dowd-LaPorte holding reserved for Glass' occasional visits. He had insisted Will and Mollie move into the home and remain as long as necessary.

Mollie raced up the stairs to her room, and a moment later he heard boy band music blasting from above. He knew she would soon be engaged in some imaginary drama with her dolls or playing an electronic game.

Will poured a slug of Crown Royal into a crystal tumbler filled with ice, then added a splash of Coke. He walked onto the deck and gazed out at the peaceful bay. The sun was warm on his face. The sounds of Mollie's play drifted down. He granted himself a moment of contentment. He took a sip of the drink and finally allowed the forbidden thought to enter his mind.

It had been too easy.

In a matter of days, he had made an astounding scientific discovery. One that had eluded every other cancer researcher. He had created a genetic cocktail that cured a cancer considered incurable. Something was missing from the picture. Could curing cancer have been this simple all along? The father in him prayed it was so, but his scientific mind suspected differently.

A thousand unanswered questions lingered. The unresolved problems with Novix. The mutated creature he'd seen pounding at the laboratory door. What happened to Shimota? He'd heard nothing and figured the man was dead. Tavey Bohanon? Also probably dead. He was certain Wayne Wilkinson had been bribed. Of course, Tamara. Where was she? He'd repeatedly called and emailed her. She hadn't responded. He contemplated the glass of whiskey and decided there were no answers to be found in it.

Will turned his attention to the blue water of the bay. Far away, where ocean met horizon, he could see a thin dark line of clouds. He saw white caps forming on the water, and felt the stiffening ocean breeze ruffle his hair. An oceanic storm was brewing, growing in strength and heading for the coast.

Mollie's musical laughter floated into his head and made its way into his soul. He smiled at the thought of his child happy and playing. He pushed away troubling thoughts, then finished his drink and went inside. Will decided he would join Mollie in her play.

CHAPTER THIRTY-ONE

Steele Pharmaceuticals
Houston, Texas

Andrew Glass held the black and white proofs at arm's length. In both photos he wore the charcoal Brioni suit, purchased to the tune of forty-five thousand dollars. The world's rarest fibers were contained in the cloth. The stitching was of white gold. The British tailor limited production to a hundred such suits yearly, although Glass was granted the privilege of purchasing one whenever he pleased. The leading man in the latest Bond feature had worn the identical outfit, and Glass thought it gave him the same chiseled look as the actor. A subtle gray silk tie above a custom-made Antonio Valente shirt completed the ensemble, which Glass topped off with a solid gold tie stud shaped like a dollar sign.

His facial expression was slightly different in each photo. In one he gazed into a distant horizon, serious of mien and carrying himself as would a diplomat or world leader. Arms crossed in a bold and confident manner. Chin thrust forward. In the other shot he adopted a more relaxed expression, staring directly into the camera with brows elevated and a tiny smile. Hands on hips. His head canted mischievously to the side, as if he weren't taking himself too seriously. Glass handed this photo to the man standing on the other side of the desk.

"This one," he said.

"Excellent choice for the cover," the layout designer assured him. "We'll embed the other shot inside the story." He was a lean and jittery man with the retro appearance of an adolescent, wearing hipster jeans and tie-dyed tee shirt sporting the logo of a heavy metal band. A shaggy head of hair and John Lennon glasses completed the look.

Glass nodded indulgently, and the young man moved swiftly from the room. This one was from Forbes Magazine. The upcoming issue would have Glass' picture dominating the cover, standing astride a globe of the world. Above his image a bold print banner reading **Man Of Steele**. The designer had proposed the clever phrase and banner, and Glass had immediately approved it.

Glass watched as the crew from Sixty Minutes bustled through the reception area. Three of them - cameraman, technician, and production assistant. They were heading somewhere in the building to set up their equipment and cameras. Glass had spent three days with the famous news magazine correspondent, herself a striking beauty despite having advanced into her seventies. She was friendly and flirtatious in the one-on-one interview, spending hours lobbing him softball questions. Gushing over the miracle of Novix and the resurrection of Steele Pharmaceuticals. Off-camera, the woman had continued to flirt as she dropped broad hints about gaining priority status for the early distribution of Novix.

The news team had already spent a day at Glass' palatial estate in River Oaks, filming the executive in various relaxed poses. Following his wife and children as they rode horses or splashed in the pool. All that remained was for the crew to finish recording background footage of Glass talking into the phone, walking busily down the hallway, or conducting a meeting. The correspondent would later overdub a narrative detailing the story of Andrew Glass' meteoric life.

Glass basked in the adulation, and the constant stream of clamoring media served to stoke his massive ego. His ever-churning brain knew that each minute of worldwide attention meant greater publicity for Novix and billions in future revenue. The drug was a phenomenon, although months from being released to the public. The Novix website had already amassed a hundred million hits.

He glanced at his watch and mentally organized his day. His busy agenda was crowded with a list of problems to address. They could wait until the film crew departed. He swiveled restlessly in his big leather chair until they called for him. For the next hour he pretended to work while the film crew recorded his every movement. Eventually the cameraman declared he had enough footage, and the crew packed up and exited the building.

Glass buzzed his executive assistant and told her to send in Scottie Bowers. He moved to a bar in the corner and poured a slug of bourbon over ice. Bowers walked into the office. The jockey-sized private investigator plopped down on a corner sofa, and Glass moved over to join him. He put his drink on the coffee table and looked expectantly at the investigator.

Bowers pulled a pack of cigarettes from his shirt pocket peeled off the cellophane wrapper. This earned a glare from Glass, so he put them away and got to business.

"You want the good or bad?"

"Start with the good," Glass said.

"All's well in Santa Cruz," Bowers said. "Connors is behaving himself. His little girl's healthy, and he's staying busy in the lab. Looks from the video feed like he's doing experiments on rats."

"No unusual communications? No visitors?"

Bowers shook his head. "Everything's copacetic. We've got him covered around the clock. We monitor what he does and where he goes. Listen to his calls. Pretty routine. He goes from the lab to the house. He looks after his little girl and plays with mice. He's drinking a little bit. That's it, boss."

"What about Rodgers?"

"Still nothing. After Guatemala, she went straight to the university and applied for a sabbatical. Took off the next morning. Hasn't been back to her apartment. Right now she's off the radar. I'm still chasing her."

Glass twisted the big West Point ring. "Chase harder."

"I'll run her down. People can't just disappear anymore," Bowers said. "There are always digital footprints."

"Then find her, goddamit, and set up airtight surveillance." Glass picked up his drink and stared at the skyline of Houston.

"What about Bohanon?" Bowers asked.

"Travers is taking care of it. Anything else I should be worrying about?"

Bowers shrugged. "I don't think so. Something bothering you?"

"No," Glass said. "I just don't want any surprises."

He waved Bowers away and the investigator hurried from the room. Glass glanced at his schedule before walking into the corporate conference room. A group of men awaited, most of them company executives and board members. Joseph Hermann. Elliot Masters beside him. Glass smiled at the attorney, then took his place at the head of the table. He nodded at Hermann.

"We have clinical trials of Novix running in six locations around the country," the scientist began without preamble. A map of the United States appeared on a video screen behind him. "A thousand trial subjects. The FDA approved us for phase three studies, which allowed us to recruit a large number of subjects."

"Any problem getting participants?"

Hermann chuckled. "That's usually a problem with clinical trials. Not in the case of Novix. We used a recruiting firm. They opened up a website, and within a day we had a hundred thousand volunteers. We've set up a blind outpatient study, all subjects fifty or older. The oldest is ninety." Hermann pointed to circles on the map representing Denver and San Francisco. "These are placebo sites. Clinical sites are located in Phoenix, New York, and Dallas. The other one's in Juarez."

Glass was becoming impatient with the droning narrative. "Cut to it," he said. "How are things looking?"

"It's early," Hermann said, "but results are encouraging. Ninety percent of Novix subjects are demonstrating mild age reversal on a cellular level. Some are starting to appear younger. A few have no beneficial reaction to the medication. None of the subjects have suffered a toxic reaction."

Glass nodded his approval. "What next?"

"We continue running the trial and gathering data. We need six more months with these kinds of results. That should clear us with the FDA for test-marketing. "

Glass waved a hand, dismissing the meeting. As the others filed out, he signaled for Hermann and Elliott Masters to remain.

"So much for the bullshit," he said. "What's the story?"

"Not good," Hermann said. "We can't get dosage strength or frequency stabilized. Only a few subjects are demonstrating mild true age reversal. Less than a percent."

"The rest?"

"No measurable changes. Most subjects are showing no reaction to the drug. Some are experiencing serious side effects."

"Such as?"

"Toxic reactions. Tissue rejection. Uncontrolled tumor growth. A few heart attacks."

"Deaths?"

"Nine so far," Hermann said. "We've altered the medical records to attribute the deaths to other causes."

Glass turned to the attorney. "Opinion?"

Elliot Masters shrugged. "From a legal standpoint, a mortality rate of less than one percent constitutes an acceptable risk."

"What about financial exposure?"

The attorney stared at the ceiling, calculating. "As an example, let's say you sell Novix to a million people, at the price point you're thinking about, and you gross ten billion dollars," the attorney said. "Estimate forty percent for manufacturing and distribution costs, you'll net six billion dollars. If one percent of your customers die, that comes to ten thousand people."

"Let's say half of them sue, which is typical," the attorney continued. "Roughly five thousand lawsuits. We contest all of them. Delay. File motions. Require consumers to sign liability waivers. Put warning labels on bottles advising of adverse effects and possible death. Your advertising people put out a campaign singing the praises of the drug. Blame the deaths on something other than Novix. We drag it out for years. I guarantee half the plaintiffs drop out. We discredit those who stay the course. A few cases go to trial, but we eventually settle for a few hundred thousand. Insurance will cover some of the exposure. I'm guessing losses at a billion dollars, more or less."

"That's five billion dollars in profit?"

"Roughly," Masters said, "but ten thousand people die."

"I heard you," Glass said, a trifle sharply. He turned to Hermann. "How long to work out the bugs?"

"Three years," Hermann said.

"We don't have three years. We have six months."

Glass had heard enough from Hermann. He jerked his head towards the door and the blocky scientist departed. Glass exhaled and raised his brows as he regarded his corporate attorney.

"Your miracle drug doesn't work," Masters said. He studied his manicured nails.

"It doesn't matter," Glass growled at his attorney.

Masters had a doubtful look on his face. "You can't sell a drug that kills people. Not with prior knowledge of its dangers. Sixty Minutes will be wanting to talk to you for entirely different reasons."

"Happens all the time in this business," Glass said. "No drug's perfectly safe. You just said a one percent mortality rate's acceptable."

"You're projecting a customer base of fifty million. Distributing Novix on that scale could potentially kill a half a million people."

"You were okay with ten thousand deaths a minute ago. So don't start moralizing. Remember we're in the pharmaceuticals industry, Elliot. People who use our products sometimes die. It's the cost of doing business."

"I'm your attorney," Masters said. "I must advise that you're at risk for criminal exposure. If Novix kills people and your prior knowledge of its dangers can be proven, you're facing prison. You're vulnerable, Andrew. There are people out there who know the truth."

Glass waved a dismissive hand. "They're being handled. I'm taking Novix to market, Elliot. End of story. We'll make our billions and handle the fallout. In a couple of years the world will forget about Novix. I'll give them something much better. A new miracle drug."

"What would that be?"

Glass offered the man a smug smile. "One that cures cancer," he said.

Elliot Masters shook his head in disbelief. "You'll have a drug that will cure cancer? In the next two years?"

"I already have it," Glass said. "In Santa Cruz."

———◦———

Steve McNeal walked up two flights of stairs and through a maze of cubicles until he arrived at the one occupied by Sydney Sinclair. She was a short and robust woman who favored tight business suits and tiny skirts. She invariably wobbled around in high heels. She was also a mile-a-minute chatterbox.

Sydney had held a dozen jobs at the Daily Sun during her twenty-year tenure. She'd started by throwing papers in her rundown Harwood Heights neighborhood. She'd been the paper's high school correspondent, and after college she'd hired on as an entry-level copy editor. Tours as a field reporter and editorial writer led to her promotion to news editor. She quickly grew tired of the stress and crazy hours. The past four years Sydney had served as the paper's medical correspondent. McNeal knew her to be smart and savvy, and she was also a buddy.

Sydney's eyes were fixed on her computer screen when McNeal walked into her cubicle. They exchanged pleasantries and gossip, and eventually he got to the purpose of his visit.

"I'm researching a story on fraud and corruption in big Pharma," he said. "I don't know much. How bad is it?"

Sydney leaned back and hooted in laughter. "As bad as it gets. The pharmaceutical industry's so corrupt it's been called the new mafia," she said. "Their practices meet the government's legal criteria for organized crime. Big Pharma's the world's biggest drug cartel, operating with the full approval of the American government."

McNeal's eyes widened in surprise. "Wow," he said. He leaned forward and made a *come on* motion with his hands. "Tell me."

"Big Pharma's the most cut-throat and profitable legalized industry in the world. It's also the most poorly regulated. It's the perfect environment for fraud and abuse, which is rampant. I did a story on this a couple of years ago. America's the most medicated country on the planet. Seventy percent of the population takes some kind of prescription medication. Half of us take more than one every day."

"Americans are also the unhealthiest people in the world. We eat bad food. Drink. Smoke. Get fat. Don't exercise. We're sicker than any industrialized country in the world. We have a massive and inefficient medical system, and every doctor in the country writes a ton of prescriptions on a daily basis. Most get 'incentives,' which are basically payoffs, from the drug companies. These companies spend billions on advertising, convincing us we need their medicines. They invent medical problems, then sell us drugs to treat them."

"Doesn't the government regulate the industry?"

"There are laws," Sydney said. "The False Claim Act. Prescription Drugs Marketing Act. Plus plain old laws against fraud and criminal behavior. But it's an impossible industry to regulate. These companies are huge and byzantine, and they circle the globe. They go to lengths to conceal their activities that approach the level of national security. The government can't match their budgets or manpower. Drug trials are a joke. They're supposed to be independent, but most are overseen by the researchers doing the study. They supervise themselves. It's crazy. And who's funding these studies? Usually the same company that's manufacturing the drug being studied."

Sydney paused for breath, then she continued. "There's the medical journal scam. They publish research studies that supposedly prove these drugs work. Nearly a million of these articles are published every year in this country. Who's checking to see if they're legitimate? Heck, I uncovered an outfit in New Jersey that does nothing but write fraudulent articles. They bribe doctors to approve them and publish the articles in legitimate journals. The drug companies pay twenty to fifty thousand dollars for just one of these articles. The doctors get thousands to sign off on them."

"Christ," McNeal said. "This does sound like the mafia. Do all these companies cheat?"

Sydney let loose another belly laugh. "They all cheat, all the time. These outfits run the biggest shell games in history. They develop and market drugs that don't work. They run fake drug studies to make us believe they're safe. They spend billions on marketing to convince us we need these drugs. They bribe doctors to prescribe them. They build production facilities in remote countries, so they're unregulated. In some of these pill plants, there's no medical professional or even a pharmacist to provide oversight. They don't even follow their own formulas. Some of them put contaminated products into their drugs." She raised a finger to Steve, then swung around to her computer, where she tapped in commands.

"Listen to this," she said. "Couple years ago, GlaxoSmithKline was fined three billion dollars for shenanigans just like the ones we're talking about. *Three billion dollars*, Steve. Ninth-biggest pharma company in the world." Sydney rotated the monitor for McNeal to see. She scrolled down the screen to reveal a list of drug companies and the sanctions they'd received.

"Nearly every big drug company's been caught, and they've paid enormous fines. Merck. Roche. Pfizer. None of them have clean hands. They pay billions in criminal penalties. The drug industry's paid thirty billion dollars in fines and penalties in the past decade alone. Every imaginable violation. I'm guessing they get caught five percent of the time."

McNeal considered asking her about Steele Pharmaceuticals but thought better of the idea.

"What about killing people? Violence?"

"They kill tens of thousands of people every year by putting bad drugs on the market," Sydney said. "One company sold a diabetes drug they knew didn't work. Supposedly killed fifteen thousand people before they pulled the drug off the market. They were fined a billion dollars. They probably made twenty billion off the drug, and nobody went to jail. As far as violence or murder, they solve most problems by throwing money at them. But I wouldn't put anything past these people. Some of the characters running these companies are bad actors."

"I remember a story," she said. Sydney swung her chair around and furiously tapped on a keyboard.

"Found it. Last year a pill-producing plant in Mexico mysteriously burned to the ground three days before a team of U.S. government inspectors was due to arrive. The plant was owned by a big Pharma player and operated by a subsidiary. Rumor was the factory was producing fake medicines and was about to be exposed. Seven people died in the fire. Nothing could be proven, because the evidence burned up. The drug company skated."

"Can you send me source information? Anything you have on all this?"

"I've got a ton of stuff," she said. "I'll shoot it over to you."

Sydney gave him a speculative look. "What are you chasing, anyway?"

"Fishing expedition," he said. "Nothing specific at this point."

"Okay," she gave him a knowing smile, "but if it's something I can get in on, let me know."

"You know I will."

"Whatever you're investigating," Sydney warned, "watch your step. Some of these characters are nasty. I'd be careful."

"People keep telling me that," McNeal said.

CHAPTER THIRTY-TWO

Crazy Canyon Trailhead
Near Missoula, Montana

The Montana trooper exited his patrol car and strode to the brown-painted iron pole that served as a barrier to motorized traffic. The blacktop road ended at the barrier, and beyond it he could see the logging trail that wound up the mountain toward the peaks of Sentinel Mountain. He studied the overgrown trail and decided it was passable for the cruiser. The trooper pushed his hat higher on his forehead and exhaled in relief. He needed to get to the Black Bear trailhead and didn't fancy a five-mile vertical hike this morning. He pulled a trail map from the glove box and determined that he could drive most of the way.

He pushed aside the pole, pulled the cruiser through, then jogged back and pulled the barrier back across the trail. He drove carefully up the steep dirt path, slowly navigating turns and cutbacks until he arrived at the junction of trails. Crazy Canyon trail narrowed to a walking path, and Black Bear trail branched off to its right. A small crowd of hikers was bunched at the intersection. The trooper walked over and patiently listened as they chattered about what was occurring up on the mountain.

The officer returned to the cruiser and advised dispatch to mobilize a chopper. He had a mile of trail to hike, and the morning sun was already warm on his back. He grabbed a bottle of water. He was young and fit, and he anticipated no problems hiking up the hill. He pushed through the little crowd and began moving up the trail, which grew increasingly narrow and steep as he climbed towards the mountain peak.

The densely forested mountain sloped upwards to his right. To the trail's left a sheer vertical wall dropped a thousand feet to the valley floor. The trooper hiked with care, favoring the right side of the path. He rounded a switchback and saw more hikers clustered ahead. Two men and a woman. The men were supporting the woman, who was slumped between them. She was sobbing, head in hands.

As the trooper approached, the woman broke free and ran towards him. She was graying and in her fifties, wearing hiking boots and a backpack. The woman appeared stricken and red-eyed.

"My husband." Her voice was hoarse from crying as she pointed towards the ledge. "Fell into the canyon."

The trooper moved to the edge of the trail and peered over. Far below, he could see the oddly sprawled body. He studied the steep and jagged slope, and considered the rocky surface where the man was lying motionless It would be impossible to hike down to confirm what he had already concluded. He looked again at the inert body and had no doubt he'd be writing up a fatality this morning.

"Anybody see what happened?"

The woman shook her head and took a shuddering breath. "He was ahead of us. He likes to climb hard to the top. We heard him shout and ran up." She was trembling. The tears started again. "I can't believe it. We regularly hike this trail. It's not that dangerous. I don't understand how he could fall."

Heart attack or stroke, the trooper was thinking as he considered the woman's age. Her husband was probably older. He nodded in sympathy. "I've called for a chopper," he said. "Mountain rescue's on their way. They'll get down to him." He pulled out a small spiral notebook and pen. "Sorry, ma'am, but I do need some information," he said. "What's your husband's name?"

"Wilkinson," she said. "Dr. Wayne Wilkinson. He's a professor at the university."

McNeal drove home with his mind humming.

He drummed his fingers on the steering wheel. His brain was operating on autopilot, absently navigating the city streets as his busy mind kept running through the question marks he'd pinned to the messy corkboard.

McNeal lived in a tall condo tower off Lakeshore Drive with a view of the water. Arriving home, he turned on the computer and saw the email from Sydney. She'd included a list of attachments. There were hundreds of pages, and he spent the evening downloading and reading them.

His instincts were screaming. There was a huge story here, one with national or even international implications.

McNeal was convinced somebody was committing criminal acts, for reasons presently unknown. It was a fascinating puzzle and he needed to fill in the pieces. He'd identified the main players. The next step was to figure out what they were doing. Why they were doing it. Their motivation. Who would profit. He needed to gather more puzzle pieces. Then he would assemble them and develop his storyline.

He began working on an itinerary. Atlanta would be on the list. He would talk to the local cops about William Bernard, the team member who'd died in the suspicious car accident. He'd attempt to interview the man's wife. Then travel to California and talk to Will Connors. Was Tavey Bohanon, the missing Paragon security man, still alive? If so, he would track him down. Wayne Wilkinson, the head of the inspection team, lived in Montana. Eventually, McNeal would make his way to Houston and interview Andrew Glass.

But first he needed to find Tamara.

McNeal walked into his bedroom and rummaged in a high closet shelf until he found the photo album. He unclipped the first picture in the album. He and Tamara. In wedding clothes. The photo was ten years old, but it represented another lifetime. McNeal barely recognized himself. He was wearing a tightly-fitted suit and skinny tie. A style trendy a decade ago. He looked young and naïve. Tamara was decked out in her wedding regalia. A short, bosom-hugging white dress and spiked high heels. A veil held by a sparkling tiara atop her wild red hair. She was blushing and radiant. As he contemplated the picture, he unlocked the box in his mind where he kept his memories of her.

They'd met at an Eagles concert. He sat behind her and saw nothing but her lovely backside because she never sat down. She spent the evening screaming out her love for the band and dreamily swaying as she sang along with them. McNeal couldn't stop watching her, and finally he climbed over the seat and stood beside her. She'd linked her arm through his, and soon they were dancing and singing together.

The connection was electric. He toppled over the edge and was instantly crazy for her. Tamara was an exotic creature from another planet. Impulsive and emotional, Totally unpredictable. His diametric opposite. Logic had no place in her life. She was all about emotions. She wore too much lipstick and perfumed every part of the body. Her clothing choices were bold and unpredictable. She read classical literature and listened to deafening rock music. Her libido was off the charts, and he'd never known such sex. They married a year later.

On the night of their second anniversary they'd made passionate love. Tamara tenderly kissed him and told him she adored him but couldn't handle marriage. She didn't want to try any longer. The next morning she packed her bags, and it was over. He was shocked and heartbroken. It was years before he let go of his anger. He watched from a distance as she roared through another marriage and divorce. Eventually he stopped blaming himself for the failed relationship.

McNeal grew to appreciate her for what she'd given him. He forgave her for what she'd taken. He still loved her, and their relationship gradually transitioned into an easy friendship. Once or twice a year he drove down to Champagne to see her.

There was a reason beyond sentiment that McNeal was examining the photo album. He thought it might provide clues to her location. McNeal had strong-armed an IT buddy at the paper to hack Tamara's credit card account. He pulled the bills from his briefcase and scanned the lists of charges. The same evening she'd departed the university, Tamara gassed up at a convenience store outside Chicago. Considering she'd driven from Champagne, it was reasonable to presume she was heading north. A charge the next day to an Italian restaurant in southern Wisconsin. Cash withdrawal a few hours later from a town further north.

McNeal flipped through the album until he found the picture. They were on a rickety wooden dock in front of a pristine lake ringed by huge tamaracks. He held a tiny sunfish aloft. Tamara stood beside him, hand covering her mouth in mock astonishment. The little cottage belonged to her uncle. They had gone there to honeymoon. The cabin was near the town of Three Lakes, in the northernmost part of Wisconsin. The tiny community was located amidst a hundred-mile-long chain of lakes that wound through the pristine wilderness. The lakes were so plentiful that many had no names.

Her uncle's place was located on an unnamed body of water thirty miles from Three Lakes. It was her favorite place on earth, and she'd spent every summer of her childhood there. She once told him if she needed to hide out, she'd go straight to her uncle's summer cabin.

McNeal pulled up a state map on the computer and studied it. He ran a search and found the website for the town of Three Lakes. He scrolled through the site and saw the little community had a five-person police force. He activated his phone and called a cop buddy. Over the years he had developed relationships with some of the Chicago cops. One he liked was Bobby Otis, a good-natured grizzly of a man who'd spent a couple of seasons on the Bears defensive line. He'd blown out a knee and retired to go into law enforcement. Over the years the cop and reporter occasionally had the opportunity to help one another in their work. They'd shared more than a few beers. McNeal considered him a friend. He advised Otis of the situation, and the cop promised he'd reach out.

McNeal was asleep on the couch when his phone buzzed. He blinked open his eyes to morning sun streaming through the window. He picked up the phone and saw it was Otis.

"A Three Lakes deputy cruised past the cabin this morning," the cop reported. "The lights are on. Smoke coming out the chimney. There's a red convertible parked outside the place."

"Probably her," McNeal said.

"My man wrote down her plate number," Otis said. "I ran it this morning. It's her."

CHAPTER THIRTY-THREE

Steele Pharmaceuticals
Houston, Texas

Night had descended on Houston.

Glass was alone in his office. A security detail was stationed on the first floor; otherwise, the building was empty. The overhead lights were off, and a desk lamp illuminated the room. Glass nursed a drink as he peered into the waiting room. A man was sitting there, calmly leafing through a magazine. Glass had a final meeting to conduct before his evening was over. He strode to the door and opened it. Bob Travers walked into the office.

"How was Montana?" Glass said.

"Nice," Travers responded with an ingenuous smile. "The last best place. Cleanest air in the world. Did some hiking."

Glass kept a stone face. "Any problems?"

"A tragic hiking accident. Somebody fell off a mountain."

"Fatal?"

"Absolutely," Travers said.

"Shame," Glass said. "What about Guatemala?"

"Cleaned up. Johnson and his crew are long gone. Video equipment's been cleaned out. We found what was left of that weasel LeDoux. Took care of his body. Recovered the jobara plant."

"Find anything else?"

"No," Travers said.

Glass smiled indulgently at the lie. He knew Travers had found two hundred and fifty thousand dollars in LeDoux's backpack. Glass didn't care about the money. It was nothing more than pocket change when larger stakes were considered. Travers had recovered the jobara plant. He was welcome to keep the money.

"Bohanon?"

"Sneaky Mick bastard," Travers said. "Slipped out of the facility with three bullets still in his body. Stole a Jeep from the motor pool. Made it to Guatemala City and got on a commercial flight to San Diego. Left a credit card trail a mile wide. I've got a man keeping an eye on him. He's not moving well at the moment. Drinking himself to death."

Glass leaned back in his chair and steepled his fingers as he contemplated Bob Travers. He considered the paradox the man represented. A stone cold killer, yet behaving with the eager beaver demeanor of a used car salesman. Travers was chubby and out of shape. Face perpetually flushed and sweating. He played the role of glad-handing people pleaser to perfection. Harmless, if you didn't gaze too long at his predatory eyes.

Glass considered him indispensable. A loyal attack dog. He likened Travers to a razor-sharp blade, a valuable and necessary tool but one to be handled with extreme care. Travers efficiently carried out any task assigned to him. He killed without complication or emotion. He had coldly eliminated Shimota. Arranged William Bernard's unfortunate auto accident in Atlanta. Pushed Wayne Wilkinson from a mountain trail in Montana. All done with casual indifference, as if he were running errands.

"Bohanon's a problem," Glass said.

Travers nodded in agreement. "He knows too much. There's the rest of the inspection team to think about."

Glass paused and ran scenarios through his mind. "Take care of Bohanon," he said. "Bowers hasn't located the woman. Once he finds her, I'll let you know how to proceed."

"Connors?"

Glass shook his head. "Not yet. He's busy curing cancer."

Glass walked to the window and stared into the parking lot, watching as Travers drove away. On his way to carry out an assassination. Glass didn't savor making these decisions, but he believed them necessary and justified. He considered himself a principled person, a man of honor. The head of a multinational corporation. Few men possessed the talent to manage such a complex organization, or the ability to act decisively in times of crisis.

His company's survival was in his hands. Glass envisioned himself a general officer leading his forces into war. The business world was a battleground as surely as the deserts of the Middle East. Corporate nations engaged in hostile actions against one another, with vast territory and mighty fortunes at stake. In this war, the combatants wore three-piece suits and traveled in private jets.

Glass experienced not an iota of hesitation about sending Travers off on his deadly errands. He was fighting a war. There were enemies at the gates. Battles to be fought.

There would be casualties.

CHAPTER THIRTY-FOUR

McNeal stuffed his shaving kit into the suitcase and started to it zipper it. He looked at the nightstand beside the bed. He made a *why not* shrug and removed the pistol from the drawer. A lethal-looking nine-millimeter semi-automatic, the weapon was flat black and smelled of lubricant. His cop friend Bobby Otis had recommended the model. McNeal weighed the thing in his hand. It felt solid and lethal. He'd never fired it. Never even carried it.

He'd impulsively bought it last year while researching a story on gang-related drug trafficking in the city's jail system. There had been death threats from gang-bangers and drug dealers. Even complicit detention officers made veiled threats. He'd brought the weapon home and put it into the nightstand, then promptly forgot about it.

McNeal dropped the 15-cartridge clip into his hand. Fully loaded. He shoved the clip into the pistol and laid the weapon in his suitcase. He rode the elevator to the parking garage and threw the suitcase into the trunk of his car. He owned an eight-year-old Toyota. A faded blue two-door with an odometer pushing a hundred thousand miles. A reliable vehicle also unobtrusive enough to provide McNeal camouflage as he traversed the city's dangerous streets in pursuit of the next headline.

It would take an hour to clear Chicago traffic. Then a three-hour drive up Interstate Ninety through Madison. Another three hours to reach northern Wisconsin. McNeal drove through a corner kiosk and grabbed a cup of steaming coffee. Traffic was light, and he quickly cleared the city. He crossed the state line and was soon speeding through splendid Wisconsin dairyland. He kept the radio off and passed the time trying to organize the jumble of puzzle pieces. The topic consumed him, and the drive to Madison went quickly. Once in the college town, he pulled into a big travel plaza for gas and a coffee refill.

Returning to the car, McNeal spotted the gigantic billboard beside the interstate. Dramatic lettering across the top of the sign: ***Novix. Drink From The Fountain Of Youth.*** Below was a montage of photos. A stooped and gray-haired woman with cane in hand. Extending across the billboard an evolutionary chart-type sequence of pictures in which she gradually grew younger. The last one featured the same woman, now a teenager. She was dancing and her arms thrust joyfully skyward. McNeal had to admire the marketing strategy. Who wouldn't want to grow younger? Who wouldn't want to take Novix?

He resumed the monotonous drive, now thinking about Tamara. He was eager to see her. McNeal had many questions for his ex-wife. Why was she hiding? Who she was running from? What had her scared? He was convinced it all connected to the story he was chasing. He was anxious to learn the details of Guatemala. Another thought crossed his mind. Tamara had no idea he was coming. Would she welcome his unannounced arrival?

He wondered if she was alone.

He felt a prickle of jealousy, then chuckled at his silliness. Tamara was a heart-breaker. She'd thoroughly stomped on his. They'd divorced ten years ago. She quickly ran through another husband, and he figured she had other relationships. He passed the miles wondering why he was thinking such thoughts. Why it mattered. Why she still held a place in his heart. Was there another reason he was so eager to see her? He gazed across the Wisconsin flatlands and thought about his life.

He'd been alone since the divorce. Immersed in his career. He allowed little time for a social life. McNeal had drinking buddies he accompanied on occasion to Bulls or Bears games. He had happy hour friends, mostly Sydney Sinclair and Bobby Otis. He'd grown comfortable in his solitary life. He once tried to own a cat, a pet that required minimal attention. He had no time for the creature, sometimes unable to locate it in his apartment. His isolation had much to do with his work, which sucked up time like a vortex and included an element of danger. He also suspected his preference to be alone had something to do with Tamara.

He exited the interstate north of Madison and continued his journey along narrow state roads. The landscape became lush as farmland fell away and was replaced with forested hills covered with sugar maple and tamarack. It seemed that every five miles he passed a lake.

He pulled into the scenic village of Three Lakes, where he got out to stretch his back. A pretty little town. A fishing mecca busy with summer traffic. This was Muskie and walleye country. Pickup trucks and fishing poles in abundance. It had been a decade since his last visit, and he wasn't convinced he could find his way to the cabin. He consulted the GPS on his phone, pulling up a map and locating the sequence of roads to follow.

It took an hour to drive thirty miles along country roads that transformed from blacktop to gravel to dirt as he traveled more deeply into the woods. He was bumping along a deeply furrowed road when the GPS advised him to turn down an overgrown lane with a rusty mailbox. He inched down the path until the little lake came into view. He spotted the peaked green tin roof of the cabin. Tamara's red convertible parked beside it. He shut off the engine and remained in the car. He spotted her standing on the dock. She was staring at the car. She looked afraid. He got out and waved at her.

Tamara let loose a cry and came running into his arms.

———◆———

McNeal stooped in front of the stone fireplace and laid a chunk of firewood atop glowing embers. He watched as orange flames eagerly rose to consume the wood. He moved to the ancient couch and dropped onto it. The same couch from a decade earlier. He'd made love to Tamara on this sofa. On the wooden porch they had exchanged moonlight kisses. Skinny dipped off the little dock. It seemed a hundred years since he'd last been here. The memories were bittersweet and not unpleasant. He'd been filled with naïve optimism. Certain he would spend his life with Tamara.

He ran his eyes around the cabin. Built a century earlier out of hand-chopped logs and mud caulking, the outer walls repeatedly coated with forest service brown paint. The green tin roof seemed new. The interior was one big room. A kitchen area and a little bathroom. A king sized bed pushed against a far wall. A river-rock fireplace took up most of another wall, the old couch in front of it. The room had grown warm from the fireplace.

Tamara was cross-legged on the floor, holding a glass of red wine. Wearing an extra-large men's dress shirt with sleeves rolled up. Silk pajama bottoms. She was barefoot. The ensemble gave her a childlike appearance. Her face was pale. Eyes reddened and swollen from crying. The shock of wild hair was subdued behind her head with a rubber band.

Tamara had drunk wine all afternoon. Overjoyed to see him and eager to talk about Guatemala. The excitement at making the journey. Her eagerness to visit the Guyama village. The wondrous scientific discoveries she'd seen at Tikal. The arboreal wonders of Serenity Gardens. The orangutan whose severed spine had been repaired, and the chimp growing younger. She told him how it all quickly changed. Her suspicions that something wasn't right. The attack on Shimota. Her terrifying foray into the jungle. The strange creature that battered down the doors of the facility.

Finally she stopped talking and stared at the wine glass. McNeal waited. He knew she had more to say.

"I need to tell you something," she said. "It might hurt you. If it does, I'm sorry."

McNeal gave her a puzzled look and nodded.

"You weren't my first husband."

McNeal's eyes widened in surprise, and a flare of jealous pain shot through his body. He started to react. Thought better of it and said nothing.

"When I was eighteen I married a guy named Billy Mackie," she said. "I'd just finished high school. He was a year older. Rode around on a motorcycle, and wore leathers. Had that slicked back hair. You know the type. Every small town has one. He had a job as a mechanic." Tamara shook her head at the memory of her adolescent silliness. "He'd dropped out of school, been arrested a couple of times, and my parents hated him. Naturally, I fell for him. We got married two months after I met him, in a little civil ceremony. He drove me home on his motorcycle."

She offered McNeal an apologetic look. "I know I should have been honest. It was a shameful part of my life. I was eighteen. The marriage lasted four months. When we met, I wanted you to think I was perfect."

"I wish you'd told me," McNeal said. "It wouldn't have mattered."

They stared at one another in silence. McNeal was curious about the timing of her revelation. Why she was choosing this moment to reveal a decade-old secret no longer important to either of them. "My razor-sharp reporter instincts tell me there's more to this story."

Tamara rose and walked to the little kitchen, where she poured from a wine bottle. "He lived in a trailer park when I met him. His place was about as trashy as it gets. After the wedding I moved in with him. Postponed college. Got a job as a waitress. We were happy enough, in the way of clueless teenagers."

"Anyway," she said, "he had a shed out behind the trailer. Told me he kept motorcycle parts in it. He kept it locked, so things wouldn't get stolen. I came home from work one afternoon and cops were surrounding the place. Guns drawn. Billy handcuffed, sitting on the steps. They were all over the trailer, and had the shed opened up. Billy wasn't keeping parts in there. The place was full of chemicals. While I was at work, Billy and another guy were cooking meth."

"You married a drug dealer," McNeal said.

"I was arrested and charged with conspiracy to manufacture methamphetamine, which was a big-time felony. They told me I was facing twelve years in prison. Of course I denied it. I really didn't know what he was doing. The cops weren't interested in my story."

"What did you do?"

"My parents posted the bail," she said. "They got me a lawyer who wanted me to take a plea bargain. Told me he could get the sentence down to five years. He thought it was a good deal. Said I'd be out in three. Didn't seem concerned that my life would be ruined. Billy was sitting in jail. I had this same attorney file divorce papers and serve them on him. The next day I got on a Greyhound bus. Went to Illinois to live with an aunt. I went back to my maiden name. Enrolled in college that way. I went on with my life. Never returned to Missouri, and I never heard anything more about it."

"Until Andrew Glass threatened to expose you?"

"First he tried to convince me of the importance of this drug Novix. How the survival of his company was at stake. They'd go bankrupt if he didn't get the drug approved.

295

When I wouldn't agree to shut up, he tried to bribe me. Offered me two hundred and fifty thousand dollars. I turned him down flat. He gave me this arrogant smile. Handed me a big envelope. Told me to look inside. It was my booking photo and the police report. He asked what my dean might think when she saw it. Said the authorities in Missouri would appreciate finding me."

"Your career would end," McNeal said, "you'd face prosecution on the drug charge. I can understand why you gave in."

She shook her head. "I didn't. Glass had me hopping mad. You know I don't intimidate easily. I didn't care about his drug or his stupid company. Didn't care who he told about my past. I told him I was going straight to the media."

"So what happened?"

"He left the room," she said. "A man named Travers came in. I'm sure he killed Yanni, and I accused him of it. He told me I was right. He said the same thing could happen to me. He showed me pictures taken through my bedroom window. Photos of me at dinner. Sitting in my office at the university. Said he could find me any time he wanted. Glass came back and again offered me the money. I told him I didn't want it. But I agreed to shut up. I just wanted to get away from that place."

"He let you go?"

"Flew me home on his private jet. I was scared to death. Afraid he'd toss me out of the plane. But he didn't bother me. After I got home, I couldn't stop thinking about Travers. He terrifies me. I figured he wouldn't find me up here." She paused and raised her eyes in thought.

"One more crazy thing. After I got back I discovered I was two hundred and fifty thousand dollars richer. Somebody deposited it in my checking account."

"Makes you look complicit," McNeal said.

"I hadn't thought of that," she said. "Now that I'm out here, it sometimes seems ridiculous. Like I'm imagining the whole thing. We're talking about a giant pharmaceutical company, a business that trades on the stock market. I can believe they'd try to bribe someone. But murder? Would they kill people?"

"What if Andrew Glass' name was *El Chapo*," he said, "and you were interfering with his multi-billion dollar drug operation. Would it be far-fetched to think you'd be in danger?"

"These people are like that? A drug cartel?"

"They operate the same way. They've got billions riding on this drug. I suspect Shimota's not the only one they've eliminated."

He saw a wave of exhaustion ripple through her body. She announced that she needed a nap, yawned and stretched, then climbed in the bed. McNeal remained on the couch and watched as she burrowed under a big comforter. The alcohol worked its magic, and soon she was softly snoring. He walked outside to the little dock. He stared at the tranquil lake and tried to piece it together.

Steele Pharmaceuticals was a company in trouble and facing bankruptcy. Its survival depended on Novix. Failure to gain approval of the drug would be catastrophic. Glass manipulated the inspection team, making sure he could control the people assigned to it. He faked research to make the drug seem effective. Used bribery, blackmail and murder to eliminate problems. The scenario explained most of the question marks on McNeal's corkboard. This was a sensational story, but he couldn't write it based solely on Tamara's claims. He had few hard facts. No proof of anything.

Tamara found him on the dock. "What do we do now?" she said.

"First, get you out of danger," he said. "The best tactic is to go public. Let the world know what's going on. Once this bullshit's out in the open, they won't have any reason to bother you. But when this gets out, we may not be able to keep the drug charge out of it."

"I don't care," she said. "I'm ready for a job change. Besides, I want to take down this bastard. Where do we start?"

"We do some digging. Get hard proof. I want to talk to the team members. Starting with Will Connors."

"You know how to find him?"

"He's living in a mansion in California."

Tamara gave him a perplexed look.

"I'll explain it," he said. "Right now we've got other priorities. I need to book a flight to San Francisco."

"I'm going with you. First class. Those assholes stuck a quarter million dollars in my bank account. I may as well spend it."

Tamara yawned and stretched her body, then declared she was ready to eat. She heated a big can of beef stew and spooned it into bowls. She filled tall glasses with icy water from the faucet. After dinner they took turns showering. She went in first and emerged later with a towel wrapped turban-style around her head. Another towel around her body. McNeal showered and brushed his teeth. He examined himself in the mirror, then took a deep breath before opening the door.

Pathetic. I'm hoping to score with my ex-wife.

If anything happened between them, now was the time. He walked into the room, then smiled and shook his head. Tamara was already asleep, snuggled under the covers. She left a pillow and blanket on the couch. He kissed her forehead, and she wished him a sleepy goodnight.

The next morning over coffee they discussed their itinerary. They'd leave immediately for Madison. On the way, book a flight to California. Rent a car and drive to Santa Cruz. They decided to drive his car to Madison and leave hers parked at the cabin. McNeal threw his suitcase on the bed and searched for a clean shirt. He laid aside the pistol.

"Can you take that thing with you?"

"In the checked bag, if it's unloaded and declared," he said. "Think it needs to be in a locked case."

"Take it."

McNeal returned the weapon to the suitcase. Tamara picked up her purse and rummaged until she found what she wanted. She held it up for McNeal to see. A pink lipstick tube.

"I had my uncle's shotgun, in case Travers found me," she said. "I also had this."

"You figured to gloss him to death?"

"No, silly," she said. "It's pepper spray. Pretty cute, huh? You think I should bring it?"

"I'm bringing my gun," he said, "bring your lipstick."

Thirty minutes later they pulled away from the cabin. McNeal steered down the little lane and turned onto the winding dirt road that would lead them to Three Lakes. Tamara pulled a CD from her purse, and soon the car was rocking with music. She looked fresh and was wearing makeup this morning. McNeal kept his eyes trained on the narrow road and failed to notice the man standing in the woods, studying them through binoculars.

"Shit," Scottie Bowers muttered.

The diminutive investigator jogged through the woods to his car. He drummed his fingers on the steering wheel until the cloud of dust the other vehicle left in its wake had settled. He pulled onto the dirt road and began to follow at a careful distance. He checked his phone for a signal, and when he got one Bowers punched in Andrew Glass' number.

CHAPTER THIRTY-FIVE

Gaslamp Quarter
San Diego, California

The walls of O'Houlihans were festooned with shamrocks and unicorns. A neon leprechaun grinned from above the bar. The bartender wore a green bowler hat and matching bow tie. The place was jammed with drunken patrons. They frequently linked arms and swayed in rhythm as they sang bawdy limericks or teary songs of Ireland. They roared in self-congratulation and slapped one another on the back at the conclusion of each song.

Travers sat with his back to the wall, facing the front door. Sipping bitter brown ale as his sharp eyes swept the pub. He thought the place ridiculous and paid no mind to the frivolity. He was content to sit at a corner table and sip the nasty beer. Packed along the bar were a dozen men jammed elbow-tight on emerald vinyl stools. Travers was interested in the man slumped at the far end of the bar.

He watched Tavey Bohanon toss back a shot of whiskey. The Irishman licked his lips and contemplated the empty glass before extending it across the bar for a refill. Travers had followed Bohanon the past three days. The man spent every waking hour in this dive and was serious about his drinking. Bohanon favored straight shots of single-malt Bushmills, a high-dollar whiskey distilled in County Antrim in Northern Ireland. He'd been born in a neighboring county, and this bar was a gathering place for ex-pats hailing from that region of the Emerald Isle.

Travers felt the phone vibrate against his leg.

He smiled when he saw it was his wife. Texting to wish him good night. He was married to a woman a decade younger. A Latin beauty who immigrated as a teenager to Texas from Veracruz, a seaside city on the Bay Of Campeche. She was new to the country and naïve in many ways. Travers loved her saucy attitude and accent. Her impulsivity and wild passion. He suspected she'd married him because of his position and money. He had a legitimate job title at Steele, as vice president of marketing. He drew a hefty salary. Travers didn't mind the idea that she might have married him for his money. He thought of her dark eyes and voluptuous body, and figured he'd gotten the better of the deal.

She knew nothing about his darker assignments, and Travers was careful to keep it that way. He loved his wife and planned to spend his life with her. They lived a good life, and she'd grown accustomed to his constant travel and unpredictable schedule. He bought her a nice five-bedroom house in a Houston suburb. They were talking about kids. She seemed happy enough, although she talked wistfully about one day returning to her homeland. Travers dialed her and chatted briefly before wishing her goodnight. He returned his attention to the bar.

Bohanon was in the process of finishing his evening. Travers watched as the Irishman eyed a shot of amber liquid and raised it to his lips. Bohanon turned the glass upside down and pushed it towards the bartender. Travers knew this was the man's sign that he was done for the night, so he threw a couple of dollars on the table and hurried out ahead of him.

Travers walked through the darkness to his car and popped open the trunk. He reached into a black gym bag and slipped on a pair of surgical gloves. He extracted a heavy lead pipe. He tapped the thing against his palm, and decided it would meet his needs. Travers concealed the pipe under his jacket and walked beneath tall and burnished street lamps until he reached a darkened alley. He turned into it and stopped at a dumpster halfway down the alley. He moved behind it and settled into the darkness to wait.

It would look like a random assault. He'd slug Bohanon with the pipe, rendering him unconscious. Finish the man with further blows to the head. Empty Bohanon's wallet and toss it into the dumpster. In the morning, the police would take a cursory look and conclude the victim was a drunk. Mugged and robbed. Not uncommon on a Saturday night in downtown San Diego. Travers would be in Houston by morning, listening to his wife chatter about kids.

He experienced no reluctance in committing this act of violence. The Irishman had earned his fate. Travers had developed a liking for the man in Guatemala. Bohanon was a competent security man despite his ridiculous brogue and ever-present flask. He was a trusted member of the team. Then Bohanon revealed himself as nothing more than a common thief. He committed acts of betrayal that threatened damage to the company. He knew far too many secrets.

Travers was careful in his preparations. He'd thoroughly checked Bohanon's background. The man had served in the Irish Defense Forces. Then a decade as a cop on the streets of Ulster. After immigrating to America, he'd hired on at Paragon Security and rose to a position of senior management. Bohanon was no civilian. Once he'd been a hard man, capable of defending himself. Travers wouldn't ordinarily take him on at close range.

That wasn't the man he was waiting to ambush. Bohanon had become a drunken sot. His skills and reflexes compromised. Recovering from gunshot wounds. Shuffling through the streets like an old man. Travers had surveilled him for three days. Bohanon spent his hours in the noisy pub. Drinking himself to oblivion. Stumbling each night down this alley. Tonight he would go down easily.

He heard the shuffle of footsteps. Bohanon's blocky frame was silhouetted by the streetlight and cast a long shadow into the alley. Travers tensed as the man began lurching towards him. He lifted the pipe to his shoulder. The footsteps grew louder, then abruptly stopped. Travers cocked his head in puzzlement. He stepped forward and glanced up the alley.

"Fuck." Travers jogged onto the cobblestone street and looked both ways. He saw no sign of Bohanon.

———◆———

Bohanon had suspected for days someone was following him. It began with a prickling of the neck. An intuitive suspicion that something wasn't right. A sense of unease that put his body on hyper alert. He began to pay attention to his surroundings. To the people around him. He stopped at a department store window and studied the reflection. He caught a glimpse of a face. Vaguely familiar. He observed a vehicle cruise past his motel room the past two mornings. He was certain someone had searched his room, although he knew an intruder would find nothing of importance. Bohanon kept everything he owned in a suitcase lying open on the bed.

Last night he spotted Bob Travers sitting at a tiny table in a dark corner of O'Houlihans. Everything fell into place. Bohanon wasn't surprised to see Travers had returned this evening.

Bohanon had prepared himself for the evening.

Tonight he drank fewer shots of Irish whiskey. He carried a heavy sap in his pocket. He turned his shot glass upside down and signaled for the tab. He glanced at the big mirror behind the bar and saw Travers walk out the door. Bohanon followed a minute later and walked his usual route, but tonight he stopped at the mouth of the dark alley. He had no doubt Travers was awaiting him in the darkness. Bohanon felt the weight of the sap in his pocket and considered letting Travers take his shot. Once he would have enjoyed it. He'd faced men in the streets of Ulster far more lethal than Bob Travers. At his best, he could easily handle the man. But at the moment he was unprepared for a fight.

Bohanon was fortunate to be alive. He still walked the earth for one simple reason. The idiot LeDoux's had chosen to assault him using a tiny .22 pistol. The little bullets had done considerable damage to bone and muscle, but they missed vital organs. Bohanon survived their impact but the slugs left him bloody and weakened. He managed to crawl through miles of jungle. Escaped the research facility. Stole a Jeep. Visited a grimy clinic in Guatemala City run by an ancient *mestizo* who called himself a doctor and spoke not a word of English. The old man laid Bohanon on a kitchen table. Offered a slug of tequila for anesthesia before extracting the bullets from his body. The *mestizo* did a surprisingly competent job. Bohanon was growing stronger by the day. But he was much too weak for an alley fight.

Not tonight.

The Irishman turned and limped away. He would deal with Travers another time.

His car was parked in a grocery store lot next to the motel. Bohanon reached into the glove box for the pistol and laid it on the seat beside him. He wouldn't return to the motel. He drove through city streets until certain nobody followed him, then he merged onto the freeway. At Oceanside, he exited onto Mission Avenue and drove through the empty town towards the shore. He found an isolated beachside lot. Bohanon pulled the silver flask from his boot and stared at the dark ocean.

He'd screwed up royally. The whiskey couldn't stop his mind from ruminating on his utter stupidity. He had a nice situation with Paragon Security. A good job with responsibility. He enjoyed the work and travel. An occasional fat bonus. But no man grew rich on the wages of a security guard. LeDoux had approached months earlier and dangled the opportunity to earn a quarter-million dollars. By committing a simple act of theft. Greed short-circuited common sense He agreed to steal a jobara plant and sell it to LeDoux.

LeDoux was a harmless idiot, but Bohanon had underestimated him. After turning over the plant, he'd taken his bag of money and walked into the jungle. Never sensing a shred of danger. Oblivious to the man behind him. Then he felt a stinging sensation in his back. He thought he'd been stung by a jungle insect. Then gunshots echoed through the jungle and Bohanon went down while LeDoux ran off with the money. Through pure Irish stubbornness he had held onto life. Crawled out of the jungle. Escaped Guatemala.

Surviving Travers would be a different matter. Bohanon had eluded him tonight, but Travers would eventually find him. The man was a stone cold killer. Bohanon stared into the night and considered alternatives. Ireland came into his mind. He didn't savor the prospect of returning to his depressing homeland. But he didn't want to die in a country not his own. He sealed the decision with a nip, then put the flask in his boot and returned to the freeway. There was a final thing he wanted to do before he left the country.

He headed north, in the direction of Santa Cruz.

CHAPTER THIRTY-SIX

Oceana Montessori School
Santa Cruz, California

"I like it here," Mollie said.

The classroom was large and open. No desks. The room was filled with chairs, couches and worktables. A dozen learning pods – self-contained areas providing materials for various academic subjects. There were math and science areas. English and literature. Art and music. Astronomy. A nature area contained living plants and crawling insects. In the creativity area, art and photography supplies. There were beads laid out in the math area for counting. The walls were covered with artwork created by children.

Fifteen students were scattered around the room, each engrossed in a chosen area of study. The atmosphere was relaxed and quiet. Mollie seemed to love it. She eagerly moved from one pod to another. Exploring. Touching and feeling in the Montessori way. Everything seemed to interest her. She saw a bookshelf and ran to it. A minute later she was stretched out on the floor, flipping through the pages of a large and colorful book.

He watched her lips move as she read. Her brow furrowed in concentration. A champagne rush filled his head. Joy was an emotion he hadn't felt in a long time. He closed his eyes and savored the sense of victory. Mollie was a living miracle. Proof that magic existed. The cancer that nearly took her had been defeated. The process had shattered his life. Her recovery had restored and rearranged it. Now he saw the world differently. His life had been transformed into something better. Gone was ambition. Desire for fame or money. Life was about Mollie and savoring the wonders of an ordinary day.

He'd fixed her a pancake breakfast this morning, then listened attentively as she chattered about a toy she wanted for her birthday. She insisted on dressing herself, and carefully chose her outfit for the day. She spent a good amount of time deciding which shoes to wear, finally selecting her favorite pink high top sneakers.

She'd missed a full year of school. Worried she might struggle in a regular classroom, he brought her this morning to a Montessori school. The relaxed pace and fluid learning environment would give Mollie the chance to catch up at her own pace. The school's administrator suggested the Montessori method would minimize any sense of failure. Mollie could focus on subjects that interested her. The official suggested that Will bring Mollie to the school for a visit.

They drove home with Mollie chattering about her day. He glanced at her animated face. Tomorrow they would return. He would formally enroll her. She continued to babble as he traversed the winding road towards the big house. He decided it was time to vacate the place. He appreciated Glass' generosity, but he'd stayed long enough. He would begin a search for a new home once Mollie became acclimated to school.

The afternoon sun felt warm on his face. Life had returned to normal. The cancer was gone from Mollie's body. She was returning to school. Engaging in child's play. Will was again engaging in meaningful research, participating in breakthrough cancer research. He liked his job. His biggest problem now was finding a permanent place to live. The future was bright. He had the sense that all of life's problems were in the past.

———————◆·◆·◆———————

Andrew Glass was standing at a podium two thousand miles away. Behind him a map of the world illuminated a huge screen. Pulsating circles representing target populations dotted the map. He proudly announced to the board that Novix would be available in every industrialized country within three years. Foreign sales were projected to eclipse those in the United States. Glass brought on-screen an earnings projection chart represented by a near-vertical upward line. He estimated profits in the hundreds of billions. Other genetic wonders were in the pipeline. Glass caused a buzz when he hinted at breakthroughs in treatment for cancer and dementia. He was facilitating an animated question and answer session when his phone buzzed.

Scottie Bowers.

Glass excused himself and walked from the room. He stood in a glass atrium as the investigator gave him a rapid-fire update from Wisconsin. Bowers had located Tamara.

Accompanied by Steve McNeal. They were at the moment waiting to board a plane in Madison. Glass rubbed a hand across his forehead as he considered this development. He knew what McNeal did for a living. He ordered Bowers to continue following the couple until their flight departed from Madison. Travers would pick them up in San Francisco.

The phone was still in his hand when it vibrated again. Travers calling from San Diego. Delivering the morning's second dose of bad news.

"Forget Bohanon," Glass snapped. "We have a more urgent problem." He advised Travers of the situation in Wisconsin. "They're boarding a flight to San Francisco. I don't have to tell you where they're going."

"Santa Cruz."

"Make sure they don't get there."

Travers hesitated. "That won't be easy. I can't just make them disappear. That kind of thing takes planning."

"Plan something," Glass growled. "Get your ass out there and take care of them."

"This is getting complicated," Travers said. "It's not a simple matter to take out two people. And what about Connors? You can't eliminate everyone else and leave him."

The line went silent as Glass thought through it.

"Him, too," he said.

CHAPTER THIRTY-SEVEN

Dane County Regional Airport
Madison, Wisconsin

The plane rose smoothly into the sky and began a gradual turn to the west as the pilot activated his electronic route for Dallas. McNeal sat in a wide first-class seat, sipping a Bloody Mary. Tamara had ordered a drink despite the breakfast hour and insisted he join her. He put aside the glass and opened his laptop, fidgeting while the software loaded. He glanced over at Tamara. She was staring out the aircraft window at cottony cloud banks while sipping her drink. Headphones were on, and she was tapping her fingers to some rock anthem.

Probably the Eagles, McNeal thought. He enjoyed the group's country-infused sound and clever lyrics, but not with the same passion as Tamara. McNeal appreciated their talent as gifted writers who created drug-inspired songs about cowboys, outlaws, outsiders and women. Tamara understood the group on a spiritual level. She believed them to be philosophers. Sage interpreters of the contemporary world. She elevated the group onto the same plateau as

Plato or Socrates. For Tamara, their songs imparted universal meaning and provided inspirational messages for comprehending love and the modern world.

The aircraft reached sufficient altitude and McNeal was able to connect his computer to the plane's onboard Wi-Fi. He began the task of sketching in biographies for the inspection team. He ordered a Google search on Wayne Wilkinson, the head of the Guatemala inspection team. Wilkinson held a tenured chair in the biological sciences division at a university in Montana. McNeal scrolled through the stream of Google hits highlighted by the search engine. He perused a lengthy newspaper article found in the Missoulian. He reached over and grabbed Tamara's arm.

"Look at this."

She pulled off her headphones and stared at the computer, then emitted a little squeal. "Oh my God."

"Wilkinson fell off a hiking trail and died," McNeal said. "His wife apparently doesn't believe his death was accidental."

"They killed him," she said, her voice tremulous with fright. She leaned close to McNeal's ear and whispered, "Travers killed him because he knew too much."

"I'm starting to think you're right," McNeal said. "This goes far beyond coincidence. Wilkinson's the third member of the team to die under questionable circumstances."

"They're trying to shut us up. They'll be coming after me. And Will. And you, when they find out you're with me." She looked nervously around the cabin, as if Travers might be sneaking up on her. "We should go to the police."

"Agreed," McNeal said. "We should tell somebody what's happening. But there's nothing we can do at the moment. Let's get to Santa Cruz. It's a couple of hours from San Francisco. I'll talk to Connors. See what he has to say. Then we go to the authorities."

Tamara stared a long time out the window before eventually returning to her headphones. McNeal noticed her flushed face and quivering chin. She was gnawing at a fingernail. He could think of nothing that might reassure her, so he ordered her another drink and resumed his internet search.

They were an hour into a three-hour flight to Dallas, where they'd connect to San Francisco. The trip became interminably long, as Tamara remained preoccupied and unable to relax. She consumed more drinks, which only seemed to increase her anxiety. She fidgeted through the brief layover in Dallas, and soon they were aboard the next flight. She ordered another drink, then promptly fell asleep and didn't awaken until they touched down in San Francisco.

McNeal picked up a big sedan at the rental kiosk and loaded the bags into the trunk. Evening was descending as they exited the airport, and soon they were heading south down the 101 Freeway. The stress of the day caught up with McNeal. Yawning and stretching his neck, he decided it was time for coffee. He pulled off the freeway into a brightly illuminated travel plaza. Tamara waited in the car, and a few minutes later McNeal returned carrying two large Styrofoam cups. He slid into the car and glanced at her. Tamara's eyes were wide with fear.

A gun was jammed into the back of her head.

Bob Travers was thoroughly pissed. He felt a vein pulsating in his temple, and his heart skittered like a jackrabbit. His neck burned as if scalded by a hot iron. He had just kidnapped two people. At gunpoint, in the middle of a fucking travel plaza in the heart of northern California. A stupid and risky move, one that might earn him a permanent billet in San Quentin.

Talk about fucking Mission Impossible. Everything about this deal was wrong. You don't just dash off to San Francisco and assassinate a bunch of people. Committing Capital Murder wasn't a seat of the pants operation. It required precision engineering. Careful planning to the smallest detail. Selection of the ideal time and place. Choosing weaponry appropriate for the setting. Striking at the perfect opportunity. Disposing of bodies. Leaving a clean crime scene. Disappearing without a trace. Creating an airtight alibi. None of those things were checked off Travers' list. He didn't even have a list. He had the sense of rushing headlong into an epic disaster.

He'd picked up McNeal and Rodgers easily enough when they passed through airport security, and he tailed them out of the city. When McNeal pulled into the travel plaza for coffee, Travers impulsively decided to act. The gun terrified them both, and neither McNeal nor Rodgers offered any resistance. They meekly followed his commands, and now they were back on the freeway. McNeal driving with a pistol jammed into his neck.

From the back seat, he ordered McNeal to follow the freeway signs for Santa Cruz. He saw a cell phone parked in a slot in the center console. He shook his head at his stupidity. He leaned forward and grabbed the phone. Swiped it open and saw it was McNeal's. He tapped the woman on the shoulder with the pistol and demanded her phone. She rummaged through her purse and handed it over to him. He removed the SIM cards and tossed them out the window. He wondered what else he might be overlooking.

Travers stared at the dense traffic streaming beneath harsh freeway lights. He felt a pang of yearning for his young wife. He wondered what she might be doing tonight. She probably had a fire going in the huge river rock fireplace that took up an entire wall of the family room. A language book open in her lap. When they last talked, she'd been working on her English and trying to teach him Spanish.

He turned his thoughts to Andrew Glass. He greatly admired the man. Considered him to be brilliant. A visionary and strategic planner without equal, always three steps ahead of the competition. Brutal and calculating, willing to eliminate anything that stood in the way of his objective. He was the general officer issuing commands. Travers his loyal soldier marching off to carry them out. He'd never experienced a shred of doubt regarding Glass' judgment.

But this deal was certifiably insane. Glass had ordered him to carry out a triple homicide. To carry it out immediately. No planning. Improvise on the fly. Glass issued the assignment as casually as ordering take-out. *Run over to San Francisco and take care of three people. Make them disappear. Get it done today. Leave no evidence. Don't implicate me.*

Meanwhile, Glass was ensconced in his penthouse office in Houston. Sipping five-hundred-dollar scotch. Secure and insulated in his corporate castle. Sending his loyal minion off to war with a casual wave of the hand. Oblivious to the impossibility of the task.

Travers began to wonder if his boss might be losing his grip.

He considered whether he might also be slipping. He'd botched the hit on Bohanon in San Diego. Then he lost the man's trail. Now he was in the middle of this mess. Clueless about how to resolve it. He pondered whether it might be time to retire from this line of work.

He put the idea away for future consideration. More immediate problems demanded his attention. He had two hostages in the front seat. So far, his plan consisted of taking them to Santa Cruz. He would secure Will Connors. He would figure out the details from there. He began running scenarios through his mind. Things that had worked in the past. Staging a fatal accident was out of the question. Too complicated and not enough time. A home invasion had possibilities. That would also require time and planning. The safest bet would involve simply making them vanish. The freeway ran close to the beach and in the distance he saw the dark waters of the Pacific. It was a big ocean. A good place to make bodies disappear.

The pair in the front seat were whispering. He ordered them to shut up. He decided he didn't like the arrangement. He was in the back seat. McNeal was driving the car. If the man had the balls, he could ruin the gig in a second by ramming the car into an adjacent vehicle. Traffic would pile up and cops would rush to the scene. He saw a rest stop exit sign and directed McNeal to pull into it. The place was brightly lit and deserted. He commanded McNeal to drive behind the cinder block restroom. He ordered the pair from the car and pushed them to the ground.

Travers opened the trunk and tossed out the suitcases. He stooped and glanced around the trunk's interior, spotting the yellow plastic release latch. He wrenched the thing off and tossed it aside, then he pulled the pair to their feet. Using zip ties, he bound their wrists and shoved them into the trunk. He noticed the woman's purse on the front seat, so he tossed it in before slamming the lid.

He was pulling from the lot when he spotted the suitcases in the rearview mirror. He cursed his abject stupidity. He might as well leave a flashing neon light to illuminate their trail. He threw the car into reverse and squealed back to the bags. He tossed them in the back seat, then worked his way back onto the freeway.

It was better, but the situation remained perilous. He was traveling along a busy interstate in a car rented to someone else. With a pair of hostages in the trunk. A routine traffic stop could spell disaster. He had an hour of driving before arriving in Santa Cruz. Travers drove carefully down the freeway, staying within the speed limit and signaling to change lanes.

CHAPTER THIRTY-EIGHT

Coastal Bay Estates
Santa Cruz, California

Travers parked the car in a convenience store parking lot on El Rancho Drive. He leaned against the trunk of the sedan and watched the Range Rover turn onto the busy street. The little girl was turned towards her father, engaged in animated conversation. He thumped the side of the car in frustration. He hadn't thought about the kid.

He waited until the SUV disappeared from sight, then he drove up the hill past estate-sized homes until he reached the one at the top. He pulled over and gazed at the house. A huge two-story the size of a department store. Tall picture windows with views of the Pacific. Three chimneys rose from the roof. A five-car garage. He'd never stepped inside a place so magnificent. An ornate double gate guarded the entrance, and Travers noticed the keypad on the gate's metal frame.

He drummed his fingers on the steering wheel, the sense of unease rising in his craw. He was exposed and vulnerable. A stranger in this affluent community. Residents would know one another and recognize him as someone who didn't belong here. The development was surely protected by electronic surveillance and private security. Cameras would be everywhere. He glanced up the winding road and figured one was recording him right now.

The thought of dumping the pair crossed his mind. Just leave them in the trunk and walk away. Catch an Uber to the airport and get the hell out of California. He quickly saw the folly of the idea. Andrew Glass was not a man who tolerated failure. Travers thought of his nice home in Texas, and his innocent wife. He knew better than to underestimate his boss' capabilities.

As he pulled to the gate of the big house, he swiped open his phone and then punched a sequence of numbers into the keypad. The gate swung open and he drove onto the property. The house was on an enormous landscaped lot ringed with tall shrubs and trees offering a modicum of privacy. He scrolled through text messages until finding the one from Glass providing the location of the electronic controller for the home's surveillance system.

Travers parked in the cobblestone driveway and walked around to the back of the house. There was a sparkling blue pool and a cabana larger than his home in Texas. The property ended at the side of the mountain. He could only imagine the enormity of Glass' wealth to own a home like this and never use it. He moved along the back wall until he saw the gray rectangular box. He extracted a pair of wire cutters from a small black bag. He opened the box and clipped a pair of cables. The home's video surveillance system was now off-line.

He returned to the front of the house and saw a keypad lock on the door. He entered the code and heard the deadbolt retract, then he stepped inside. He did a quick walkthrough, affirming the place was unoccupied. Opening a door off the kitchen, he saw stairs leading downward. He flipped on a light switch and went down to the landing. There was a deadbolt lock on the door. Travers ran his hands along the threshold and found the key. He pulled open the door and walked into a large cellar. Hundreds of dusty wine bottles lined the walls. No windows. Bare light bulbs with pull chains provided lighting.

He returned to the car. He pushed a button on the key fob and the trunk obediently popped open. Tamara was holding a pink lipstick tube in her hands. She sat up and smiled, then raised the tube to her lips.

Travers chuckled derisively. "Going to a party?"

She smiled again, then she shot him in the face with the pepper spray.

The tube carried a tiny payload, most of which dissipated during its short journey to his face. Some cayenne pepper got to his eyes, and Travers felt the burning sting as it made contact. He staggered backward, blinking and rubbing furiously at his eyes. The pair was scrambling to get out of the trunk. Travers pulled the pistol from his pocket and stepped in front of them.

"Fucking bitch." He raised his fist to strike her but thought better of it.

He roughly herded them into the house and down the stairs into the cellar. He forced them to their knees and bound their ankles with zip ties. He remembered the rental car was still out front. Still rubbing his stinging eyes, Travers raised the garage door and pulled the car inside.

He returned to the living room and waited for Connors to come home.

———◆———

"**W**e get to pet a shark," Mollie exclaimed. "They have dolphins and baby seals. And a whale skeleton."

Mollie was fascinated with the ocean and pestered Will every Saturday to take her to the beach. She loved to race ahead and splash in the foamy waves breaking on the shoreline. She built sand castles with her little pink pail and bucket. She walked barefoot along the shore, digging for sand crabs and studying them before releasing the creatures back to the water. She declared her intention of becoming a marine biologist, although Will doubted that she had any idea what that meant.

She continued to chatter as he drove towards the ocean. Today Mollie was going on a school field trip to the marine museum by the Monterrey Bay. She continued to regale him with information about the museum as he pulled into the parking lot. He spotted the cluster of kids, and Mollie jumped from the car and ran to join them, shouting a high-pitched goodbye to her father. He watched as teachers herded children through a ticket window and into the museum, then he set off to carry out his task for the day. It was time to leave the mansion on the hill. While Mollie spent her day at the marine museum, he'd go house-hunting.

He had already compiled a list of small homes and condos in the area, and he spent the morning with an agent.

The task was proving harder than he'd figured. Rentals in this town were small and expensive. He walked through a condo with two small bedrooms, a single bathroom, kitchen and living room. The tiny place rented for four thousand a month and could easily fit inside the family room of the corporate house. By lunchtime he had crossed all the prospects off the list except one. He drove across town and spent five minutes looking at a bungalow built in the fifties. It was a couple of blocks from the beach and more expensive than the condo. Its proximity to the beach caused him to hesitate before reluctantly crossing it off the list.

He planned to cook on the grill tonight, so he stopped by the high-end grocery store to pick up a steak and salad fixings. He tossed a package of hot dogs into the cart. Mollie preferred them to steak any day.

A man approached as he was pushing the cart towards the register. The man was middle-aged, ruddy-faced and favoring his right leg. The face was familiar, but Will couldn't place him. The man limped up to Will's cart, then grinned and stuck out his hand.

"Ah'm Tavey Bohanon," he said, "ya knew me in Guatemala. Ah'm hopin' ta have words with ya."

Will raised his brows in surprise, then he took the extended hand. Of course he remembered Bohanon. Will hadn't forgotten the tenderness the man had shown Tamara after her traumatic journey to the Guyama village. Will had developed a fondness for the Irishman during their time in Guatemala.

"Let me get another steak," he said.

———•———

Travers stepped from behind the door when they walked into the house. He confiscated the handgun tucked in the small of Bohanon's back. He bound their hands and pushed the men onto the couch. Pulling a chair from the kitchen, he sat down in front of them.

"I know you have a kid," he said to Connors. "Where is she?"

"On a school field trip. I'm supposed to pick her up at seven."

"She'll be all right," Travers said. "I don't hurt kids." He pulled the pair to their feet and forced them down the stairs into the cellar.

Travers went back upstairs and located the bar. He found a bottle of 30-year old scotch and poured a generous slug into a heavy Waterford glass. He walked outside and sat by the pool. Alarm bells continued to clang in his head. His own voice was stridently screaming danger and urging him to walk away from this mess. He had four people trussed and locked in a wine cellar. Scheduled for immediate elimination. A little girl due home in four hours. He took a strong pull of the scotch and tried to piece together a plan.

Travers drained the glass and returned to the bar for a refill. He didn't know what the fuck to do. The job was impossible. Too many complications. Too much risk. If this thing went south, his ass was squarely on the line. It was time to think outside the box. Was there another way? A smarter move?

Something sprang into his head. A niggling of an idea. He allowed the thought to germinate and grow, sipping the single-malt while trouble-shooting complications. Running through worst-case scenarios. Risks and rewards. The elements soon clicked into place like a line of red sevens spit from a whirling slot machine.

His last perfect job.

He activated his phone and called Andrew Glass.

———◆———

They huddled close together on the pitch-black cellar floor, grasping one another for warmth and comfort. All efforts at escape had been exhausted. The fumbling attempts to help one another out of the zip ties. Scooting through the blackness, searching with hands for anything to cut off their shackles. Trying to force open the door. Brainstorming escape plans.

Now they were quiet, each pondering their fate.

Will was thinking about dying and leaving Mollie alone in the world. Terrified by thoughts of what might happen to her. Travers swore he didn't hurt kids, but Will had no confidence he was telling the truth. The man was a murderer. It wasn't a stretch to figure he was also a liar. The thought of Mollie at the man's mercy brought forth a white-hot surge of rage and fear. He'd nearly broken his wrists in a fruitless effort to tear them out of the restraints. Rage had gradually given way to hopelessness.

The last year ran through his mind like the riffling of cards. Mollie's diagnosis. The wasting of her body. Her trust in him. His crazy dash around the world. The miracle he found in Guatemala. Her astonishing recovery and the precious sense of normality they'd discovered the past few months. He didn't want to leave his child alone in the world.

He wondered who would care for her. Who would tell her of his death, and who would console her.

Bohanon leaned his head against a cold concrete wall and wished for a final taste of Bushmills. He allowed into his mind images of the wide meadows and rolling hills of the Emerald Isle. He would never again see his homeland. His brothers and sisters. He remembered the foolish choices of his life. The good things he had thrown away. The men he had harmed. Women who wanted to love him. His preference for the warm embrace of whiskey, which comforted him far more than the arms of any woman. He had always believed he would die at the hands of another, and now the moment had arrived. Bohanon breathed deeply and accepted his fate. This dark room was an appropriate place to receive his reward for a wasted life.

Tamara could see the arcing curve of her life slicing like a fluorescent comet through the cellar's darkness. She bowed her head and counted the people she'd hurt and disappointed. The list was quite long and populated exclusively with men. Her great talents involved hurting those who wanted to love her and lying to herself. Now bound in a dark cellar and awaiting her executioner, she understood the vastness of her failure as a human being. The extent of her immature selfishness. Always thinking only of herself, she chose to run from intimacy and disappoint every man who dared care for her. She smiled in bitterness at the irony of the moment. Two such men were beside her in this cellar.

She had betrayed Steve McNeal out of pure selfishness. She broke his heart because the thrill was gone and she couldn't handle the daily grind of marriage. She simply grew tired and walked away, giving no thought to the emotional devastation left in her wake. He had found a way to forgive her, and this act of selflessness served only to inflame her guilt. She had nearly fallen into the same pattern with Will Connors. At least she found the sense to halt the relationship before stomping on his heart. Tamara made a silent vow. If she survived this nightmare, she'd change her life. She would become a better person. She would make amends.

McNeal was absorbed in his own thoughts. He had run through every possible escape scenario. Broken a wine bottle and used a wedge of sharp glass to saw at the zip ties. Shimmying around the cellar, exploring every inch of it and searching every crevice for a weapon or tool. Slamming his body against the heavy door. He spent time considering the possibility of rescue. Would someone come searching for him? The only possibility would be Reed Tobias, his boss at the paper. He replayed conversations in his head, trying to remember if Tobias knew his itinerary. He gave up on the idea. Tobias knew nothing about the cabin in Wisconsin. He had no idea McNeal had gone to California.

McNeal felt something shift in his mind. A surrender to the inevitable. An abandonment of hope. He began composing the story he might have written. It wouldn't be him, but someone would one day chronicle the story of Novix. Of Andrew Glass and Steele Pharmaceuticals. McNeal decided the cellar scenario would add a nice element of drama. His death would make interesting reading. He squatted in the blackness and realized he was part of a story someone else would write.

CHAPTER THIRTY-NINE

Steele Pharmaceuticals
Houston, Texas

Tall chrome doors on the private elevator slid open and Bob Travers walked into the penthouse office. Glass stood at the bar holding shots of whiskey. They clinked glasses and drank. Travers moved to the leather couch and wearily dropped onto it. Glass could see fatigue on the man's face. Eyes were lined with weariness, and his face shiny with perspiration. Clothes were rumpled.

"Nice job in California," Glass said. "You saved my ass. You saved the company."

Travers tilted his head and gazed at the ceiling, lips curled as if remembering something distasteful. "Long day."

"How the hell did you get it done?"

Travers shrugged. "Better you don't know."

Glass understood. The less he knew about what happened in Santa Cruz, the better. That fact that Travers was extorting him for another million dollars was only a mild irritation. The man had called this afternoon and demanded more money. On top of the sizeable bonus

Glass was already paying him. Travers wanted his money tonight. He also announced he was quitting his job at Steele. Effective immediately.

Glass stoically accepted the news. Travers was a good soldier. He had dirtied his hands many times so those of his boss could stay clean. Travers had cleaned up the mess on the West Coast. Glass could now move forward with Novix and begin raking in billions. The million dollars the man demanded was pocket change. He had earned the money. And the right to walk away. Still, Glass hated losing the man's services.

"You sure you want to give it up?"

Travers nodded wearily. "I'm finished killing people."

"Any chance of one last job?" Glass spread his palms entreatingly. "I'll make it worth your while. Another million."

"Who are we talking about?"

"Hermann. The only one left who can hurt us."

Travers raised his brows and considered it. "Okay," he said. "One last job. Then I'm done."

Glass smiled appreciatively. He reached under his desk and rolled out a small travel suitcase. "Take a look," he said. "Tell me how it feels to be a millionaire." He pushed it towards Travers, who lifted the suitcase onto the couch and opened it.

"That's a lot of cash," Glass said. "I won't be offended if you want to count it."

Travers began stacking bundles of cash on the couch.

Glass walked to the sliding door, stepping onto the balcony and into the night air. It was well past midnight. In the distance he could see the lights of Houston's harbor and the dark ocean beyond it. He hadn't been on the yacht in weeks. The weekend might be a good time. He'd bring along the wife and kids. He stared out at city skyline and anticipated the serenity of the water.

Travers stepped behind him and struck Glass in the head with the lead pipe. Glass collapsed to the floor, and Travers bent to study his face. He hefted the man by the arms and dragged him further onto the balcony. He looked over the railing. The concrete parking garage was twenty stories below. He lifted Andrew Glass to his feet and leaned him against the railing, then he gave a push. Glass teetered, then fell backward and went cartwheeling towards the earth. Travers didn't bother to watch the landing.

"There's your one last job," he said.

He walked into the office and finished his drink, then he wiped clean the glass. He went to the couch and gathered up the stacks of cash and stowed them in the suitcase. Travers removed a small bug detector from his pocket. He activated it and carefully swept the office. The device alerted on a smoke detector mounted on the wall. Travers pulled it apart and found the tiny video camera. It alerted on a fountain pen on Glass' desk. Travers threw the camera and pen into the money bag.

He walked onto the balcony, gazing into the sky and wondering if he had forgotten anything. He went through his mental checklist. The corporate offices were deserted this time of night. Glass allowed no surveillance of his private elevator and office. Travers had located the devices Glass himself had planted. He was driving a car stolen at the airport. There might be other loose ends, but he decided they wouldn't matter.

He pulled a burner phone from his pocket and called the Santa Cruz police department. He informed the operator that hostages were held in a foothills mansion. He provided the address before breaking off the connection. He crushed the phone beneath his heel and tossed it into the bag.

He studied his watch and calculated the time it would take to drive home. The wife was busy packing. Tonight they would travel along the coast until they reached the Laguna Madre Bay. Tomorrow morning they would cross the border at Brownsville. He anticipated no problems carrying the cash, as travelers were rarely searched crossing into Mexico. A good day of driving would get them to Veracruz, and his wife's noisy family. He would change his name and learn Spanish.

He'd live a millionaire's life on the coast of Mexico.

It sounded like a nice way to retire.

CHAPTER FORTY

Chicago Daily Sun
Chicago, Illinois

Part One of the three-part story broke in the Chicago Sun's Sunday morning edition, in a six-page insert located behind the front-page section. Parts Two and Three were published on subsequent Sundays. McNeal entitled the first installment **Fall Of A Titan**. The story led with a narrative on the death of Andrew Glass, whose twenty-floor plunge from the Steele Corporate Tower made worldwide news and fueled intense speculation about the cause of his death. The Houston coroner's office had provisionally classified the death as a suicide.

In riveting detail, McNeal spun the story of Andrew Glass' meteoric life. He described the escalating chain of events that culminated in the man's leap from the executive suite of his own office tower. McNeal hinted that the executive's disastrous leadership of Steele Pharmaceuticals might have driven him to suicide. Glass wouldn't be the first corporate head to jump from a tall building in the wake of monumental financial failure.

McNeal included a profile of Steele Pharmaceuticals, providing a timeline that ran from the company's glory days to its current free fall. Investors were fleeing from the stock and the bottom had fallen out of its market position. The Securities And Exchange Commission announced it was renewing its investigation into fraud and stock manipulation. Days earlier a company spokesman announced that Steele was filing for chapter eleven reorganization and a temporary chief executive officer had been appointed. A corporate purge was underway, already claiming the company's chief legal counsel and head of research. Steele also launched a public relations campaign aimed at distancing itself from the legacy of Andrew Glass.

In the second installment, McNeal told the story of the Tikal Project. He described the research center hidden in the depths of the Guatemalan jungle. He introduced the world to the FDA inspection team, and told of the genetic wonderland they discovered in Renewal Gardens. He told readers about Gus, the orangutan whose spine was miraculously repaired. Sheila, the ancient chimp genetically regressed to adolescence. He revealed the pattern of deceit and fraud uncovered by Yanni Shimota. The unethical and illegal research carried out by Joseph Hermann. The mutated lab animal that escaped from the facility and terrorized the jungle.

In a blockbuster revelation, McNeal exposed the truth of Novix. He confirmed that the drug was actually capable of restoring youth. Then he revealed the drug's terrible paradox. Novix held the promise of extending life but could potentially kill those who used it. He detailed the fraudulent manipulation of the drug's clinical trials to conceal its malignant potential. McNeal used a metaphor in likening the drug's effect to a surgeon announcing the operation was a success, but the patient died. The story wove together the silken strings of the complicated web of deceit – the fraudulent research, the company's financial instability, and the rush to bring Novix to market before Steele Pharmaceuticals fell into bankruptcy.

In the final installment, McNeal provided the human element by introducing readers to the key players. He profiled Will Connors and described his heroic quest to save his daughter. McNeal included a sidebar on Mollie and her astounding recovery from terminal cancer. He added a picture of the little girl smiling in adoration at her father. McNeal wrote about Connors' desperate race to create the drug that saved his child. He hinted at a possible breakthrough in cancer treatment. McNeal included biographies of the story's other principals. Tamara Rodgers. Yanni Shimota. Wayne Wilkinson. William Bernard. He paid particular attention to the suspicious circumstances surrounding the deaths of Bernard, Shimota and Wilkinson.

In an epic finale, the third installment included a step-by-step narrative of his kidnapping. He described the terror-filled hours in the wine cellar, and his eventual surrender to the inevitability of death. McNeal thought this passage might represent the finest writing of his career. He vividly laid out the details of their abduction and the helpless hours spent in the darkness of a car's trunk. He detailed the events that led to their rescue. Colorful paragraphs profiled Bob Travers – their kidnapper, suspected murderer, and unexpected benefactor. He described Travers as a mystery man who'd vanished without a trace. California law enforcement had issued an arrest warrant charging Travers with multiple counts of felony kidnapping. At the time of publication, he remained at large.

McNeal described in rich detail his rescue from the cellar. The percussive sounds of boots pounding down the stairs. The door flying from its hinges. Blinding flashlights. Bulky figures in silver body armor rushing into the room, military-grade weapons at the ready. His profound relief at the realization the intruders were police officers.

McNeal was satisfied with the story. He had uncovered a criminal conspiracy with tentacles extending to the top of the corporate world. Helped prevent the distribution of a medicine with potentially catastrophic consequences. Exposed a huge pharmaceutical company as nothing more than a crime syndicate, and Andrew Glass as a thug in a Brioni suit. The story was dramatic and sensational, and it succeeded in focusing public attention on Big Pharma practices. It was irresistible to cable news, which was running endless analysis and debate. The story was put into syndication and reprinted in papers around the country.

Now that he'd put his story to bed, McNeal felt the sense of loss he invariably experienced at such times. He had the feeling that a grand adventure had just ended. He planned on taking a two-week vacation from the paper. Then he'd begin looking for another story to write.

On a sunny summer morning in July, Will moved into the little bungalow near the beach. Mollie was adjusting to the routine of school, and she'd found playmates in the neighborhood. She drew stick figures of her family and affixed artwork to the refrigerator.

Will stayed on at Dowd-LaPorte. Steele's new management team recognized his talent and offered him a permanent position. He gradually regained his intellectual curiosity, and he set about perfecting the medicine that saved Mollie's life.

He still thought about Tamara. Eventually, he would look her up. That would be a task for another time. Right now he was busy raising a child, resurrecting his career, and tackling the routine tasks of a normal life.

He awoke each morning looking forward to an ordinary day.

AUTHOR'S NOTE

During the morning hours of June 6, 1944, Army PFC James Homer Hobbs waded onto the sands of Normandy Beach. He walked into battle alongside his comrades and minutes later was struck down by heavy shelling. PFC Hobbs was posthumously awarded a Purple Heart and Silver Star. He sacrificed his life in defense of our nation. He was twenty-six, and my mother's youngest brother.

On March 5, 1945, Marine Corporal Ellsworth Patterson Huddleston stepped onto another sandy beach, this one rimming the Pacific island of Okinawa. Within hours, he fell before enemy fire. Corporal Huddleston was posthumously decorated for his bravery. He made the ultimate sacrifice in defense of our nation. He was twenty-seven, and my father's youngest brother.

Each of my parents lost a brother to war. I struggle to comprehend the depth of their sorrow and grief in the face of such tragedy. Seven decades later, my mother was still unable to speak her brother's name without spilling tears of grief. I was born following the war and never had the privilege of knowing these men. My parents chose to honor their memory by bestowing their names upon me. It has taken me a lifetime to fully understand the gift they gave me.

In tribute to these heroes, I write as Ellsworth James.

ACKNOWLEDGMENTS

Thanks to Ms. Vikkie Cossio, my amazing and talented niece who read an incomplete and abandoned draft of Third Messenger. Her enthusiasm and insistent demand that I "write more pages" inspired me to resume writing the story. Thank you, Vikkie. This story wouldn't have been completed without your support and encouragement.

Many thanks and much appreciation to Ms. Jane Bornstein, my dear friend and the world's best unpaid editor. Your corrections, suggestions and commentary contributed immeasurably to the polishing of the story. Thanks to you Ms. Jane for your energy, enthusiasm, and intelligent feedback.

Everyone should be blessed with such a partner as my precious wife Kathleen. My *sine qua non*. You are the love of my life, my inspiration, and my constant encourager. Your love forms the bedrock of my life. Your belief in me is astounding and has inspired me to accomplish things I never thought possible. You provide the indispensable "red pencil" for my stories. Your relentless editing and fearless suggestions have challenged me to become a better writer and contributed immeasurably to making Third Messenger a story worthy of publication.

Thank you, my darling. **F.A.T.E.**

Thank you for reading Third Messenger. It's a thrill to know that others are reading the story I invested a chunk of my life creating. I do appreciate it. If you feel the desire to contact me or comment on the story, please visit my website: www.ellsworthjames.com. I would love to hear from you. My next novel, **Winslow's Journey**, will be available in the Summer of 2019.

Printed and bound by PG in the USA

USA2019PGTL